THE UNDERDOG APPEAL

AN ENTERTAINMENT

BY

VLADIMIR VOLKOFF

RENAISSANCE PRESS

MACON, GEORGIA—1984

Library of Congress Catalog Number 84-61532
ISBN: 0-914707-02-7

Printed at Braun-Brumfield, Inc.
Ann Arbor, Michigan

1

"Wally," he said, "you think it'd be O.K. if I went and bumped off old Saint What's-his-name for ten thousand bucks?"

"Now Chirpie," I said, "don't be hasty. Whoever he is, he might be worth more. Especially with inflation."

*

That was in poor taste? Agreed. But consider this. First, I thought it was a joke anyway; second, I hate people calling me Wally.

"Besides," I added, "you got it all wrong. You get bumped off first and become a saint later."

I don't know why I wasted my sophisticated humor on Chirpie. I should have known better.

"He's no saint either," said Chirpie. "It's just his name. He's some kind of French freak who hates our guts. By rights he ought to get bumped off for free. No offense to you, Wally. Still there's that ten thousand . . ."

You can say one thing for Chirpie: he's a patriot.

"My dear boy," I said, "I did not imagine for one second you were talking seriously. But if, by any remote chance, you are, would you mind starting from the beginning?"

*

That was unfair of me, I confess. You may have noticed I didn't. I mean: start from the beginning. In fact it was my job with Munchin and Munchin to tell beginning authors: "*Don't* start from the beginning. Remember what a fellow called Horatius said: *in medias res,* which means: let's have some action! Start from the middle, with a nice, factual, juicy, first paragraph, and then flash your way back into the boring preliminaries." Which, incidentally, is precisely what I did: as an introductory sentence, "you think it'd be O.K. if I went and bumped off . . ." is really not bad at all, if I have to say so myself. But you see, Chirpie was not supposed to be writing a book; he was supposed to be asking my advice about an important matter, which was the only reason why I had joined him in that filthy beer joint of his, and so I think I was justified in demanding logic, not style.

Maybe I'd better introduce Chirpie.

I don't know what his I.Q. is and frankly I don't care: neither should he, since he is clearly not going to survive by his intelligence. If they have negative I.Q.'s, I mean below zero, that's where Chirpie's belongs. And physically, he looks the part, every cubic inch of him. Broad-shouldered, yes, but distinctly on the short side, with no neck to speak of, heavy, thickset and slow, he used to have a sort of Frankenstein beauty about him as long as he had a crew cut. At that time, if you were charitably inclined, you could even have taken him for some kind of elite commando boy. But now that he had decided to go fashionable (Chirpie's sense of timing!) and that his dull yellow hair hung around his head like a wet mop, there was no chance of your taking him for anything but what he was: a moron.

The only advantage of his new hairdo was that it practically hid his eyes, and by his eyes you could have guessed what he was even with the crew cut. He never opened them entirely, but kept peering at you from under heavy, drooping, reddish eyelids. There was only one occasion in life when he would firmly close one eye, widely open the other one, and use it on space and distance as an expressionless, precise, deadly gimlet. But at that time you would definitely prefer him to be looking at anything but you. . . .

Which brings me to how on earth I, of all people, should be saddled with the acquaintance, and even enjoy the confidence of, Mr. Charles W. Chirpwood.

I know this will be difficult to believe, but at a certain period in my life I happened to frequent a very ordinary American high school, which, at a certain curriculum level, happened to offer a

choice between two electives: band and R.O.T.C. Now what was I
to do? I certainly wasn't going to blow my lungs out into any silly
trumpet, and there were about umpteen drummers to one drum,
so I landed in what I considered to be the lesser of two evils.
Chirpie, on the other hand, didn't belong to, he *was* the R.O.T.C.,
or rather, since he couldn't jump a fence, scored poorly in drilling
and held all detailed maps to be his personal enemies, he was one
section of the wretched business, the main one if you will:
marksmanship. By some whim of Fate or by some mysterious
compensation of Nature, Chirpie was and is one of the two most
stupendous marksmen I ever met. In fact, he is *the* most
stupendous marks*man*, since the other one is a markswoman, but
that will come out later. Even I don't ask my authors to start from
the end.

Being an exceptional marksman, Chirpie quite naturally was the
pet student of our officers, N.C.O.s, and others. But being clumsy,
moody and stupid, he nevertheless got into a few scrapes, on
which occasions I was charitable and patriotic enough to lend him
a helping hand. Of course, the authorities expressed their appreciation gradewise, which was pleasant enough, as far as it went,
but mainly I earned the everlasting gratitude of Mr. Charles W.
Chirpwood, and though at the time I thought this was something I
could very well do without, I was mistaken: if I am now in a
position to type this story on a luxurious electronic Adler, with a
glass of Glenlivet at my elbow and Mistigri's delicate form
silhouetted against the inimitable blue backdrop provided by the
Mediterranean Sea, I owe it all—indirectly, of course—to that
unprepossessing individual.

Let me recall a few of those episodes. Once Chirpie couldn't get
out of a ditch in which he had insisted upon hiding from the
"enemy." Once he got lost in the mountains because he thought
that the N on his compass would invariably point out the North.
Once, during so-called intelligence exercises, when we had to deal
with "prisoners," he handcuffed himself to a chair and lost the
key. Once—this was his most serious escapade—he took the colonel's young wife for a waitress and began pinching her, which was
the only thing he knew how to do to women. For some reason I
undertook to pull him out of the ditch, to retrieve him from the

mountains, to find a duplicate key for the handcuffs and explain to the irate superior officer that Chirpie's sex life was limited to his passionate attachment for his rifle, and that his pinching was to be considered complimentary and above all Platonic. Upon which Chirpie declared, in his disgusting vocabulary, that we were "buddies," and set about to render me a few minor services, like shining my boots or expertly cleaning my gun.

In later life, having no gun to clean and being reconciled to the idea of shining my own shoes, I did not encourage him to pursue the relationship. However I allowed him to call me from time to time, and when he didn't understand his insurance policy or his bank's statement, he would invite me to Mack's Shack (!) for a tasteless, ice-cold beer, and I would endeavor to make everything clear for him.

"I sure appreciate it, Wally," he would effusively proclaim. "Always knew you were my own special buddy."

So, when he called me that morning and suggested a visit to Mack's Shack, adding in mysterious tones "that this was a real emergency," I gave no second thought to it. Maybe Chirpie had lost his job as a shopping center security man, maybe he didn't know how to buy a money order to send to his mother in South Georgia: anyway I had too much trouble of my own to worry about his. But I told him I would come and help him with his emergency. I guess we all need to be kind to somebody from time to time, and I considered Chirpie as my "neighbor" in the Christian sense, although I certainly wouldn't have wanted to see him becoming one in the geographical one.

And now here he was, talking about political assassination.

After some effort and more beer, I finally elicited from him the following story.

That fall, he had participated in even more turkey shoots than usual and won most of them. Incidentally, Chirpie is, I believe, the greatest turkey consumer in the world, since he feels in duty bound to eat up all those he wins. Two men had followed him from turkey shoot to turkey shoot. The only remarkable thing about them appeared that they did not care to compete, but just watched and compared notes. He had scarcely noticed them, although they had had a beer together here and there, the men never allowing the champion to pick up the check. He had forgotten all about them when suddenly, yesterday night, they rang the bell of his dingy efficiency apartment.

What did the men look like? Well . . . According to Chirpie, they looked like Laurel and Hardy straight from Macy's, which seemed to mean that one of them was big and fat, the other one thin and short, and that they both were reasonably well-dressed.

What were their names? Well . . . At first Chirpie shamefacedly confessed that he had neglected asking them, but then he rallied and observed with a sly look that doing so would have done no good since they would certainly have given false names. He had a point there.

What did they want? This was where the story became interesting. According to what I elicited from Chirpie, the scene had gone approximately this way.

To begin with, the thin man, rubbing his hands together and oozing with benevolence, had wished a good evening to Mr. Chirpwood, had inquired after Mr. Chirpwood's health, and had expressed pleasure at seeing Mr. Chirpwood again.

The big man had then added: "Yep. Long time no see."

The thin man had then gone on to describe at some length how much they had both missed Mr. Chirpwood's company, and how often they had observed to each other what a fine marksman and a wonderful overall person Mr. Chirpwood was.

At that point Chirpie had suggested their dropping the formalities and calling him by his nickname, which they graciously acquiesced to do. Thereupon Chirpie had made another suggestion concerning a drink, but the thin man, who clearly was the orator of the group, had looked somewhat shocked and declared that they were not allowed to drink when professionally engaged. The big man had then added that this was not a damned social call.

The thin man had then mentioned that the purpose of their visit was to put a very interesting business proposition before Mr. Chirpwood, sorry, he meant Chirpie. He also mentioned that this proposition would not have been made if the investigation which they had concluded had not brought results so emphatically in Chirpie's favor.

Chirpie was at the same time flattered and somewhat disquieted at learning that he had been made the object of an investigation, whereupon the thin man hastened to assure him that the inquiry had been absolutely satisfactory on all three points of interest.

First, Chirpie had no police record, paid his rent and utilities at the earliest possible date, had never written a bad check in his life, enjoyed good credit, and, although he was not married, abided, according to his neighbors and minister, by the highest moral standards that could be desired.

Second, judging from high school records and evidence obtained from employers, Chirpie was a very smart fellow indeed. (Here I raised one eyebrow and Chirpie confessed he had been surprised himself on hearing such reports of his cleverness: "I guess I was underestimating myself," he said.)

Third—and this point was the most important of all: "Yep, it's vital," agreed the big man—it had been ascertained that Mr. Charles W. Chirpwood was a good citizen. "If there had been the faintest ground providing the slightest suspicion of the tiniest little bit of hesitation in the wholeheartedness of your allegiance to the United States," began the thin man, and there he had to stop for breath, "we would have forgotten all about your marksmanship and moral qualities, and somebody else would have been called upon to fulfill the sacred duty which is going to bring you ten thousand dollars."

After this mealy-mouthed introduction, the thin man had produced a copy of the *New York Times* containing a short article about the notorious European politician, Serge Saint-Fiacre.

"They let me cut the article out," Chirpie proudly announced, as if they had entrusted him with a secret document. "Here."

He fumbled in his pockets and came up with a reasonably dirty newspaper clipping which he proceeded to spread out on the beer-stained counter. I read the thing without touching it. It ran as follows.

"NEW INTERNATIONAL PARTY CREATED IN EUROPE.—On Thursday 14th, French born Serge Saint-Fiacre held a press conference in Paris, France, to announce the creation of the European Party. Party representatives for Italy, West Germany, Belgium, Luxemburg, the Netherlands and Great Britain were present. 'If Western civilization is to survive,' said Saint-Fiacre, 'all

European nations have to merge into one so as to be able to hold their own against such giants as the U.S., U.S.S.R. and China. Although the fact is generally recognized, present European governments secretly sabotage the project, for a truly united, socially-concerned Europe would not tolerate present injustices. Obviously American interests lie in the same direction as those of present European ruling classes but not in the same direction as those of the peoples of Europe, and the new Party can expect strong American opposition to its ideals, but it will triumph in the end.' Asked whether the European Party expected to achieve victory by legal means, its leader replied with Gallic bravado that all means were legal when one was fighting in the better interests of the people. It is unclear on how many votes the new international party can count in any of the interested countries, but there is little doubt that, if it is to follow its leader, the European Party, whatever its positive program, will take a strong anti-American stand. To heavy applause, M'sieur Saint-Fiacre declared that 'to European peoples the U.S.A. now looks like the most dangerous country in the world. Experience has shown that America may intervene in our internal affairs at any time, and a recent declaration by her President, according to whom such interventions would always be for our own good, is obviously not of a nature to reassure us. What happened in Iran, Vietnam, Cuba, Brazil, and more recently in Cyprus, Ethiopia, Chile, can happen any day in Paris, Bonn, London, Rome, Brussels, The Hague or Luxemburg. The European Party,' concluded Saint-Fiacre, 'is Europe's only hope of freedom.'

"Serge Saint-Fiacre, born in 1935, is a relatively well-known figure in the wings of French politics. He has been a commentator on state-owned TV and has written articles for mildly socialist newspapers. He also owns a printing business. He has been decorated with the Legion of Honor (France's highest distinction) but usually refuses to wear it so long as certain social abuses have not been corrected in his country."

I had already heard about the European Party and was not impressed.

"So what?" I said.

"So the bastard ought to be killed," said Chirpie, whom I had always known as a gentle, humane creature, who, as the saying goes, couldn't hurt a fly, although he tore out the bull's-eye from a target with five shots.

I tried to reason with him, because, at that time, I hadn't yet grasped all the advantages the noble house of Munchin and Munchin and yours truly could derive from his folly.

"Listen," I said, "if all bastards were to be killed, the world would be faced with a serious problem of underpopulation."

"This one's anti-American," said Chirpie.

"*Non sequitur,*" I said, "which means: don't talk nonsense. If all anti-American bastards were to be killed, the world would still be faced with a serious problem of underpopulation. The only special point about this particular anti-American bastard, if I understood correctly, being that by his death you could come into ten thousand dollars."

"That's right," said Chirpie, innocently enough.

"And you are asking me, of all people, to decide *hic et nunc*— which means: in this dirty joint—whether Mr. Serge Saint-Fiacre will go on living his bastardly life or will die at your hands?"

"You have the funniest way of pronouncing the guy's name, but . . . yes, that sure is kind of what I'm asking you to do."

"Chirpie, you can't be serious."

"Wally, I'm dead serious."

"Well, 'dead' might be appropriate. How did Laurel and Hardy ask you to execute him?"

"They didn't ask."

"You mean *you* suggested it?"

"Sort of. When I read that article, you know,"—for one second Chirpie's eyelids were raised and I saw a dull fire smoldering in his pupils—"I told them plainly: 'that bastard ought to be killed.' And the thin fellow, Laurel, he said: 'That is exactly what we came to see you about.' And then, casual like, he mentioned the ten grand."

"The thin one is Hardy, Chirpie."

"I always thought it was Laurel."

"It doesn't matter. What did you answer?"

"I don't remember. I guess I looked surprised, you know."

"I know. I don't have your abilities, but I would have looked surprised too."

"I mean: it's the first time someone comes and asks me to go international."

I'm afraid I gaped.

"Chirpie! You don't mean to say that you . . . that you have already . . . gone *national,* do you?"

"Not exactly. That's what makes it so weird, you know. I realize I'm a pretty good shot, and I win all them turkey shoots and all that, but I didn't think they had already heard about me in Europe."

I patted him on the shoulder, but, to tell the truth, by now I could have done with some patting myself.

"Now, Chirpie, let's be sensible. Did you gather the impression that these gentlemen came from Europe?"

He shook his mop of a head.

"They were Americans all right, but they wanted me to go to Europe with them. So you see. They said Europeans don't have the kind of marksmen we have in this country."

"What else did they say?"

"Well . . ." he pondered "they said they would pay all expenses, and I could keep the rifle if I wanted it. 'Course I want it. And I'm going to make them pay for the most expensive damn rifle available. You know, it could be a . . . or a. . . ."

Here Chirpie became technical and I interrupted him.

"Chirpie," I said. I didn't exactly know how to ask my question. You see, the whole story sounded absurd to me, but then, with a fellow like Chirpie, *anything* is possible. "Chirpie," I said. Of course, I was supposed to know all about his professional life, but I hadn't always responded to his calls for advice, and one time might have been enough. "Chirpie. . . ."

"Yeah," he replied with some testiness, "I know my name's Chirpie. So what?"

I lowered my voice and looked around to ascertain that none of the distasteful characters sipping their beer around us were listening.

"Chirpie, you're sure you never actually . . . killed anybody?"

He grinned one of his old guileless grins.

"I'm positive."

But then he added darkly:

"Not yet."

"Chirpie," I said, "since you're asking for my advice, here it is. Forget about the whole business, which is probably a sinister joke anyway. If the men come again, don't open your door and tell them you are going to report them this minute to the F.B.I."

Chirpie smirked.

"A lot of good that would do if they are F.B.I. themselves," he said. "Anyway, Wally, I guessed all along you were the wrong person to turn to. Being half French, you can only sympathize with that bastard Saint Something-or-other. For all I know, you might even be a Roman Catholic yourself."

"As a matter of fact, I am. Was, I should say. And if you knew all along I was the wrong person to turn to, why the hell did you call me?"

I was angry, but his next remark disarmed me completely. He dipped his nose into his glass, sighed a deep sigh and murmured forlornly:

"There was no one else."

So I felt responsible again for the poor fellow and asked him what he thought would happen to him after he had bumped off Saint-Fiacre.

"All that will be taken care of," he boasted. "The men will arrange for me to escape and come back here. A private jet, I guess, or a nuclear submarine. I will just take a short vacation from my job and no one will be the wiser. Even you, if I hadn't told you, would think I had just gone down to Columbus, Georgia. The only thing those men insist on," he added, "is exactly what I want most: secrecy. The newspapers will be full of me and no one will know who 'me' is. See what I mean?"

Yes, I saw what he meant, and I also began to see something completely different. It would be the joke of the century if it worked, and though there were heaps of reasons why it ought not to work, still it might. Just to see how he would react, I said:

"The newspapers won't be full of you. Nobody in this country gives a damn if you murder ten Saint-Fiacres tomorrow."

His brow darkened, which, I felt, was a good sign.

"Maybe they won't care about Saint-Fiacre, but they'll know a job well done when they see it," he mumbled.

On that point I held my ground.

"No one will know how well the job was done," I said. "They won't even know it was done at all. Your countrymen and mine are bloody isolationists. On the other hand, if these people mean what they say, if they really want the European Party out of the way, there is no reason why you shouldn't make an honest profit by it, since you are obviously qualified for the job. Only don't take ten thousand. Take twenty, two in advance, and all expenses paid, naturally."

He looked bewildered.

"Twenty grand? I'd do it for the fun. And to get my hands on that rifle they promised."

"Maybe you would, Chirpie, because, between you and me, you are a damned fool and you know it. But take my word for it: if they offer you ten to start with, it shows they are ready to pay at least twenty. And as for the two thousand in advance, that's just to prove they are not trying to pull a joke on you. Besides, this is the way all serious business is done, Chirpie: 10% in advance, it's regular."

"You think so?"

"I most emphatically do. Since you asked my advice and I'm advising you to do exactly what you would have done anyway, at least do it my way. You'll be the better for it, I promise."

"I know you always were my special buddy, Wally."

"So I am."

I was radiating energy now. I needed him to obey me very strictly if the improbable stunt I had in mind was to have the slightest chance to come off.

"Now, listen, Chirpie. Those men came yesterday, right?"

"Right."

"When are you going to give an answer?"

"Tomorrow night. They are coming to my place. Maybe you could come too? That would help. You could do the bargaining. I would even let you have a small commission, if you got that twenty grand for me, Wally."

"Don't talk nonsense. What would I do with the commission you could afford to give me? Tip my janitor? No, Chirpie, you've got to let me talk some sense into that hairy head of yours. Did you tell the men you were going to consult somebody?"

"No. I just asked for time to think it over."

"Are you sure you didn't tell them anything about me?"

"Yeah, I'm sure."

"Good. When you called me, could anybody have overheard you?"

"Don't guess so. I called from a public booth, at the Plaza."

"That's excellent. Don't ever call me from your home. Now, when you came here, were you followed?"

"Followed?"

"Yes, followed."

"What would they follow me for? They are hiring the services of an expert, Wally, you don't seem to understand that."

"I understand it perfectly. Well, I'll check. As soon as you've finished your disgusting beer, get out. I'll pay, don't worry. Then take a leisurely walk around the block."

"Walk?! Maybe it's raining!"

"Too bad. You won't melt. Come back to the parking lot, and then take a walk around the block in the other direction. Got that?"

"I got it, but what. . . ."

"Don't argue with me, Chirpie. You know I'm working for your own good. After that, get into your car and drive straight home. Tomorrow morning call me from a pay station and I may have news for you. Out you go."

Natural authority is a great thing. Chirpie obeyed me to a T. While he walked, I stood outside, leaning against the wall of Mack's Shack in the shadow. I don't know the first thing about surveillance, but my distinct impression was that no one bothered to follow the poor moron, which I had expected anyway. So, after seeing him off, I went back into the odious place and dialed Amarantha's number.

It was a long shot. A very long shot. But *Fortuna audaces juvat*, which means: when you're in trouble, get out!

2

Amarantha's low-pitched, languid voice answered in a bored tone:

"Hello."

"Hello, Amarantha. This is Walter."

"Oh, too bad."

"What do you mean: too bad?"

"I mean I hoped for somebody interesting."

"Would you find me more interesting if I invited you to have dinner at the *Midnight Sun*?"

She considered the point and yawned delicately into the telephone:

"Well, maybe."

I could not suppress my excitement.

"Listen: something came up which could be the scoop we have been looking for."

Her tone became slightly acid.

"So that, in fact, what you suggest is that *I* invite *you* to have dinner at the *Midnight Sun*?"

Since she was, among other things—which, by the way, are frankly none of your business—my employer, her surmise was not devoid of good sense, but I retorted with some heat:

"Not at all. You know perfectly well that I may be a cad, but I am not a stingy cad."

Now that is perfectly true. In fact, I am not a cad at all, and as for stingy, numberless flower merchants, valets and waiters, perfume dealers, owners of good eating places, fine lingerie saleswomen all over the world, without mentioning hotel porters, pullman attendants, taxicab drivers and in general all "tippable" personnel, would have laughed outright at the bare idea that

Walter de Walter was stingy! To this list I would gladly have added jewelers, fur specialists and private yacht riggers; unfortunately, at that time, I had not yet acquired the means to attract the attention of these gentlemen. Anyway, "stingy" was out of the question and Amarantha knew it, none better. What she didn't know, of course, was that my checking account, which Munchin and Munchin had replenished nearly two weeks ago, had lapsed back into negative figures, and that I would have to pay the *Midnight Sun* bill with a Diners' card. The card had been taken out in my name by Munchin and Munchin, so that I could settle my expenses with it, whenever I was supposed to dine some famished author at a fried chicken place, which meant that, in the long run, Amarantha Munchin would have to pay for our dinner. Since by that time it would have become tax-deductible, I didn't worry. Anyway, I'm not the worrying type.

"Oh! no," said Amarantha very sweetly. "You're not a cad, Walter dear. Just a little caddish. Meet me there at nine, will you?"

And she hung up. "Meet me there" clearly meant that she was willing to dine with me but didn't want to commit herself for the evening. And that in turn could mean either that she was still undecided about what she would do later that night, or that she wasn't, but I wouldn't be the one she would do it with. And if it weren't me, it would probably be Billy-boy B. Bopkins III, which solution didn't appeal to me, for more than one reason. For a split second I had a vision of hiring Chirpie to rid this nice country of Billy-boy B. Bopkins III: it would be such a nicer country without him, and Chirpie would certainly give me a discount. Still, not being sure that Chirpie would accept a Diners', I decided against it. Besides, I'm not the bloody type. So I just called the *Midnight Sun* and made reservations for a party of two.

The *Midnight Sun* is a Scandinavian restaurant. Don't let that mislead you. It is true that to succeed in the restaurant business in this blessed country it is usually enough to prepare barely edible dishes, mark them about ten times what they are worth and call them by a foreign name, preferably misspelled: your patrons will eat anything, and pay lavishly for it, provided they think it is exotic. As a matter of fact, for tasting, Americans don't use their taste buds: they use their imagination. But the *Midnight Sun* does not rely too heavily upon that characteristic, and although you are supposed to eat things like reindeer, they are decently cooked, the service is solemn and fairly efficient and they don't serve their Burgundy chilled. By Southern standards, it is what you would call de luxe.

I arrived early and climbed on a bar stool. Just to snub the bartender, I asked for an unblended Scotch. Of course, they didn't have any, so I sighed and settled for a gin gimlet straight up, with Beefeater's. In Europe I would have done the opposite: asked for a gin gimlet, verified that they didn't know what I was talking about, and settled for Scotch.

Sipping the cocktail, I reflected on the situation.

I had met Amarantha Munchin at a rather smart party in New York, a few months earlier. What was I doing in New York? Well, that's a somewhat indiscreet question, but I will tell you. I was waiting for a certain storm to blow over. It does not really matter where the storm had originated or what had caused it. Let's put it this way. I am by no means a dishonest man, but I generally don't agree with most bankers' way of doing business, and most bankers don't agree with mine. So misunderstandings are bound to arise, and since bankers are more powerful than I and feel no qualms about abusing their power and calling in various officials to straighten things out, I have been known to emigrate a few times during my short thirty-two years of life. By the way, this is a family tradition. We like to move from one continent to another, and my father, for instance, enjoyed the privileges of citizenship in seven different countries: the United States, France, the United Kingdom, Monaco, Ethiopia, Liberia and Honduras, if my memory serves me well. Anyway, things had sunk so low that I was actually looking for a job. Not that I like working: for some reason it makes me tired. But other prospects were nonexistent and it appeared that I would have to earn my bread, preferably with some caviar on it.

Amarantha Munchin, at that time, had just become general director of Munchin and Munchin Publishing Company. The other Munchin of the two was her father, who had finally been retired to a nursing home. Was it because Atlanta, Georgia, is not the best place to do publishing business in, or because Mr. Munchin had been practically out of his mind during the last years of his directorship, I don't know, but the position of the firm looked rather gloomy and its future gloomier still, when Amarantha took over. In fact, the rats were already leaving the ship, and the sinking business was seriously understaffed. To Miss Munchin's mind, that brilliant cosmopolitan Walter de Walter appeared as the man who could save the situation.

"So far," she told me, "we have been publishing mainly religious literature, but religion does not seem to sell as well as it used to. What we need are new titles, new authors, something with an international flavor, to cater to Atlanta's new international interests. To find all these, we need a competent scout. How does $36,000 sound to you for a beginning? Of course," she added very sweetly, "since you are not familiar with publishing, we would ask you to do some editing chores besides the scouting, to compensate for your lack of training."

So far publishing had been very far from my usual pre-occupations, and the word "scout" had made me think about ruddy-cheeked, peak-hatted little boys tying and untying knots, but I discovered that most publishing houses do use scouts whose job it is to ferret out juicy manuscripts or promising authors. And so I accepted the ridiculous salary and whatever fringe benefits came with it.

To put it mildly, the success was neither immediate nor over-whelming. I succeeded in persuading Munchin and Munchin to translate and publish a completely incomprehensible novel called *La Femelle transcendentale* (in English it gave: *The Transcendental She-man*) and even to invite the author, young Hervé Savaryn, over from France for a launching week-long spree; but although Hervé Savaryn was an excellent friend of mine, he failed to sell more than one hundred copies, which, as Amarantha acidly re-marked, barely paid for the toothpicks. After that, I decided that we would be safer with classics, and we produced a luxurious edition of Aretino, with reproductions of the original drawings, which very nearly brought a pornographic suit against us; this we managed to dodge, but the religious sales collapsed completely. I suggested making a new translation of all the Fathers of the Church, which would have assured us at least forty-four nonpornographic volumes, but Amarantha, grown wary, put her foot down. I tried literature for youngsters; we found acceptable authors and artists; the commercial outlook was rosy; I got a raise; Amarantha ordered a dozen new dresses from Frohsin who was still in operation at that time; but we had forgotten one thing: few youngsters read and those who do don't read books for youngsters. After this third fiasco, I began to wonder if literary scouting was really my cup of tea and to fear that Miss Munchin would soon begin wondering about it too.

The worst was yet to come and, sure enough, it came, in the person of Bill B. Bopkins III, the third of the noble lineage of Bopkinses to insist on the ridiculous nickname Billy-boy.

Bopkins was the chairman of the board of B.B.B.B. Publishing Company, Inc. He was fortyish, over two-hundred-poundish and over six-feet-sixish. A big bully of a man with a booming voice who had footballed his way through college, but obviously did not lack sound business instincts. He published exclusively comics, and prospered. I don't know which came first, his meeting Amarantha at a publishers' convention or his decision to enlarge his business by means of a merger with another one, but I was faced with both at the same time and I liked neither the one nor the other. One thing was very clear to me. Amarantha was a realist and she knew that of the few assets Munchin and Munchin had to offer, she was the most desirable one. In other words, she would not surrender her person to Billy-boy if she didn't make up her mind to surrender also her business, and she would not accept the business merger if she didn't clearly see her way to a matrimonial one. Since I would rather wash dishes at a country club than serve in any capacity under Mr. Bill B. Bopkins III known as Billy-boy, my situation was perfectly clear-cut: either I succeeded to save Munchin and Munchin *in extremis*—which means: by the skin of its teeth—or I would find myself incomeless in a very short time. And I doubted that Billy-boy would even leave me the Diners'.

Now, I'm not very good at figures, but I knew this: the only way to save Munchin and Munchin was to find a best seller for it to publish. And since there is no known way to conjure up a best-seller—a book can be completely ungrammatic and horrendously dirty and still not sell—you will probably agree that I was in what,

I believe, is known as a quandary. It would be funny indeed if my old pal Chirpie helped me out, if only by postponing the merger and giving me time to find that elusive best seller.

I had reached this point in my meditations when Amarantha made her entrance. Amarantha never plainly enters like me and maybe even you: she sails regally into a room and waits for a red carpet. She usually gets it. As soon as she had crossed the threshold all male heads turned her way and all female heads turned the other way. As to maître-ds' and head-waiters' heads, something worse happened to them: they collided and seemed to explode, such was these gentlemen's haste to demonstrate their obeisance. Amarantha waved them away and marched toward me.

Amarantha is tall, though not a giant; she is slender, though not transparent by any means. Her figure is ideal and has got that quality which makes a woman look like a model, only much better. I suppose in older times they would have said that she looked like a goddess. That night she wore a long, simple, oh! so simple, black, silk jersey dress. Hardly any ornaments to speak of, in fact, just one: a heavy diamond brooch pinned at the lowest end—and, thank heavens, it was pretty low—of her décolleté.

"Hullo, Walter," she said, in that deep, silky, husky, studied voice of hers, and it was pleasant to know that I was the most envied man escorting the most hated lady of the whole restaurant.

Of course, they gave us a much better table than the one they had reserved for us, and hovered around us like a swarm of obsequious bees. Amarantha—I could never cure her of the habit—spoke directly to the maître d' instead of relaying her orders through me, but you must remember she was, among other things, my employer, and I felt obligated to show some tolerance concerning her poor manners—ordered akvavit—she always orders the right thing in the right place, while I delight in doing just the opposite—and then disappeared behind the menu, which looked like an oversized edition of the Bible. Finally, after some consideration, we ordered smoked salmon to begin with, and then roast duck with cherries, I submissively following my employer's cues.

"I'll leave the wine to you," she graciously concluded.

She is not very knowledgeable in wines, I must say, and has the good grace not to insist upon her own preferences. Instead of ordering two different wines, which would have been appropriate, I decided to show some deference to Munchin and Munchin's Diners' account, and ordered champagne (Veuve Clicquot Brut 1964) which was not exactly inexpensive but would compliment the duck as well as the salmon. Finally, we were left more or less to ourselves, and Amarantha leaned across the table toward me. Another man's heart would have, at that point, missed a beat, but I had already recognized the businesswoman's glint in her eye, and, not being a fool, did not attempt sentimentality at that point. On the contrary, I raised my glass of akvavit—she had ordered some of the awful stuff for me too—and said:

"Well, Miss Munchin, this appears to be the right time to drink to the solution of our mutual problems."

And I drained the glass at one gulp, which is the proper, and really the least unpleasant, way to do it.

"Another of your French friends in need of an American publisher?" asked Amarantha.

I allowed myself a grin.

"My dear Amarantha, this one is as American as you could wish."

And because, after all, I'm a decent fellow, and it was her money and her father's business, not mine, I told her the whole story, without embellishment.

She listened. You have to grant it to Amarantha: she is a good listener whenever she thinks there might be something for her in what you have to say. Obviously not one detail of my narrative skipped her attention, since, once I was through with it, she twirled the stem of her glass for a few seconds and then snapped:

"You were wrong, as usual."

"What about?"

"Hardy's the fat one."

She was definitely not going to give me a complex over that. I grinned:

"Well, of course."

"What do you mean, of course?"

"My dear girl, don't you feel how pedantic, boring, old hat, in one word provincial, it is to know which is which? Surely that is one of the typical points on which any really presentable person ought to be wrong."

I got her perplexed. Amarantha belongs to what is supposed to be the cream of society in Atlanta, Georgia, and the word *provincial* annoys her no end. Besides, she never knows when I'm serious and when I'm not, which, I am afraid, was at that time my main hold on her interest. The only thing she could do was to look superior, like an offended egret, and switch subjects.

"They couldn't have been F.B.I.," she said.

I agreed. I had never heard that it was part of the F.B.I.'s job to recruit patriotic snipers.

"So that makes them hoodlums."

I disagreed.

"There are less respectable institutions than the F.B.I., who are still supposed to work for the government. What about poor old C.I.A. which these days really begins to look like the dying lion someone mentioned somewhere? No passing donkey could refrain from kicking it in the ribs. What about D.I.A.? S.I.A.? N.S.A.? L.V.F.? F.T.P.? R.S.V.P.?

"Walter," said Amarantha with a shrewd look, "you are making them up."

"I am. That's precisely the point. Some of them are so secret we don't even know their names, but we know they exist."

"Are you trying to tell me that the American government is planning to murder Saint-Whoever-he-is?"

"Well, there was a time when most governments were in the habit of murdering a few saints every morning. And the American government has been planning to murder Castro, who is no saint. And Saint-Fiacre is not a saint either: it's just his name. So you see."

"Don't try to confuse me, Walter. Do you really think that if the American government seriously wanted to get rid of an obnoxious European politician, they would hire your friend Chirpie to do the job? Surely some of those X.Y.Z. fellows can shoot!"

"I suppose they can and I suppose you're right. But you see, it is not really important who wants Saint-Fiacre dead, so long as my friend Chirpie does do the job."

"I don't understand. Anyway what does all this have to do with us? You want to warn Saint-Fiacre, get a reward and invest it in my company?"

"No, my dear. You miss the point completely, which is not surprising, since you are the chairman of the board and not an underpaid scout."

"Walter, if this is some crazy way of asking for a raise. . . ."

Her black eyes sparkled angrily. They are never so beautiful as when she thinks someone is trying to get money from her.

"No, my dear girl. This is rather a crazy way of bestowing a favor on the crumbling house of Munchin and Munchin. And, if I am not mistaken, on saving it from utter destruction or an infamous merger."

"Will you be so kind as to get to the point?"

"I will be so kind. As your scout, I am supposed to look for juicy material for you to publish. Such material can be fiction or non-fiction. It can also be fiction presented as non-fiction, e.g. *The Penkovsky Papers,* Khrushchev's *Memoirs,* and, who knows, maybe even *The Diary of Anne Frank.* The normal sequence of events is, in that case, the following. Something happens that arouses the interest of the public. Then somebody writes something about it. Then somebody publishes it. Then it sells like hell (which incidentally sells pretty well these days) and everyone involved becomes very rich, with the exception of the fellow who was stupid enough to be first in line and do whatever was done in the first place. You are a publisher and need to see things from what I'll call the Contract Point of View. Well, in the normal sequence, the contract is signed after the book is written, or, when the manuscript has been commissioned from someone, at least after the event takes place. Which has a lot of disadvantages. Most real events are so crudely planned, they have such unpleasant endings, they take place in such a haphazard way! Of course, a good writer does what he can to bring the most pleasing episodes into focus, to erase unsavory details, to ensure that the right actions had the right motives, that the proper words were said at the proper moments, but still he has to tell the truth from time to time, and you'll agree that, from a publisher's point of view, it is an unsatisfactory way to work. Tinkering, patching, repainting, fixing, don't you feel how clumsy and outdated all this is? And why so? Because the writer still writes *post factum,* which means: after the cat has been let out of the bag. Just imagine what an elegant job a writer could do if the facts were still his to fiddle with, if Penkovsky, for instance, could have been saved, and maybe Anne Frank too, so they could have been married in the end?"

Having delivered this impassioned speech, I drained my glass and replenished it. With her perverse habit of picking at details when she was not sure about the heart of the matter, Amarantha said:

"You know perfectly well that Anne Frank wrote her own diary."

"Yes, my dear, but think how much more satisfactory it would have been if somebody who could change her fate had written it for her."

"It certainly couldn't have sold any better."

"No, but she could have written a few more books which wouldn't have sold badly either."

"Well, I suppose you'd better go on."

This was said grudgingly, but I could feel Amarantha was beginning to get interested.

"Now," I said, "we have to consider what subject is the most popular, or, to use terms a publisher can understand, sells best."

"Sex," said Amarantha unhesitatingly.

I had to agree to that.

"And next?"

"Violence, I suppose."

"I would be more specific, Amarantha: death. From Agatha Christie's country houses to the bullrings where El Cordobés used to operate, the main character is still the gentleman with the scythe. The Romans were less coy about it: they had real gladiators and could kill them for pleasure just by turning their thumbs down. We have to make do with TV serials, detective novels, wrestling matches. But the thrill is the same. The fascination is the same. We enjoy a higher blood pressure and nothing sends it as high as the contemplation of death. I do not mean passive death, death accepted, submitted to, endured, but active death, known as murder. Does my eloquence begin to make sense?"

She didn't answer, and I went on.

"Murder appeals to us even when it is the fruit of imagination. We are eager to believe that Ian Fleming disposed of all those enemy agents James Bond is supposed to have killed. But a real murder is bound to create an even greater sensation. When you think how many writers, rewriters, editors, subeditors, film makers, have made a living out of the various Kennedy murders, you begin to suspect a syndicate of quill drivers and secretaries of conspiring against the whole family. As a matter of fact, the death of a certain secretary in a certain body of water could even point in that direction."

"This is far-fetched."

"It is far-fetched because most people lack imagination to do the fetching. But you know as well as I do that publishers' scouts were material witnesses at Martin Luther King's murderer's trial. Those publishers knew that such a murder would make a good story. Do you follow me so far?"

"I do."

"Fine. Now, my point is this. As soon as a murder is committed, it becomes the common property of all publishers. But I, being The Ideal Scout, am able to provide Munchin and Munchin with *an option on a yet uncommitted murder.* I think this is an opportunity which no publisher in his or her right senses would dream of letting escape. It could so easily find its way to another publisher's office."

"You don't have to be so graphic, Walter."

"Sorry. I didn't mean to blackmail you into accepting, Amarantha. In fact I thought you would actually like the idea."

She looked quizzically at me. She didn't really understand me; therefore, her feelings for me were a curious blend of distrust and admiration. Her background and mine were so different that she could never really tell what I was or wasn't capable of doing. At times she would decide I had no ethics at all, but then I would refuse to eat fish without a special knife and fork, and she would realize that I was not, after all, completely immoral. She never felt altogether safe with me, which was the reason she hired me, of course.

"You mean," she said slowly, carefully picking her words, "that you would really let it happen?"

"Murders don't happen, my dear. They are committed."

"You would really let it be committed then?"

"Why not?"

"Don't you believe that life is sacred or something?"

I laughed outright.

"Aren't you enjoying your duck?"

"Human life, I should have said."

"Human life is the least sacred thing you could think of. Believing that human life is sacred is nearly as vulgar as believing that money is sacred. It is there to be spent, gambled with, enjoyed, squandered, sometimes even turned into useful things, but certainly not to be worshipped."

"I thought you were some kind of a Christian."

"Well, to worship anything but God is distinctly unchristian, isn't it?"

"So you would let this Mr. Saint-Fiacre die without lifting a finger?"

"On the contrary. I will lift quite a few fingers to let him die more profitably than he has lived."

"More profitably for whom?"

"For Munchin and Munchin: who else? Oh! and Walter de Walter too."

"Wouldn't that be something like being 'an accessory after the fact' or something like that?"

"Rather, 'before the fact,' I should say."

"Wouldn't that involve some risks?"

I signalled the waiter to bring me the menu so I might order dessert.

"My dear Amarantha," I said, "you would run no more risks than now, having dinner with a disreputable character like myself and contemplating a merger with a disgusting character like Billy-boy. The risks would be run by me, and I would gladly run many more to prevent the said merger."

You see, I was really rather fond of Amarantha.

"What will you have for dessert?" I asked.

She shrugged her beautiful naked shoulders. She had not heard my question and murmured very low:

"A murder for a book. . . ."

"Some books," I quipped, "are much worse than some murders."

"I'll buy that," she said.

And Amarantha seldom buys anything she doesn't think has a good resale value.

3

You know very little about Amarantha Munchin if you think that I carried the day that easily, but I did carry the night, which was an encouraging sign—besides being rather nice.

For a few hours I must confess I forgot all about Chirpie's projected murder and our intended best seller. Not, thank goodness, that I tend to become sentimental in a horizontal position, but I have always felt that, when paying homage to a lady, it is rude to think about something else. Moreover, Amarantha was not exactly the girl to make it easy for you to think about something else.

So it came as rather a shock to me when, having lit a cigarette—I could never cure her of the filthy habit—she suddenly observed in a very matter-of-fact voice—quite different from the one she had just been using:

"It won't work."

"What won't work?" I asked sleepily.

"Moron shooting completely unknown character. Who will want to read about it?"

"Oh! but we'll change all that, Amarantha. That's the advantage of working before the deed is done."

"What do you mean: change all that?"

I sat up. I saw that she would insist on talking it out now, although the time (and place) didn't seem exactly appropriate to me.

"All right, Amarantha. I grant you that Chirpie being a moron, and Saint-Fiacre completely unknown in this country, at a first glance seems rather unfortunate. In fact, it is the other way, because we can much more easily make them into the murderer and murderee that will appeal to the public. Also I know how provincial people tend to be, and I realize that the murder of any American nonentity would strike them more than the assassination of a European leader whose obnoxious activities may well change the course of history. But, on the other hand, if the assassination took place closer to us, it would be more difficult to make it appear what we want it to look like. So, on a whole, we are rather lucky. You and I do have a few friends in the press, and there is still some time to focus as much interest as we can on Saint-Fiacre. As to Chirpie, it is his interest to remain anonymous, and so we can mold him into any figure that we find suitable. You see, the main thing is to give the public a murder that they can enjoy. A real fun murder, if you see what I mean."

"What is a real fun murder, Walter?"

"There are two kinds of real fun murders. One in which you sympathize with the victim, and the other one in which you sympathize with the murderer. Robert Kennedy's and Martin Luther King's murders sold well because they belonged to the first category. But our murderee being an anti-American foreigner with a difficult name, I think our best bet is the second category."

"You mean people will want him dead just because he does not like us?"

"No, Amarantha," I sighed. "People have become too progressive for that kind of common sense, healthy attitude. It's all very well for Laurel and Hardy to want Saint-Fiacre out of the way because of his anti-American feelings—if that is indeed their reason—but the public will want something else. We said earlier that sex and violence were best sellers, but you know there is something that outsells them both."

Immediately the business woman was on the alert:

"What is that?"

I shrugged. "Whatever you want to call it . . . let's say: virtue."

She nearly giggled.

"Virtue! Fancy you, Walter dear, talking of virtue! And with virtually nothing on too!"

"My dear girl, my costume has no bearing upon the matter. I never prided myself on belonging to the majority. What I'm trying to say is that the majority is childishly attached to virtue. Not necessarily to chastity, but to justice, to fairness, to the love of freedom, especially in the more revolutionary form of revolt against injustice, unfairness, tyranny, etc. It is what we psychologists call the Robin Hood Complex. And nowhere is it more developed than in our United States. For some Freudian reason there is nothing an American likes more than an underdog. If we want the public to like our murder, we have to commit it in the name of The Archetypal Underdog. Now what widely known underdogs can you think of?"

"Negroes."

"Right."

"Indians."

"Yes. Sometime ago they were villains, but now they have been turned into underdogs. Go on."

"Well . . . the Jews are still supposed to be underdogs, aren't they?"

"Definitely. Who else?"

"The Palestinians are trying for the part."

"You got the idea. Go on."

"Women, I guess."

It would make a cat laugh to suggest that Amarantha Munchin belonged to an underdog group, but, on the other hand, women have been known to claim the underdog status. The underbitch status, I should say.

"All right," I said.

"Sexual perverts, inverts, whatever."

"True."

"Oh! and underprivileged people."

Amarantha's vocabulary is much more up-to-date than mine.

"What we used to call the poor, yes. Who else?"

She couldn't think of anyone else. I suggested poets, but being a publisher she had to disagree. Then she suggested artists. She was right. Whatever their merit as painters, the French Impressionists were clever enough to play up to the middle class underdog sentimentality and to persuade their contemporaries and ours that it is a great misfortune to be an artist. But an artist committing a murder would not appeal to the majority, I felt, even if it were done in the name of justice, fairness or love of freedom. Most people would guess that being an artist *and* a murderer would be a case of *over-*, not *under-*, privilege. Murder considered as one of the fine arts sounds all right in cultured surroundings, but on the broad, popular market, it would smell of overdogs rather than underdogs. So we left artists to their own devices, and added to our list farm hands, students, and finally mixed breeds, such as mulattoes and the like, since being an under-mongrel is definitely worse than being an underdog.

"And that's it, I think," said Amarantha.

"Fine. None of them sounds too appealing to me, but we'll see what we can do. Tomorrow I'll read up on Saint-Fiacre and try to find if he ever oppressed any of the aforesaid minorities. And now, if I may, I would like to sleep a few minutes before I have to get up at an unearthly hour to clock-in at the office."

I didn't really have to clock-in, and so Amarantha felt no qualms about poking me in the ribs ten minutes later, when I was already dreaming about three beautiful mulatto girls with flowers in their hair, whom I was entertaining—or rather who were entertaining me—on the deck of a gleaming white yacht I had bought with the proceeds of our best seller.

"Walter," she said, "will Chirpie write the story?"

"No, silly. I'll write it myself."

"You're not a writer."

"If only writers wrote books, we would have nothing to read, besides Shakespeare, Dostoievsky, Tolstoi and a few others. Come on, you are a publisher! You ought to know it doesn't take a writer to write a book!"

I turned on the other side and went back to sleep. She woke me again.

"Walter, before we embark on anything, we have to know what is the real motive."

"We're much better off not knowing. If we knew, it might cramp our style."

"At least, we have to know for sure that these men are not actually working for the government."

I yawned. She had a point. Munchin and Munchin didn't want to interfere in official business. Neither did Walter de Walter.

"I'll investigate," I said, without having the slightest idea how to set about it, but Amarantha was apparently impressed with my spirit of decision since she let me sleep through what remained of the night.

*

Chirpie reported the next morning by phone.

"Wally," he began, "I'm gonna ask for a Browning Olympian."

"You do that," I said, "but before you do, I have to see you."

"O.K. I'll buy you a beer at Mack's Shack."

"No, Chirpie. Some place where I can't be seen talking to you."

He suggested the men's room used by the janitors and security men of the shopping plaza where he worked. That made sense to me because I knew nothing about clandestine meetings besides what I had seen in the movies, and I happened to remember that the first meeting in *Our Man in Havana* does take place in a buen-retiro. So, I mentally placed myself under Graham Greene's protection and said I would drive over immediately. The secretary watched me leave with an ironic expression on her pretty, insignificant face: she knew I spent as little time in the office as I could, but what she did not know was that, for once, I was really leaving on company business, on business which could transform Munchin and Munchin into one of the leading publishing houses overnight . . . or nearly.

My Alfa Romeo—I always drive a European car when I live in the States—took me over in a few minutes. It was fun to be walking between two rows of brilliantly lit show windows full of expensive things, and then to duck suddenly into a narrow, dark hall with brick walls, a concrete floor and a smell of garbage. At the end of the hall was the men's room. Except for Chirpie it was unoccupied and we had a nice little chat.

The speech I made can be summarized as follows. *If* everything went according to plan (meaning if I didn't discover that the whole project was government initiated), Chirpie was not only to agree to do the job that had been suggested, which would bring him twenty thousand dollars—not counting the Browning Olympian which, he informed me, was well worth another thousand or two—but he was also to keep me informed concerning everything he did, and, at the last moment, start taking his orders from me and not from his actual employers. Although not very bright, Chirpie was quick to see that then he would risk losing the money. I had foreseen the objection. First of all, he was to demand that half the sum be paid in advance.

"But you said 10% was customary."

"Because I didn't think of how much expertise was needed. Anyway you were ready to do it for ten thousand in the first place. And second, if you do as I tell, I will promise you twenty thousand more, which, since you will lose the second ten, will make a total of . . . ."

"Forty?" he asked hopefully.

"Thirty."

"What will I have to do?"

He peered at me from under his reddish eyelids.

I remembered his yearn for publicity and how I had disappointed him by telling him no one would be interested in Saint-Fiacre's death. Well, that had to change if I still wanted to prevent a merger between Munchin and Billy-boy. I explained that if he followed his employers' directions, they would probably help him escape, but they would insist on his keeping the whole business very quiet.

"If you do it my way," I said, "everybody will hear about what you have done, because you will tell them yourself."

He grinned. "I don't want to go to jail, Wally. I can't tell anyone about it, except a special buddy like you."

"You will not go to jail, Chirpie. You will have a press conference, with journalists from the *New York Times,* and the *London Times,* and *Le Monde,* and *Die Woche,* and the *Corriere della Sera—*"

"And the *Atlanta Constitution?*"

"Well, of course, Chirpie: and the *Atlanta Constitution.* All asking you questions. And you will be standing there with a black stocking over your head, telling them about it. And then I will help you come back to Atlanta, Georgia, and for some time you will go on working here as a security guard, because people must not guess that you have suddenly come into a lot of money, and after that you can do whatever you please."

"I'll go to all the turkey shoots in the country."

"Right. And win them all too."

I clapped him on the back. He was really a pathetic figure with his long hair and the peaked cap on top of it. But the revolver at his side looked quite businesslike and I knew he could use it. Not as well as a rifle maybe, but well enough.

"Where will the second twenty thousand come from?" he asked.

I had wondered if I would have to tell him right away. I obviously had to.

"From a book."

He looked incredulous.

"Twenty thousand bucks from a book? What book?"

"A book I am going to write and you will sign."

"With my own name?"

"No. With a fancy name."

"Like the Batman, or something?"

"Something along those lines."

"I like the Batman."

"We will discuss it."

"What will the book be about? About how I bumped off old Saint-Fulcrum?"

"Precisely. But you understand you must not tell Laurel and Hardy about the book. We keep that between us."

"Who do you take me for? Some damned idiot?"

"Of course not, Chirpie."

"And that book will be worth twenty thousand dollars?"

I nodded complacently.

"It will be a very beautiful job," I said, "and I write a very beautiful style. So you see."

I had already made the computations, starting from my own share. I wanted a minimum of one hundred thousand, and since the author generally gets about 10% of the total receipts, I wanted the book to bring in a minimum of one million. What with the hardcover and the paperback editions, we would then have to sell a minumum of some two hundred thousand copies. Surely, with a real murder and an adequate story we could do better than that! If we sold one million—counting the translations, it was not improbable at all—I would be an independent man if not a rich one, and

Chirpie's twenty thousand could be expended by Munchin and Munchin without the slightest problem.

"Will there be pictures of me?" asked Chirpie.

"You don't want to be recognized, do you?"

He looked crestfallen.

"I don't like books with no pictures."

"We could have a picture of you with the black stocking over your head," I said hastily.

"And with the rifle?"

"With the rifle too."

He smiled contentedly, like a child.

"It's going to be a beautiful book, eh, Wally?"

"Yes, a jolly book, Chirpie."

"I want to give it to my old woman for her birthday."

"But you mustn't tell her who wrote it."

He was annoyed with my stupidity.

"Look here, man, I told you already I am no damn idiot. I'll tell her I bought the book for the pictures."

"That's right, Chirpie. Now let me explain how we will communicate."

So long as he stayed in the U.S., there was no problem. He could always call me from various public phones. But, if the assassination was to take place in France, as seemed probable, I had no way of knowing how closely Chirpie would be watched. I began by making him memorize a telephone number. It was Nénette's number and I'll tell you all about Nénette—"all" is a little presumptuous, I'm afraid—a little later. I also explained that he had to let it ring three times, then dial again, let it ring two times, dial again and wait for the answer. All that went in rather easily. It was much harder to make him understand the complicated system of tokens that the French use for their public phones instead of coins. Who knows, with inflation we may have to resort to these tricks too in this country, but I hope we'll at least have only one kind of token and not two. But then his employers, whoever they were, might not let him use a phone, might even never leave him alone. Still they presumably would have to move him from place to place. In that case, he was to write little messages that he would hide in old cigarette packs which he would crumple and throw on the ground. That trick I knew from an Eric Ambler novel. Of course, if he were brought to France in a sealed container, kept in an underground jail, taken out of it in a cage five minutes before pressing the trigger and then disposed of "with extreme prejudice" as unprejudiced people like to say, my beautiful plan would not work. But what was the point of fearing the worst when the best could very well happen?

I was in the midst of these considerations when I suddenly realized that at the same time I was helping plan a murder, I might very well be saving my friend Chirpie's life. Should I tell him about it or should I behave modestly and keep it quiet? I didn't know who those Laurel and Hardy characters were, I didn't know what their ulterior motive was, but it seemed like a safe bet that they were after secrecy, and anyway there are few people who give you twenty thousand when they can get away with giving you ten. It was obviously to the two gentlemen's advantage to bump off Chirpie as soon as he would have bumped off Saint-Fiacre. In other words, Chirpie would definitely be safer following my plan of escape than theirs. Not that Chirpie's safety was an all important consideration. Nevertheless, if I could do both of us a good turn at the same time, so much the better. But ought I to frighten Chirpie at this point by disclosing my sinister suspicions to him? I decided to wait.

So I skipped the suspicions and went into the matter of passports. Did Chirpie have one? Yes, naturally he had a passport. He was a marksman of international reputation. Didn't I realize he needed a passport more than some other people? He was getting very superior indeed. I didn't mind. I was very glad he had a passport. I explained that he should send it to me, through the mail. Laurel and Hardy would be sure to ask if he had one, and he would say no, and apply for another one. Was that clear? What would he say to the people behind the desks? He would tell them he had lost his first passport, but he would be sure to tell L. and H. that he never had had one. Had that sunk deep enough?

I made him repeat his lesson several times in a row. And then I made him promise to call me in the afternoon to repeat it once again over the phone. I had never suspected I possessed so much patience but apparently I did. We shook each other's hand—mine

ached for two hours—and parted after I had given to him a password which would ensure that our future messages would be received as authentic. I didn't really think we would need a password, but they always seem to have them in books, and so we
agreed that anyone coming to see Chirpie and asking him if he had
been born under the sign of the Capricorn (which he had) would
be a "friend" if, to Chirpie's affirmative answer, he responded by
saying: "And I was born under a stop sign." It was pretty corny,
but it was easy to remember, it made Chirpie laugh and it sounded
innocent enough if uttered in the presence of "enemies."

Having had a spot of lunch, I drove to the Alliance Française
and leafed through all the magazines they had. Saint-Fiacre was
mentioned in most of them, and in *Match* I even found a photograph of the man. Rather short and thin, he had a triangular head
with small piercing eyes, which would have suggested a snake, if it
were not for the big pointed ears, which distinctly suggested
Mephistopheles. Snakes and devils being cousins, the mixture was
not exactly pleasing to the eye, at least to most eyes: to mine it was
very pleasing indeed. As I said before, I am not sentimental;
however, I would have been unpleasantly surprised to find out
that my intended murderee was a hearty-looking chap with an
innocent grin on an honest face. It was much more satisfactory to
observe that Saint-Fiacre looked like a sly and venomous scoundrel. His high and deeply furrowed forehead, his eyebrows which
went off at a curious angle, his pointed cheekbones and chin, his
carnivorous teeth rather indecently exposed in a wolfish smile,
definitely had character; but as to innocence or honesty, they
didn't seem like subjects he would have majored in. He had been
photographed at a cocktail party on some billionaire's lawn, and
he stood glass in hand, the fingers of his other hand spread out in
an expressive, Gallic gesture. But all that didn't give me much to
go on. According to the small articles about him and extracts from
his speeches, he never had run the risk of antagonizing Negroes,
Jews, homosexuals, mulattoes, women, students, economically
unstable citizens, or any other category of people whom I could
hope to present as underdogs. You must understand that Serge
Saint-Fiacre was a leftist, and although his physique was quite
acceptable for the part I intended to cast him for, his ideas

appeared to be objectionably commendable, if that makes any
sense at all. Give me a rightist any day! They at least can be made
to look as if they sympathized with oppression, reaction, tyranny,
fascism, jingoism, discrimination. Of course, there is the other
bugbear: Communism, but although in the countries they have
taken over the comrades seem to have made mincemeat of quite a
number of various underdogs, they still manage to appear as
underdogs themselves in all other countries, and it would not do at
all to try and sell a book telling, in sympathetic terms, about the
assassination of a red or pink leader in a democratic, or sup-
posedly democratic, society.

I was rather discouraged. The only people Saint-Fiacre ever
criticized were the rich, the powerful, the established. Obviously
he had discovered the Underdog Appeal before I did.

I went back to the office and learned that Amarantha had left to
play golf with Billy-boy. I borrowed the secretary's car and let her
have my Alfa Romeo to entertain her boyfriend in or with,
whichever. I went to a department store and bought some perfectly ugly clothes. I changed into them in the men's room. Then I
went to a wig store and bought a wig. I looked perfectly disgraceful with black, vulgarly stylized hair, a yellow shirt, green pants
and a red Escort. But at least, if I were spotted, I would give the
opposition something to remember as clearly as possible, something which looked as different from the real me as the red Escort
from my lotus-white Italian beauty. Then I drove over to Chirpie's
apartment house, parked in what seemed to me a tactically well-
chosen place, and prepared to wait.

First, Chirpie came back from work, around six, and gave me
the satisfaction of walking very close to my car, even throwing an
idle glance at its occupant, and not recognizing me.

Then, about an hour later, an old battered Maverick, recently
repainted green, parked on the other side of the street, and two
characters emerged from it, whom I immediately recognized as
Chirpie's two mentors. One was indeed tall and big, the other
small and lantern-jawed. The first one looked very stupid; the
second one very nasty. They didn't make me think of Hardy and
Laurel because there was something deliberately obnoxious about
the way they walked, looked around themselves, slammed the

Maverick's doors. But they obviously were some kind of comedians, playing prearranged parts. At a guess, Mr. Laurel was the boss and had hired Mr. Hardy for his physical appearance, as an effective offset to his own. They didn't look like government agents, and I didn't share Chirpie's enthusiasm about the way they dressed. Their suits looked fairly new but they were poorly cut and made of poor material.

I jotted down the license plate number as soon as they had disappeared into the building and then went over to the car in the hope that they would have forgotten to lock it and that its interior would reveal something about them. They had carefully locked it and the only thing the interior revealed through the glass was a lot of dirt and cigarette stubs. I might have tried to pry one of the windows open with a coat-hanger, but I am not very deft at that kind of thing. Besides, I didn't want to have to explain my behavior either to Mr. Hardy or to a policeman. I went back to the Escort and settled down to wait once again. At one time I had considered providing Chirpie with a tape recorder and asking him to record the conversation, but I had decided against it: Chirpie would tell me in his own words what passed between them and there would be no risk of his checking in their presence to see if the tape recorder worked properly.

After about an hour the two gentlemen strutted out. There was something very distasteful about the way they walked: it was boastful and stealthy at the same time. I pitied Chirpie for having fallen into their hands and congratulated him mentally for having me to protect him against them.

They drove off, and I tried to follow.

But it was the first time in my life I was playing that game, and I had decided to be so cautious that I lost them at the second turn. At least nothing indicated that they had noticed they were being followed, and I decided I would consider that as a positive result. Anyway I had obtained what I had come for: the license plate number.

Now what do you do with a license plate number, unless you are a policeman or a private detective with good connections, especially if you want to remain anonymous and unnoticed? Well, you do what my father used to say is the best solution in any situation: you hire a professional. But that could wait till tomorrow. I finished the evening off with a couple of drinks and a sandwich somewhere. I had a few friends in Atlanta, naturally, but not enough to be invited to dinner parties every night. Southern hospitality does not seem to be what it was, or it may have been overrated in the first place.

The next morning I had a conference with Amarantha, or maybe I should say that she had a conference with me, since I had very little to say. I told her that I intended to hire a private eye to look into the license plate business, and she agreed to pay him (she was already paying for the wig and the gaudy clothes). Then she asked what I had found on Saint-Fiacre, and I confessed that I had found nothing. Saint-Fiacre was no chauvinist, male or otherwise, no anti-Semite, no racist, no sexual square, no student shooter, no capitalist. Rather, he seemed to be making a comfortable living off his pathetic appeals in favor of all the underprivileged of the world: surely there was nothing wrong with that.

Amarantha looked both scornful of me and pleased with herself; the tip of her tongue darted between her lips painted a deep strawberry red.

"I am surprised at you," she said. "You are supposed to be so clever, Walter dear, *and* a scout! And you missed an absolutely revolting point. I don't know how it could be used against him, but it is perfectly obvious that your Saint-Fiacre is a cruel, insensitive, arrogant kind of man."

"Hurrah!" I exclaimed. "Who said that?"

"He proved to be so himself. Haven't you read his speech about progress?"

She obviously had been doing some research on her own.

"Yes, I have read it. What of it?"

She produced a notepad and read what was clearly a quotation from the famous speech:

"*. . . And if we want to keep our country, I mean Europe, on the highway of progress, we have to stop being permissive, indulgent, sometimes even tolerant. As that reactionary thinker Gabriel Marcel has said: 'It is not children who degenerate, it is parents who resign.' Childhood deserves respect? True. Youth deserves freedom? True again. But that does not mean that childhood and* *youth should not be informed, educated and sometimes disciplined. Our ideals of freedom, equality and fraternity should be hammered into the heads of our young ones at any price. The jungle begets society, society begets tyranny, tyranny begets revolution, revolution begets freedom. Let not freedom beget the jungle!"*

There was a look of triumph on Amarantha's usually languid face.

"So what?" I said. "It all seems rather sensible to me."

"Because you yourself are a reactionary at heart, Walter. Can't you feel how this idea of disciplining children strikes a truly modern person? It is odious! Just odious! The commentator didn't miss it."

"What did he say?"

"That Saint-Fiacre, with all his liberal talk, was a typical, ruthless, adult chauvinist, that he probably believed in beating hell out of small children with straps, whips and a special French instrument which sounds like a cat-o'-nine-tails and is, strangely enough, called a *martinet,* pronounced *martinay,* and that it was no wonder if, with that kind of ideas, he was so deeply anti-American. So there you are."

On first impression, I was frankly disgusted with Amarantha's find. All right, so Saint-Fiacre might believe that a good spanking could do a mischievous boy no harm, he might even be a disciple of King Solomon and profess a "Spare the rod, spoil the child" kind of doctrine. What use could that be to us? On second thought, I decided that I might be in the wrong. After all, I was only partly American, and I hadn't even noticed the passage in question, but Amarantha and the commentator had reacted violently to it: we would be working primarily for an American audience and their reactions counted more than mine. Personally, my contacts with American children had been scanty; most of them had made me yearn for a good, limber birch rod properly macerated in pickle which I would have used not so much on their as on their parents' hides, and that really goes for quite a few modern European parents too, but maybe my reactions were so strong one way only because sound American reactions were just as strong the other way. It would really be rather delightful if we could unleash a flood of good Anglo-Saxon Dickensian child pity against that great Underdog-Appealist, Serge Saint-Fiacre. I was still not enthusiastic, but I was beginning to feel tempted. At that time, of course, I did not realize how close to the bull's-eye Amarantha had inadvertently hit.

"Has the man any children of his own?" I asked. "Is he even married?"

"The journalist doesn't say."

"Give me that paper, please."

I reread the quotation and began to feel much better. I took a pencil, deleted a few words, did not add a single one, and returned the paper to Amarantha.

"What do you think of this?"

Now the quotation read thus:

". . . We have to stop being tolerant. As that reactionary thinker Gabriel Marcel has said: 'It is not children who degenerate.' But that does not mean that childhood and youth should not be disciplined. Our ideals should be hammered into the heads of our young ones. Let not freedom beget the jungle!"

"What does it mean?" asked Amarantha.

"It means, as your journalist very aptly put it—we will steal the expression from him—that Saint-Fiacre is a dirty adult chauvinist. Children, according to him, are made to be disciplined, pommeled, brainwashed. Yes, this is an excellent quotation. The trouble is we won't find many so good. But one little sniff of that kind of thing may be enough. We can add as many of our own as we wish so long as we have this one to fall back upon. 'As Mr. Saint-Fiacre has repeatedly maintained, in particular in his speech on progress—' You know the stuff. But the children of Europe will get up on their frail little legs and declare: 'No, Mr. Saint-Fiacre, we shall not be disciplined, pommeled and brainwashed any longer. For too many centuries we have suffered in the ghetto of the nursery. The hour has come when we shall demand our sacred rights.' I've heard there have already been a few recriminations among teen agers this side of the ocean: we will see to it that Europe does not fall too far behind. Amarantha, I truly believe you've got something."

I was still ruminating Amarantha's quotation whose value to us had been so brilliantly enhanced by my pencil—I swore I would never despise editors any more: that little bit of editing could save us all from Bill B. Bopkins III—when Chirpie rang up. He sounded absolutely dejected.

"What is it, Chirpie? They don't want to cough up?"

No, it appeared they were quite ready to cough up. They had readily agreed to double the amount they first offered, and to pay half of it in advance. The money would be delivered in cash, and Chirpie would pretend he had lent it over the years to a friend who had suddenly come into a fortune and repaid the ten thousand. I advised him to exchange the bills before banking them: they could be stolen money. He thanked me for the advice, but remained disconsolate.

"Come now, Chirpie, what's the matter?"

The matter was that Messrs. Laurel and Hardy refused to let Chirpie buy a Browning Olympian. They absolutely insisted on his getting a Ruger.

"Isn't the Ruger a good gun?"

"Wally, you don't know what you're talking about. A Ruger 77 bolt action is one of the finest rifles ever made."

"Then why don't you want a Ruger?"

"Oh! I don't mind a Ruger, but I want the Browning Olympian."

"Why don't they want you to have one?"

"I dunno."

He was nearly crying into the phone.

"Is it because it is more expensive?"

"Well, it is, about five times as much as the Ruger, but I said I would buy it out of my own money, I mean out of the ten thousand they'd give me, and still they said no; I had to use the Ruger."

"Any special Ruger that they already have?"

"No, a Ruger I could buy where I wanted. I'll go to old Sam and order one from him. But I wanted a Browning Olympian!"

"Are there any other good rifles?"

"Sure. Winchester 70. Remington 700 BDL."

"Did you suggest using one of those?"

"Yeah, I did."

"What did they say?"

"It had to be a Ruger."

It didn't make sense. I know some publicity stunts which require your using a special kind of vacuum cleaner, but obviously Ruger couldn't use Saint-Fiacre's murder for publicity. "The gun that killed an anti-American adult chauvinist"? Absurd.

"Listen, Chirpie," I said. "When everything is finished and you are back here with a lot of money, who is going to prevent your buying the Browning?"

That dried his tears. He thanked me with effusion and hung up.

I opened the yellow pages and began looking for a discreet private detective. I didn't want to get involved with the large out-fits, who could afford to become inquisitive about me. I wanted to be able to give a false name, pay cash, and receive my information without anybody being able to trace whom it went to. Finally, my choice fell on the Snipe and Boudin Agency—"No job too small or too big." It is, I know, somewhat strange that I chose that particular agency, but there were reasons. One, I felt a little bashful asking professionals such a simple thing as tracing the owner of a car and that "No job too small" business put me at my ease. Two, the address was Pryor Street, which meant that Snipe and Boudin were not fancy, expensive, independent agents of whom I felt rather shy, but poor beggars who would be happy to earn a few bucks and ask no questions. Finally, I may have been favorably impressed by the second partner's name being obviously of French origin: after all, I do have quite a few drops of French blood myself. Whatever the reason, I decided to do business with Snipe and Boudin.

At first, I intended to call them on the phone, but then I changed my mind. I didn't want to give them any number at which they could call me back; and, besides, I had never seen a live private dick and I was curious. So I borrowed the Escort again, changed into my disreputable outfit and drove to Pryor Street. For some reason I had decided to give my name as Harold McIntosh.

Pryor Street is crowded, noisy, smelly, run-down. The Agency was located in the dirtiest of all its buildings.

In the hall several empty bottles of peach wine were scattered. The wine itself had not gone very far. It had sojourned for a brief time in the stomach of some drunk and then had been liberally poured on the floor. The stink was abominable.

A prehistoric elevator took me up two floors. A brass plate covered with fingerprints told me I was entering into the offices of the Snipe and Boudin Detective Agency.

A huge room with a high ceiling had been partitioned into several small cubicles. In the first cubicle an elderly secretary in a miniskirt was playing hostess. Her teeth were long and yellow.

"May I help you?" she said.

"Er, yes," I stuttered. "I just wanted to ask if Mr. Snipe could be so good as to help me find the owner of a car. My name is Harold McIntosh, and I . . . I have seen it parked very often a block away from my house. Especially when I come home unexpectedly. Now Mrs. McIntosh and me not being on the best of terms. . . ."

The old hag interrupted me with some impatience.

"You'll tell all that to Mr. Snipe. You know the license plate number?"

"Yes, of course."

I took a pencil and a notepad that was on her desk and jotted the number down. It was, as I recall, CKW-861.

Then she screamed:

"Mr. Snipe! There's a man here who wants to see you. About a car."

She was waving the sheet of note paper on which I had scribbled the number.

The door opened and a short, thin, lantern-jawed man came in. He was our Mr. Laurel.

"Hullo," he said. "I'm Joe Snipe. Nice to meet you. What can I do for you?"

Behind him, I caught a glimpse of the bulky figure of our Mr. Hardy. Undoubtedly, he was the junior partner of the firm.

"Here's the number of the car," said the hostess, and she went on waving the sheet of paper under the very nose of Mr. Snipe.

4

"So what did you do?" Amarantha asked when I told her the story.

"I snatched the paper, told the old hag that I was used to conducting my own business and gave Snipe a good talking to. Then I walked out with the paper in my pocket."

"A talking to? About what?"

"Oh! I don't know. When you're embarrassed, it's generally the best way out. Abuse the poor fellow until he doesn't know if he is standing on his feet or on his head."

"But what could you tell him?"

"Nonsense. That he had no business hiring old witches to play the part of hostesses. That he was a despicable crook running a lousy establishment. (Establishment, as you know, is now a dirty word.) That he had no business tricking honorable people into visiting that hovel of his. That if he wanted to get drunk he ought to learn how to use a bathroom. And so on. He really didn't understand what was happening to him. And before he could think of something to say, I was out."

"You don't think he suspected anything?"

"He probably suspected I was crazy."

"Don't you think he will recognize you if he sees you again?"

"I don't intend to let him. You see, I didn't really enjoy his company."

"So where does that leave us?" Amarantha leaned back in her presidential chair and began nibbling at a pencil with her small, sharp teeth.

"In my opinion," I said, "it leaves us in the clear. Snipe and Boudin do not look like G-men. Of course, there is nothing impossible about some government agency using them as go-betweens, but if you ask me, it is improbable, especially after the ludicrous happenings at Watergate and other places. I don't mean that the government has laid off all secret activities, but they must be terribly afraid of being compromised, and to associate with a firm like Snipe and Boudin would compromise anyone. I believe we are safe."

"Safe! Walter dear, what do you mean exactly by safe?"

"Safe to assume that this plot to assassinate Saint-Fiacre is not an official proposition and consequently that we may risk turning it to our advantage."

Amarantha Munchin is not an adventuress, neither is she a coward. Anyway whatever physical risks were involved would be run by me, not by her, so, after I had sworn to her that even under third degree pressures I would not reveal the part she was taking in the whole business, she gave me the green light.

We began to prepare for what I, in my mind, called Operation Holy Hansom, that being the exact translation of the name Saint-Fiacre.

The preparation was threefold.

As far as Chirpie was concerned, little was to be done for the present. He was expecting his new passport, which would take a few weeks. Laurel and Hardy, or, I should say, Snipe and Boudin, had been a little annoyed at his not having one, but they had not offered to provide him with a false one. He was still a little sad about the Browning Olympian, but I finally found a way to console him when he told me that the Ruger was an all-American rifle whereas the Browning was manufactured in Belgium.

"Can't you see that it will be much more pleasurable to dispatch the anti-American bastard with an all-American rifle? You don't want him to die a death "made in Europe," do you? You want to sock it to him with a good U.S. bullet from a good U.S. weapon, don't you?"

As I said before, Chirpie is a patriot, and that finally soothed his hurt feelings.

"Yeah," he said with a bloodthirsty drawl, "a good U.S. bullet in his dirty French noodle. That'll teach all them Krauts!"

The geography was vague but the spirit was excellent and I let it stand at that.

Since I intended to go to France at the same time as Chirpie, we decided, Amarantha and I, that I would take a vacation from Munchin and Munchin and indicate that I was going to spend it in Europe. If questioned at a later time, I didn't want to appear having lied to anyone, because that would have suggested premeditation. When he learned I was taking a holiday, Billy-boy roared with laughter.

"Already worked enough, eh? Well, I'm glad things seem to have blown over a bit."

I was a little disconcerted by his knowing so much about me. As a matter of fact nothing had blown over, only France was not the country whose climate disagreed with me, but it was interesting that Billy-boy should have made inquiries about me. Even Amarantha didn't know I had been in trouble, or at least wasn't supposed to know it. I didn't doubt that Billy-boy had imparted to her any information he might have gathered. In fact, the imparting might very well have been the ulterior motive for the gathering. That meant that Billy-boy was somewhat afraid of me, or of my influence over Miss Munchin, which made me feel good.

"I don't know about blown over," I said. "I just happen not to be a work horse like yourself. Six months at the grind is enough for me. I'm rather better at resting than at working anyway."

"It's a matter of grit!" said Billy-boy.

"Or of grits," I replied.

Billy-boy didn't like this thrust at his hard-working deep-country origins. I'll admit it wasn't quite fair play, but his innuendoes about things blowing over hadn't been either.

The last and most important thing that remained to be done was somewhat preparing public opinion. I wanted people to be a little more acquainted with the name Serge Saint-Fiacre than they were, and I also wanted some of them to be able to say "I told you so" when he would die a victim to his adult chauvinist opinions. Moreover, some probability to our version of the events had to be managed. Remember that we didn't know who actually wanted to get rid of Saint-Fiacre: it could be for political or for private reasons; and whoever was behind the plot could either want to remain unknown—in that case our claim to the murder would remain unchallenged—or, on the contrary, he might want to make some sort of publicity of it, as, for instance, the Palestinians. In the second case, there would be a rather ridiculous contest "We did him in—No, we did" in which the advantage would be on our side, since I hoped that we would have Chirpie by that time, but not such a great advantage that some preparation wouldn't come in useful too. That meant a trip to New York, at the expense of Munchin and Munchin, and although I don't particularly like the dirty, hostile, mercantile city, I do have a few friends there, whom it would be nice to look up.

So, one morning I flew into Kennedy, and as soon as we had landed, I called George Broker, who is a journalist and nevertheless a very nice fellow.

"George," I said, "I have just landed on an Air France flight from Paris." (I had taken the shuttle to the international arrivals building.) "I've got an intuition that you are going to come and pick me up." (I hate driving in heavy traffic and taxis give me claustrophobia.) "You might even," I added generously, "buy me lunch."

"Walter! Old fellow! I'm glad to hear your voice! D'you have anything for me?"

"Nothing we would want to discuss over the phone, George."

He whistled. "It's that good?"

"Not bad. But let me be honest about it, George. It's not something I could give you free."

He whistled again. "Oh! you mean it's *that* good!"

I was known to be fairly liberal with the little tidbits of information that came my way.

I sighed. "Times are hard, George, and I have to work for a living."

"Quite a change, eh? Poor fellow. You were not raised that way. Well, let's hope for better times. And I shall certainly be very happy to wine and lunch you."

"And to pick me up."

"I'm on my way."

George Broker is the dearest fellow. He is fortyish, baldish, he wears very thick glasses, he is something of a prude, not one bad feeling ever crossed his soul, and he thinks everybody is just as kind and honest as he. With all that he is not a bad journalist, quite the opposite. As I remarked to Amarantha, good feelings sell exceedingly well and George possesses that tremendous advantage that his are absolutely sincere. He is not extremely patriotic where America is concerned, but tell him what Ruanda's flag looks like, and he will wave it with gusto. He is absolutely straight, but he wrote a series of magnificent articles for the defense of lesbians' rights. He was expelled from Egypt for taking Israel's side during the Six Days War, and later from Israel for writing a sympathetic paper about Palestinians. Sympathy, that's his key word. And sympathy is very often better than perspicacity when you want to get the whole picture, at one glance. In George Broker's case it even paid well. I certainly had no scruples about that lunch, which I knew would be simple but good.

Some time later George arrived in one of his crumpled grey suits, shook me by the hand with great effusiveness and asked anxiously:

"So! How are the prostitutes?"

I said that George was a prude and I am still saying it. If you think that George had ever had any personal interest in prostitutes, you are completely off the mark. I don't think he has ever talked to one besides politely saying "No, Madam; thank you very much, I'm sure." Not that he despises them: he has just never had the opportunity to exercise his sympathy where prostitutes are concerned. What he was referring to was a quite different matter. Some of you may remember that approximately at that time, under the guidance of their labor unions, French prostitutes had first gone on strike and then occupied several churches in order to impress the government with their seriousness about whatever it was, civil rights, social security, sabbaticals, I don't know. Finally the whole business boiled down but, for a few days, violence had been in the air. Now, George Broker is a very sweet, peaceful person; the sight of blood makes him faint; not only wouldn't he hurt a fly, he wouldn't hurt a flea either; but, nevertheless, he is a guerrilla warfare freak. Don't feed him; give him a guerrilla war somewhere in the world: he will be happy. And although prostitutes did not seem very promising from that standpoint, he still hoped that there would be some fighting around the rue des Martyrs in Paris.

"Back at work, I assume," I replied. "George, will you help with my luggage?"

George dutifully carried my leather bags into the trunk of his very old Mercedes, and we plunged into the grey cloud of stinking, polluted air, that New Yorkers tell you no sane person could do without. We left the bags at my hotel and then repaired to some joint in the Village, whose name I don't remember. I mean: anyone can roast a piece of beef and do reasonably well. I didn't bother to go over my rigmarole concerning single malt whisky, since George knew it already and I didn't expect to meet the waiter again, but ordered a gin gimlet straight up right away. George had a martini, and he let me choose the wine, which was reasonably good (Côte-de-Beaune Village in case you're interested). But it was only after lunch, when George was seemingly engrossed with an enormous pie and I was sipping an acceptable expresso that he finally looked straight at me through his thick, benevolent glasses and said:

"Well, Walter, how much?"

Our rules were as follows. I would quote a price. He would or would not express interest. Then I would tell my story. If he thought he could do something with it, he would pay cash and I would not tell the story to any one else for a week; if he thought he couldn't, no money would change hands and he would never tell a living soul what he had heard from me free of charge.

"For you, one thousand."

"O.K. Out with it."

I had to begin with background information.

"You know, my dear George, that France traditionally is a country where the word Family means a lot and where the *pater familias*—which means good ol' Dad—has virtually had a right of life and death over all its members until very recently indeed." (That was untrue, but *virtually* is a very good word.) "You realize that Napoleonic law allowed the husband to beat his wife, which he did frequently, and then both parents would conclude an alliance and have a go at the children. Physical punishment has always been considered as perfectly normal in France, and I don't mean solemn caning or symbolic paddling. Many parents keep special whips, called *martinets,* to punish their children with, and . . ."

George interrupted. "How d'you spell that?" he asked, and took a note. The fact that he had taken his notebook out was encouraging.

"I myself," I went on, "sat once at a table where the father had a riding crop by his plate, and whenever one of the eight children did something to displease him, for instance, opened his mouth to speak, or held his knife incorrectly, the father—a very distinguished gentleman, by the way—would land him one on the wrist, and the child would immediately say 'Thank you.'"

I had actually witnessed the scene, and must confess that it had made an unpleasant impression on me, although certainly not to the extent that it made me cry, but big tears welled in George's blue eyes.

"Poor kids," he muttered, "poor kids," and took a note.

I hate children being referred to as kids; if I had any, it would make me feel like a goat; but, for once, pleasure at the sensation I was creating took precedence over my annoyance.

"Also," I continued, "when I was a student at a very fashionable school run by Jesuits—that was before my father came to this country—I remember very clearly one of my classmates being kicked from one end of the hall to the other by his tender Papa, only because he had made some bad grades that quarter."

"Poor, poor kid," mumbled George. "Was the father an alcoholic or something?"

"I don't know if he was an alcoholic or not. The only thing I can tell you is that he was a baron."

"Goodness gracious! A baron!" exclaimed George, as if he had so far believed barons to have a monopoly on patience and sweetness of temperament.

"Another friend of mine, a girl, if it matters, on the day when she was twenty-one—which made her an adult, you know—received a beautiful present from her father, a signet ring, I think it was. And he congratulated her nicely on her coming of age and added: "But don't imagine that will prevent my slapping your face if you deserve it."

"Poor kid," said George, and made yet another note.

"Well, you can imagine that by the year 1968 of Our Lord the situation was rather explosive." (Journalists adore explosive situations.) "The Revolution broke out, and it was truly a revolution of the young against adult chauvinists." (I noticed with pleasure that George made a note of that happy expression.) "For a whole month the Revolution raged." (Yes, it did, although to my mind a Revolution which keeps on raging for a whole month and does not make one victim was not very serious in the first place, but we didn't have to go into that.) "As you know, even progressive parties, even Communist workers refused to help the young people of France vindicate their rights. And still they fought. They occupied the Sorbonne, they made speeches in the classrooms, they made love in the library, in short they behaved with understandable rashness. The whole costume room of the Théâtre de France was torn to pieces. The pressure had been too much. The disorder which everybody could see, and which was only a natural reaction against the order of yesterday, played into the hands of the government. An amnesty was proclaimed; some superficial reforms were granted; high school students were sometimes allowed to smoke in the classroom and were not forced to stand up every time a teacher came in. . . . That was about it. The Great Youthful Revolution of May '68 had somehow petered out, because the rebels had no leaders, no organization, no logistics, no doctrine, no arms: only their faith in themselves and their bare hands. They were abandoned by everyone and so they had to submit and bide their time."

George is an articulate fellow himself; nevertheless, he was taking notes; he obviously thought that some of my formulas would sound right in his article.

"Now," I went on after ordering a Rémy Martin from the waiter, "the backlash began. When students were demonstrating on the streets, there was little adults could do against them, short of machine-gunning them on the Champs-Elysées. But now, each student was back in his home, at the mercy of his father, his mother, his teachers, and the concierge, who is generally also a policeman. They couldn't take them when they were united, so they took them one by one. And being frightened, the adults resorted to all those old methods of oppression which they knew so well: 70 hours of study a week, thrashings for poor grades, kneeling on peas. . . ."

"Kneeling on what?!"

"On peas. Dry peas, naturally. Try it. It's a very good method of persuasion. Licking dusty floors, going to bed without dinner, slaps in the face for the least show of spirit. . . . All that was very well in another century, my dear George, but in our days, with the media being what they are, it just won't work. As all tyrannies, adult tyranny feels that its end is near; so it becomes ten times more tyrannical; and so it will be destroyed."

"Amen. Do you think there will be a guerilla war?"
I lowered my voice.

"That's exactly the point. The young people of France see every-day in the paper or on the TV screen that the only means which allows the weak somehow to put themselves on an equal footing with the strong is violence. Not disorderly violence, which is obnoxious and ineffective, but organized violence, which is very effective indeed. There are enough how-to books on the market to teach them all the basics of clandestine work, sabotage, assassina-tion and the like. Photocopying methods make it easy to com-municate with hundreds of people at the same time. The young people have been oppressed and so they have become deceitful. Now these secular habits of deceit are going to be put to good use. Leaders are emerging. Weapons are being stocked in secret places. Networks are forming on a very strict need-to-know basis. You know how cruel young people can be. . . ."

"That does not surprise me. After all they've been through, poor kids. . . ."

"Well, this cruelty will now serve. Boys will cease tearing off butterflies' wings, they will go and strangle their grandmothers. Do you believe that, George?"

"You do express it with a lot of feeling. I didn't even know you had it in you to feel so strongly for them. But we all know what children are capable of. So you expect a kind of *Clockwork Orange* guerilla war?"

"No, not *Clockwork Orange*. Organised. Systematic. With committees—they call them soviets—of young people condemning adults to death and executing the sentence. You have to realize that guns and explosives being what they are, a fourteen-year-old boy is just as dangerous as a thirty-year-old man. There is nothing that we do that they couldn't if they were taught. And they can teach themselves. No," I shook my head, "I think that some very dark days are in store for France, George. And then for the rest of

Europe. And why not for this country too? You can hide a .22 pistol in a school bag, a hand grenade in a lunch-box. It is as easy to blow a detested teacher skyhigh as to put sneezing powder on his desk or glue on his chair. I can imagine what family dinners will look like a few weeks from now. The mother serves the soup and wonders if the daughter hasn't poisoned it. The father looks up from his newspaper and wonders if the son is not implicated in the murder described on the front page. Think what the Hitler Jugend did during the last days of the Third Reich! The young are always ready to sacrifice themselves, and how do you fight a war against your own children who tell you: 'Come and kill me'?"

I leaned back on my chair and George leaned forward across the table.

"Walter," he said, "do you actually know of any such organization?"

I nodded.

"*The* organization," I corrected.

"What's its name? Can you tell me?"

I appeared to hesitate. "George, I know I can trust you. It would make it very awkward for me if anybody ever learned that you got the name from me."

"Nobody ever will. I promise. And you can tell those kids of yours that I understand and sympathize. If they revolt against such oppression as you described, it shows they are just good, plucky kids. That's all they are. Right?"

"You wait till they begin kidnapping old gentlemen from rest homes and burn their toes to get their safes' combinations."

He winced. "I hope it won't come to that. But I feel like you do, that a guerilla war is probably unavoidable. Now, the name?"

I lowered my voice to a whisper and, having gulped down the remains of Rémy Martin:

"*Les Enfants de Mai,*" I said. "The Children of May."

And the name was somehow so aptly found, it was at the same time so innocent and so sinister, that I couldn't help shivering. George made a note.

*

From then on, and until George's article was published, I was in honor bound not to disclose anything about les Enfants de Mai to anyone for a whole week. But that didn't prevent me from calling a very dear friend of mine, Olivia Trent. She was not free for dinner but could manage it for supper. I took her to a very exclusive club to which I had belonged earlier and where the personnel knew me for a generous member. The fact that my dues had been left unpaid for quite some time was indifferent to them: on the contrary, they knew that I would tip them liberally enough to make it worth their while to serve me in spite of my irregular position. So we sat at a little table by an old-fashioned bay window on the fiftieth floor and had all Manhattan glittering in the night at our feet. There were roses at the table, and also a bottle of Heidsieck Monopole '64.

Olivia is really very beautiful, as intellectuals go. She has a smooth, oval face with sleek, golden hair very neatly arranged in a cute little bun; she wears very large round glasses; they are so thin that I suspect she doesn't really need them but likes the stylized look they give to her face. She is also very successful in her field and radiates good feelings, although not of the same kind as George. If his speciality is sympathy and his hobby guerilla war, her speciality is admiration and her hobby brilliant young politicians. I remembered she had done very well by J.J.S.S. (in case you don't know who J.J.S.S. is, it shows she didn't do well enough) and I thought it worth while to invest part of George's thousand dollars in an evening with her.

"It's really rather nice here," she said looking around. "I've always wished somebody would invite me here but they tell me you have to be a member."

"Well, yes," I said. "We don't want just anyone to be able to come and spoil the view, or drink the rinse-water, you know what I mean."

She didn't pretend she was unimpressed, which was really very nice on her part. Olivia is a good girl and as honest as a successful person can afford to be. I told her I was just back from France—a scouting expedition.

"Did you find anything interesting to publish?"

"One or two trifles. I don't know if my boss will like them. You know how publishers are. They want to be sure that something will sell. I don't blame them: after all, it's their money. And a book that will sell in France probably won't sell in America. So . . ."

I changed the subject, and we chattered away about mutual friends: who had left whom and who had moved in with whom, that kind of thing, and then, when the bottle was already half empty, I went back to more intellectual themes.

"You know, Olivia, what annoys me very much is what I found in France that would be of real interest is not a book, not even a manuscript, but a subject for a book. Only who would write it?"

"Why not you, Walter?"

"Oh, I couldn't. Not my style at all. Maybe I could dash off a thriller, or a play, but this would take research, dates, footnotes, indexes—Not for me, thank you."

"So you mean it would be a serious book? What about?"

"I guess you haven't heard about Serge Saint-Fiacre?"

"It does ring a bell."

"The President of the European International Party."

"Oh! yes. What kind of man is he? Did you meet him?"

"Not personally. We have common friends. I should rather say, acquaintances. They rave about him. They think he is going to be one of the great statesmen of the century. I've looked a little into the matter, and I do not doubt that we'll hear more about him pretty soon."

(That, at least, was true.)

"How old is he?"

"He was born in '35."

"So he's really quite young for a politician," said Olivia with curiosity—professional curiosity, of course—beginning to bubble.

I shrugged my shoulders and took her hand.

"I'm not really interested in politicians. He would make a good subject for a book, I think, or even for a series of serious articles. But not at all in my line. Do you know I missed you very much, Olivia, when I was in France?" I added with a tender inflection in my voice.

She took her hand away.

"Tell me about Saint-Fiacre."

"He's somewhat of an idealist, I'm afraid. Says he does not wear his Legion of Honor because there is not enough honor left in France. That kind of fellow."

Her eyes shone with admiration. I took her hand again. This time she let me hold it, but when I sighed and began expounding on how happy I was to see her again, she interrupted me with some impatience.

"Yes, yes, but what are his political ideas?"

"He thinks that all the peoples of Europe should unite against their governments. Not that he is a Communist, not at all, but he feels that the balance of power in the world can be established only if Europe unites."

"Everybody feels that."

I caressed her hand gently and she didn't object, so long as I went on talking about Saint-Fiacre.

"Yes, I'm not saying that is very original. But what is, is this. He thinks that, although all European governments *say* they want to unite, they *do* exactly the opposite. He proves rather convincingly that all the people who at present wield power and enjoy wealth would lose everything they have if Europe suddenly became one nation. It stands to reason: there would be only one government, only one parliament, instead of several. Same thing for the Army and the Navy. Only one general-in-chief instead of about ten. So, according to him, present governments have been sabotaging unified Europe for a quarter of a century, and it's time they should stop."

"But of course!" Olivia exclaimed. "Why did we never think of it? It's the only possible explanation! For twenty-five years, even more, all those *established* men have been pretending they were ready to destroy their own *establishment*. But they would have had to be real idealists to do it! So they conspired among themselves *not* to do it!"

"Yes, that's what Saint-Fiacre says." My hand crept on to her arm. "That the Europe of peoples is still a dream, whereas the Europe of the governments is already a fact, although a secret one. He calls it the European paradox: heads of nations agree secretly never to agree publicly, they unite on the sly in order never to unite in the open. He really has a few strong words about it."

I had made up some of the strong words, but what did it matter? The opinions were truly S.F.'s. Olivia would not make a book of it: she was definitely incapable of writing a book, but she would write an article, and people would talk about it and quote it with glee: although France and the U.S. are still Allies, I believe, and although history binds them rather close together, there are few things American journalists enjoy more than trouble in France, or French journalists more than trouble in America.

Anyhow, I had done what I could and what else I did that evening does not concern this story and must remain strictly off the record. If Olivia may have found some encouragement for her admiration for Saint-Fiacre in whatever feelings—sporadic feelings, by the way—I may inspire her with, that has no real bearing on the matter. Neither Olivia nor George are gullible people. What I had told them was the truth, or so close to the truth that it might have been the truth. It is true that French parents do beat up their children from time to time; it is true that the children, while they are children, sometimes resent the treatment (although they are generally grateful for it later); it is true that the so-called May Revolution was entirely operated by teenagers; it is true that Europe takes a long time in the making; it is true that many people stand to lose many things when it is finally made; it was true that Serge Saint-Fiacre made an excellent subject for an article. If George and Olivia served me well, I didn't serve them badly either, and when, after two more days in New York, pleasantly spent with old friends squandering George's contribution, I flew back to Atlanta, I felt that everyone had gained by what I had done, with the possible—and hoped for—exception of Mr. Bill B. Bopkins III.

5

Nothing much had happened in Atlanta during my absence. Chirpie had bought his Ruger. It was walnut, he informed me, real American walnut, and it weighed 6½ pounds, and it was 42 inches long. The caliber was 308, whatever it means. I am a fairly good shot myself but all these technicalities bore me to death. I was interested to learn, though, that after letting Chirpie buy the Ruger for himself, Snipe and Boudin had confiscated it from him. It would be sent to France, they exclaimed, in a box full of golf clubs. Chirpie would have preferred to carry it himself, but Snipe managed to persuade him it would be rather risky trying to carry a Ruger 77 aboard an airplane—"Yep! Very risky!" added Boudin—and Chirpie bowed to their experience. They even took the scope from him—a Leopold 6 power.

"So we'll have to do the sighting in in France, I guess," he concluded.

Amarantha was kind to me although a little nervous. Mr. Bopkins was becoming more and more insistent about a merger which represented security, and she couldn't tell him what her last hope consisted in and why she was always postponing her decision. At the same time, she didn't want to discourage him, because she only half-believed in the possibility of success. I tried to be with her as much as I could. For one thing, it was rather pleasant, and for another, I was afraid that she would blurt out our secret to Billyboy if he caught her in a moment of defenselessness: so I tried to keep all her moments of defenselessness for myself; the advantage was twofold.

Finally, Chirpie telephoned to say that his passport had arrived. Snipe was due to call him that night to ask about it. Must he tell him? Of course, he must. The next day he called again.

"We're leaving day after tomorrow, Wally. I'm gonna fly on a real jumbo jet right across the ocean to where the Limeys are."

"Are you flying to England then?"

"No, to Frog-country. No offense meant to you, Wally. I never believed you're really French, you know. You're much too nice."

"Thank you, Chirpie. Do you remember the company and flight number?"

All he remembered was "Delta," but that didn't matter. The office secretary is very efficient. I asked her to call Delta for a Mr. Chirpwood who was flying to France and had got confused about his connection. She neatly typed all the data for my absent-minded friend. So that was that. It had been just playing so far, but the real adventure was about to begin.

Let me give you here a word of explanation. I don't pretend to be more honest than the next fellow, and I had been known to live by my wits, but I'm not an adventurer, and I did realize that murder is serious business. To tell you the truth, even the first time I put on that beastly wig, I felt my heart sink a little and had to fight back a ridiculous fear that I would be arrested by the first cop who saw me—whether for wearing a wig or for planning the assassination of a politician, I didn't know. My short and unlucky attempt at surveillance had given me all the thrills of James Bond, and as to the scene in Mr. Snipe's office, when I had all but thwarted my own plans at the very beginning, it said more for my presence of mind than for my ability at doing clandestine work. So, when I realized that things had really begun moving, that, if I didn't want to make a fool of myself, I had now to go through with it, my heart sank just a little lower, and I wondered for a few minutes if it wouldn't be better to leave Munchin and Munchin to its own devices, or rather to Mr. Bopkins's, and to start looking for some more respectable way of earning a living, like courting a rich widow with a rich temperament or even advertising toothpaste. But there was something in my blood that made me shrink before the idea of shrinking, back out before the idea of backing out.

I remembered in time the family motto, *Nil Obstat*, which means: I'll cross that bridge when I come to it, or, more precisely, I'll tolerate no obstacles. Incidentally, that motto was borrowed from us by the Roman Church, which prints it on most of its publications to indicate that it sees no objection to the material therein. Since it definitely would see quite a few objections to the material contained in this book, I have even contemplated the idea of printing the family motto on the first page, just for the fun of it, but the charming young woman who looks over my shoulder while I am typing tells me it would not be in good taste, and I tend to agree with her.

In any case, I intended to remain as far from the murder as I could, and as to the press conference that I wanted to organize later on, there was no crime in that, and a lot of fun. The only point on which I would be at variance with the law was, as far as I could see, the fact that I did not intend to tattle on poor Chirpie. Well, too bad for the law. I would be very careful and pretend I had known nothing in advance.

I wanted to arrive in France before Chirpie, and I asked our very efficient secretary to arrange for a convenient flight. This time our very efficient secretary did not deserve her reputation: we were already in the shoulder of the season, she was told—the shoulder! who can have thought of such a ridiculous expression—and all seats were booked. It took me a trip to the company's office and some flirting with the pretty clerk—fortunately she was Cuban; Americans sometimes prefer their conscience to my sex-appeal—to get everything settled.

I packed my things in my leather bags—Lancel, naturally—kissed Amarantha good-bye, promised her a gallon of *My Sin* in small bottles (you should always buy perfume in small bottles), promised her that whatever happened she would not be involved (I might be a cad, but I am, after all, for better or for worse, a gentleman of sorts), did not promise that I would be faithful to her (she didn't count on that), and made her promise me once again that Mr. Bopkins would not learn anything from her about our plans:

"He would make a cartoon of it all," I told her.

She did not smile. "I still am not sure it is not just a cartoon, you know," she said.

I had prepared a surprise for her. "*A propos* of cartoons," I said lightly, "you should open *Time* magazine. There is one there that you should like."

Olivia had been as good as my word. That very morning I had

read a long article by her, describing the career and ideas of Serge
Saint-Fiacre. Where did she get all the information I had been
looking for in vain? At any rate I was sure, knowing Olivia, that
she had not made it up. I suppose there is something to be said
after all in favor of professionals. She had dug up a whole biog-
raphy, numerous quotations and even three pictures. On one of
them he was haranguing a group of workmen in overalls. He
himself was in shirt sleeves and in suspenders; his triangular face
looked more triangular still because of the open jaws; in fact it
made me think of the front end of a shark which had been used for
publicity by a fairly recent best seller that Munchin and Munchin
did not publish. On the second one, he was voting. His hand was
still on the envelope that was being slipped into the receptacle
provided for the will of the people; but his face was turned toward
the audience, and it wore a very sly, very self-satisfied smile, with
eyes twinkling and the corners of the mouth turned upwards,
somewhat after the fashion of alligators. Snake, wolf, shark, alligator, I am being rather incoherent but I am just trying to convey
what I saw. I might add that his alligator's smile, with lips closely
knit together, looked as if it had a zipper to open and close it.
Mainly to close it. Meanwhile his ears were still pointing upward,
Mephistopheles-like. In other words, he looked just a little bit out
of the ordinary for a Latin type, but frankly obnoxious when you
considered him with Anglo-Saxon eyes. On the third picture, he
was bent in two over the hand of some Countess who played in
European society the part of what the French call a locomotive: in
other words she was one of the unhappy few who have saddled
themselves with the ridiculous duty of setting the fashion. As
everyone knows, they retaliate by making the fashion as ridiculous
as they can. On that picture, most of what you could see of Saint-
Fiacre was his behind, and I must say he had an unpleasant behind. Something tense and mean about it, something nearly feminine and at the same time vulgar. . . . Obviously it was not the
behind of a gentleman, which was all right with me. As a matter of
fact, I had had a rather weird feeling looking at Monsieur Saint-
Fiacre's shrewd, calculating, impudent, intensely alive face and
thinking that I would be instrumental in bringing about its dis-
solution; I had even wondered what this face would look like with

eyes closed, dead; but the behind made me forget all about these unhealthy ideas. Obviously Monsieur Saint-Fiacre was pressing the two halves of his behind very closely together, which always speaks for a distrustful, cowardly, villainous kind of character. That kind of behind deserved whatever Fate had in store for it. I loathed the Countess for giving her hand to kiss to such an obvious bouncer.

Amarantha took *Time* from my hands, and I walked toward the door without looking back. The secretary—who was odd-job woman with Munchin and Munchin—drove me to the airport. She was not bad-looking and I kissed her good-bye too, and promised her a quart of Chanel N° 5. The flight was uneventful and the next morning here I was at the Charles de Gaulle Airport, presenting my American passport to the smart police officer with the small moustache.

The passport business will bear some explaining. Being my father's son, the name that figures on my *French* passport (I hold double nationality, and although the Americans do not recognize my Frenchmanship, the French accept my Americanhood whenever I use it) is Walter de Walter. Whenever the Americans saw this passport—and they did from time to time—they took me for a full-blooded Frenchman and listed me under D: De Walter. My *American* passport read otherwise and I have to explain why. When my father, Hubert de Walter, came over to the United States and decided to become a citizen, he had to sign a form solemnly forswearing any title of nobility he might have held. This is standard procedure, and there is not one shoe-shine boy from Sicily who, on becoming an American citizen, has not forsworn all his titles. My father had no title, but he had the "de," which is sometimes interpreted as a sign of untitled nobility. He was reluctant to abandon it altogether, but he also wished to abide by the rules of his new adopted country (I ought to say: one of his new adopted countries). My father was very good at abiding by rules—and making the best of them. So he changed his name, Hubert de Walter, to Hubert D. Walter, and my official *American* name is Walter D. Walter, listed under W in all phone books, police records, and the like. I found such an arrangement rather convenient. To go back to my story, it was now a matter of history that Mr.

Walter, an American citizen, had left the U.S. and entered France. Whatever other trip he wanted to take could be taken under the name of M. de Walter, French citizen, with no one being the wiser.

The first thing I did after going through customs was to walk up to a phone and dial Nénette's number. Three rings and I hung up. I dialed again. Two rings and I hung up. I dialed again and let it ring.

This, as you may have guessed, was a code. But do not deduce that Nénette was engaged in any spying or counterspying activities. The activities Nénette was—and I devoutly hope still is—engaged in were of an entirely different character. In many respects she was a very old-fashioned girl. Exactly as if she had been living in the middle of the nineteenth century, she had one "pocketbook lover" and a succession of "heart lovers." In other words, she lived in a pretty little apartment in the seventeenth district (by cranking your neck and running the risk of falling off the balcony you could manage to catch a glimpse of one of the corners of the Arc de Triomphe) at the expense of a Monsieur Gillet who had a jewelry store on the Rue de la Paix. This Monsieur Gillet was quite an elderly man and had very little use for a mistress, but he kept one because it was done. From time to time though, he would come to the apartment (never without calling first) and let Nénette minister to his waning needs. Also, from time to time, he would take her to dinner or even on a weekend to Deauville, to show his friends that he too had a mistress. He took great pride in Nénette's prettiness, and also, strange to say, in her circle of intellectual acquaintances. "My little friend is not a whore as some other people's," he would say. "She reads Jean-Paul Sartre and has even met him at a party." I, for my part, would not swear that Nénette had ever read two lines of Jean-Paul Sartre, but she probably did meet him at some cocktail party or other. Since her protector was not very exacting, Nénette found herself free most of the time and she put that freedom to good advantage. Not financially though: let it be understood that Nénette was an honest girl: she saw nothing wrong in being paid for work but she would have been horrified at the idea of accepting money for pleasure. Whence the "heart-lovers." The word *heart* may well strike some of my American readers as funny, but unjustly so. The French do have some very crude words concerning all the physical functions of the body, but they have no expressions corresponding to our words "sex" (considered as an activity), "sex-appeal," "to have sex with someone," etc. For them, everything is *l'amour,* and if anyone were to be surprised and even a little doubtful about heart-lovers being replaced on an approximately weekly basis, let me reply that the French have foreseen such an objection since they coined the phrase "an innumerable heart." Such a heart was the one that belonged to Nénette, and M. Gillet didn't object, so long as she could be at his disposal at a few hours' notice. Not to hurt anyone's feelings, Nénette had devised that telephone code, in order to know which one of her heart-lovers was calling. Only heart-lovers with some time's standing would receive a code-ring, as a mark of recognition for their services; others got only her number, but, unless she was very bored, she rarely answered un-coded calls. Mine, I am proud to say, she answered with great speed.

"Walter! Darling!" (She always called me *darling,* which she pronounced *darrlene.*) "What time is it? You woke me up."

"Just after twelve. I'm sorry to have called you so early but I couldn't wait to know how you are."

"I'm great."

"I know that, but how do you feel?"

"Feel great too. Where are you?"

"Charlie's airport."

"Going to spend some time in Paris?"

"A few days."

"Why don't you move in with me?"

"Are you alone?"

"No, as a matter of fact I'm not. Hey, Didi, wake up! Wake up, you brute. Wake up, I say. No, not now, Didier. Not now. Some other time maybe. Can't you see I'm in a hurry? For goodness' sake, get your pants on and run. Monsieur Gillet is coming to lunch. That's better. Faster now. Give me a kiss. Mmmm! I love you! Good-bye. What was I saying?"

"You were very kindly suggesting . . ."

"Yes! Of course! Where did you say you were?"

"At the airport."

"Brought a car with you?"

"Not by airplane, silly. I'm going to rent one."

"Oh! I'm disappointed. I love American cars."

"They also can be rented."

"D'you really think so? What do you want for lunch? Snails? Americans always want snails."

"I'm not all that American, Nénette."

"Oh! yes, you are. You just play the Frenchman."

Now, that was a success. Because it is true that in the U.S. I do play the Frenchman, but in France I always play the American. To be told that I played the Frenchman really showed how good I was!

"So, what do you want for lunch?"

"You."

"That's for breakfast, you idiot!"

It was good to talk again to merry, inconsequent, absent-minded, crazy, charming Nénette.

"Whatever you have in the fridge."

"No, *darrlene*. Today is not a whatever day. We must celebrate your homecoming. I'll go and get something."

"All right. What kind of wine will you want?"

That she considered carefully. Being a true Frenchwoman, she knew there are only two serious subjects in life: wine and cuisine.

"How about half a bottle of white and a bottle of red?"

She meant dry white of course.

"What kind of red?"

"Oh! just anything."

She meant: not too light, not too full-bodied either, and not too expensive, because the meal would be simple and should not be overwhelmed. We hung up. I rented a light blue Lincoln-Mercury Continental Mark IV and hit the road. In the U.S. I drive only European cars, but in France I am not above showing off in one of our comfortable monsters. Not in a Cadillac though. There is a saying in France that only pig-farmers would think of driving a Cadillac: it is so showy.

Nénette was standing on her balcony and waved to me as soon as she saw me. She wore a light demi-saison pink dress with huge white flaps to the collar and an interesting inter-flap view.

Nénette, I must add, was, or rather is, a very cute, if not exactly pretty, young woman, on the short side, with artistically tousled black hair, a small, well-formed body and the tiniest feet, which, to me, is a very important point.

The old-fashioned elevator deposited me on the sixth floor in a little less than six minutes. Nénette was waiting for me on the landing and we embraced very tenderly, whatever that young woman who is looking over my shoulder may think of it. With all due apologies, I am faithful if I am not constant and I am not going to say I didn't have a tender spot in my heart for Nénette: I did.

The lunch was very simple. Duck pâté, with which my Puligny-Montrachet went very well; steaks with green peas, which my simple Beaujolais-Village complimented rather nicely; a small slice of Livarot; fresh strawberries and a cup of coffee completed the meal. The brandy we decided to take in the bedroom.

It was already after three in the afternoon when we began to talk business.

"Nénette," I said, "I'll need your help."

"Anything!" she answered.

"First, you have to pledge yourself to utter secrecy."

"What? not even to my bosom friends . . .?"

She has two dozen and I don't blame the males among them.

"Not even to them."

She sighed. "All right then. I'll be mute."

I knew she could be, from past experience. There was no better chum in the world than Nénette, whatever else she might be.

"I'll need a legman I could trust."

"What's wrong with mine?" she pouted.

"Your what?"

"Legs."

Since we were talking a kind of English—many Frenchwomen do talk English, after a fashion—, since she obviously didn't know the word *legman,* and since hers, at that moment, were exposed from hip to toe, she did have a point. I explained what a legman is.

"I'll pay well," I said, "but I want the fellow to be trustworthy, not a coward, not a babbler, and able to run fast or fight back if need be. Not that I expect any fighting. There will probably be more running to do."

"From or after?"

"After, I hope. From, it could happen."

She wrinkled her nose as she does when she tries very hard to think. She doesn't wrinkle it every often.

"Well, there's Fifi," she said. "And Popo. And the Viscount. And Didi of course. And Vava. And. . . . First, you must tell me for whom you work."

"Myself."

"I don't believe you."

"Do I look like such an altruist?"

"I'm sure it must be for the C.I.A. since you're American."

I had never contemplated working for that agency. I'm neither idealistic nor crooked enough. But, on the spur of the moment, I decided it might serve to cover my tracks if I were thought to be employed by that organization. So I said very firmly:

"No, Nénette, I am not working for the C.I.A."

She laughed. "Your nose moves," she said, and kissed it. Your nose is supposed to move in France when you are lying. "Just imagine! How awful! A dirty C.I.A. agent in my bed, when I am a pure little Marxist."

"You are a Marxist?"

"Well, yes. Anyone who is anyone is."

"What?"

"A Marxist."

"Of the Groucho variety, I assume."

"Shut up. You mustn't make fun of Marxism. It's quite the rage. The Viscount is a Maoist. I am a staunch Muscovite. We quarrel."

"In bed?"

"Don't be impertinent. We know better than that, I assure you. The Viscount isn't half bad. Well, if you're working for the enemy, I think you need Fifi."

"Why Fifi?"

"For one thing he is a Trotskiite, and everyone knows Trotsky was in the Americans' pay. Then I imagine he could really get tough if he had to. He is the best. Take Fifi."

"What if I'm working for the opposite side?"

"It doesn't matter. He's still the best. Anyway he says he is a Trotskiite. I don't think he even knows who Trotsky was."

"Do you know who Marx was?"

"Yes, I do!" she said proudly. "He is the one with the large Santa Claus beard, not the one with the small goatee, and not the one with the big moustache."

"What does Fifi do for a living?"

"Anything. Reads manuscripts for publishers. Cleans windows. Babysits. Washes cars. Teaches Latin and Greek. Works as a legman for the C.I.A."

"Is he . . . one of yours?"

"Well, yes, naturally. Not lately though."

"Does he have a code?"

"No. He's one of the uncoded ones."

"Never graduated? I see. Nénette, you'd better give him a code if you are going to allow me to use your phone for my operation. Now, don't say yes without thinking. I can go to a hotel or to another friend, but I like you better. Still, I wouldn't like to get you into trouble. Are you sure your phone's not tapped? We are told that half the phones in France are."

"Mine isn't."

"How do you know?"

"Easy. I called the Viscount—or was it somebody else? I don't remember—and talked to him for an hour about murdering Mitterand. We had all the details pat. It really sounded professional."

"So?"

"So they didn't arrest us. So the phone is not tapped."

"They may not have taken you seriously."

"Oh! Come now! They would at least have called us in to ask us for explanations."

"What would you have said?"

"That we were checking to see if our phones were tapped."

What she said made sense and I decided to leave it at that.

"Now listen, Nénette. I know you are going to jump, and, given the circumstances, the perspective might be interesting, but hear me out. I don't want you to embark on a wild goose chase without getting anything out of it. This business is going to bring me, I hope, a good deal of money. It is only fair that I should . . ."

I was on expenses, you see, and Munchin and Munchin, although not as rich as the C.I.A., still could pay a few bills before launching its best seller. Nénette closed my mouth.

"No money between you and me," she said.

"Why not?"

"I wouldn't love you any more. I would think you were M. Gillet," she added giggling.

"I wouldn't be paying for your love but for your help."

"But I would help you because I love you, *darrlene*."

"It wouldn't even be my money."

"What? C.I.A. money! That would be fun! But no, I can't accept. Just show me some."

"Some what?"

"C.I.A. money."

"But, my dear, it's just ordinary money. . . ."

"Oh!" she pouted. "I thought it might be different. Stink maybe. . . . It does not matter. No, *darrlene*, you are allowed and even encouraged to take me to restaurants, nightclubs, even theatres (not the Comédie-Française, though: it's reactionary) but you will not give me one centime. If I hang for you, I want to hang free."

"That would be rather a feat. And why is the Comédie-Française a reactionary theatre?"

"They play only classics! How much more reactionary can you get?"

I knew enough about Paris restaurants, nightclubs and even theatres to guess that Munchin and Munchin would have found it more economical to pay Nénette a salary or a flat fee, but I like a good meal and a good show myself, so I didn't insist. Anyway I couldn't have persuaded her. When Nénette says no—which she does very seldom—she means it.

6

We woke up around seven. It was time to call Fifi. He had no phone and could only be caught at his different haunts. This time, it was at a janitor's to whose son he was giving a Latin lesson. I said my name was Turner. Could he speak English? Yes, he could, with a curious accent: a mixture of British and Mediterranean. He had been recommended to me, I told him, by one of his previous employers: the name didn't matter. Would he be ready to put himself at my disposal for a few days? That depended on what he would have to do. Legwork. He didn't know the word either and sounded insulted: "You've come to the wrong address, Mister." I hastened to correct him. I added that there might be some danger, although none was expected. He wanted to know if I was going to rob a bank. I said not at all, it was rather like intelligence work. He began to ask whether it was for *les Amerloques* or for *les Cocos,* but then said he didn't want to know. It was all the same to him, provided he was paid. I said we could discuss that face to face. He offered to meet me at a small café which he knew. But I had made up my mind to be very cautious, and I suggested that we meet at a café where neither of us was known, so that if at some time he wanted to babble, it would be more difficult to trace me. He agreed and we made an appointment for eight o'clock, at the Café de Presbourg on the Avenue de la Grande Armée. This is not a distinguished place by any means; lots of people come and go, and nobody would notice us.

Nénette was going to a party that night. The invitations were for nine o'clock, which meant, since were were in France, that it would be very bad form indeed to arrive before ten, and eleven would be just about right. That would give us time for dinner, since she was good enough to take me as her escort. We would meet at half-past eight or nine—time is never very precise with Nénette—at Fouquet's.

I parked the Continental in a garage off the Avenue de la Grande Armée and walked nearly half a mile to the Café de Presbourg. I had given my description to Fifi: five feet eight, rather slim, dark hair cut fairly short, smoke-blue suit, light-blue shirt with buttoned down collar. (I only wear the beastly things in Europe, of course.) Fifi had given me his description: tall (he couldn't count in feet), thin, blond, long hair, fake suede coat, bluejeans. We had no trouble recognizing each other. We sat at a table in a corner, and, while we waited for the waiter (in many cafés it properly is the patrons who should be called "waiters"), we tried to outstare each other. I don't know if I corresponded to Fifi's image of an underground boss, but he certainly did not correspond to my image of a tough Trotskiite or of an effective legman. Tall he was, yes, but lanky, with a concave chest; his hair was very long; he used a rubber band to hold it together which gave him a vaguely eighteenth century look; his skin was unhealthily pale and he had blue spots under the eyes. When his scotch and my martini had been brought (I didn't fuss with drinks in that kind of place and ordered what the French call a martini and is a plain glass of vermouth) he raised his glass to his lips, looked at me in a half-languid, half-supercilious manner, and said:
"So?"
He wasn't going to out-so me. I took a very matter-of-fact, slightly stern, very American tone:
"What's your name?"
"You called me Fifi on the phone."
"You have to do better than that."
"All right. I'm Philippe."
"Philippe who?"
"Philippe Calmar. What's your name?" he asked rebelliously.
"I told you: Turner."
"What's your first name?"
"Mister."
He swallowed hard.
"How much are you going to pay me?" he asked, drinking up his Scotch fast, as if preparing to leave.
"Eighty a day."
"Plus expenses?"

"Naturally."

"Ninety."

"Done. But I have to warn you: there are twenty-four hours in a day."

"What about sleep?"

"If you really can't do without it, I'll tolerate some."

"I see. What exchange rate?"

That was a shrewd question and it inspired me with some respect for Fifi's aptitudes, for there are many different rates, and you can easily cheat somebody of half you owe him if you know how to do it.

"American Express."

"Fair enough. Paid when?"

"At the end of each day. Or when we meet. Or deposited in a post office box daily. I don't care."

"Make it general delivery, so I don't have to pay for the box."

"All right with me. But you know the French law forbids sending money through the mail. If they grab the money. . . ."

"Wrap it in carbon paper so they can't see what it is."

I had already learned something from my legman.

"I could send you ninety in dollars every day and not bother about the exchange."

"Fine. Now, what would I have to do?"

It must be understood that I had never been a case officer before, that I had never been in command of anything. So far I thought I hadn't done too badly, but I had to keep it up if I were to get Munchin and Munchin's daily ninety dollars worth out of Philippe Calmar.

So I told him what he would have to do tomorrow in a very terse, no-nonsense kind of style. It was hard to do, since at the same time I had a nearly irresistible crave to laugh at myself, because, after all, I am partly French, and the French feel that anything the smallest bit solemn is hilarious. To visualize myself in a solemn part was doubly hilarious. But I managed to explain what I wanted with a straight face.

"Do you have a car?" I finally asked.

"If you want to call it a car. A 1955 2 CV. I find it's a poetic means of transportation."

"Yes, but does it run?"

"It gallops."

"How fast?"

"The motor's new."

"All right. See you there then. Tomorrow."

I paid the check, as was proper, and went out, without looking back. I walked about three hundred feet on the sidewalk of the Avenue de la Grande Armée and then threw a glance over my shoulder. Lots of people hurrying this way and that way, but no sign of Fifi. Either he was very good or he was not good enough. I walked some more and looked back again. Nothing. Of course I wanted Fifi to be loyal to me, but I also wanted him to be resourceful, and if he were not taking this opportunity of learning something about me, he was a fool: I would have to look for another legman. Fortunately I had told this one a cock-and-bull story which had no relation to what he was really supposed to do for me, and the rendezvous I had given him could betray nothing. I felt rather complacent about my own trickiness.

I came to a street branching off to the left. I turned into it without trying to hide what I was doing and then slipped very fast into a doorway. I didn't have very long to wait. Fifi turned the corner and hurried his step. He walked so close to me I could have caught him by the sleeve. He was screwing up his eyes and peering into the darkness. I didn't move. I wanted to see what he would do. He took a few more steps and then stopped. Obviously he was sure that I was not in front of him any more. It was time for me to pounce on him before he pounced on me.

I walked up to him. "Fifi," I said, "I am paying you to spy on other people. Not on me. Whom do you take me for anyway? A damned amateur?"

He looked down at me for a few seconds. Then he smiled his supercilious smile, took a step back and made me a courtly bow, complete with legs crossed and the little flourish of the hand.

"Now," I said, "you walk away while I watch."

My authority had been established. He walked away with dignity, but obviously defeated. I was very pleased with myself as I watched him disappear into the darkness.

As I expected, Nénette was late. I picked up an American newspaper at a newsstand near Fouquet's and refrained from ordering anything. It is rude to order before the lady has arrived. It is rude to read too, of course, but I had an excuse. I was expecting, rather impatiently, George Broker's article. I was not disappointed. Although the cautious fellow did not use all the information I had given him—for instance, he never gave the name of the organization "Les Enfants de Mai"—he did paint an appalling picture of children-parents and student-teacher relationships in France, told my little stories about physical punishment, and—that was the most important—dealt at length with the backlash supposed to have followed the '68 mini-revolution. *"No blood was shed at that time,"* he wrote, *"but what happened in May '68 may well have been the general rehearsal of what is going to happen very soon. Violence is loathsome wherever it comes from, but responsibility must lie at the door of the initiating party. France, as everybody knows has no Santa Claus figure; instead it has two figures, the Père Noël one, who brings presents to 'good' children, and the Père Fouettard or Father Flogger, who brings rods to 'bad,' i.e., unhappy children. Let us say this. The tradition of repression is very strong in France. Repression, as everyone knows, breeds rebellion. If at any time soon the lid were to burst open and if the secular image of le Père Fouettard were to be pulled down and smashed into fifty million pieces, a country which has done so much for the civilization of the whole world, while remaining itself so backward in some respects, may very well find itself on the brink of a guerilla war."* Good old George! I would have to provide him with a little more evidence, and he would be at it again pretty soon. Naturally it was all couched in prudent terms: *may, if, at any time, on the brink of*—But I didn't mind that. The good work had begun.

Nénette was just an hour and a half late. So we had a bite at Fouquet's, walked to the garage where I had parked the Continental, and arrived in style at the party, rue François Ier. Of course there was no place to park, so I left Nénette at the door and drove for some time, looking for what the French call "a battlement." Eventually I found one and had only half a mile to walk back, so everything was in order.

The party was given by one of the many private radio stations in

France. In fact, some stations are not even in France: they are located in the surrounding countries, but the work is done in Paris, and the parties are given in Paris. This time it was in honor of a young man who had made what he called a "retrospective reportage" about the horrors of war. Everybody said that he had proved to everybody's satisfaction that war is awful, just plain awful. I don't think originality should be preferred to anything, but I confessed loudly enough that I would be much more interested to see someone prove to everybody's satisfaction that war is great, just plain great.

"Shut up!" said Nénette. "Everyone here knows you work for the C.I.A. So don't try to shock them by pretending you are a warmonger. You're worse."

I'm afraid that for a second I gaped at the idea that "everyone here knew I was working for the C.I.A." but then I decided this was as good a cover as another one, and let myself be introduced to scores of people who shook my hand and didn't believe for a second I was working for the C.I.A.

"When it's whispered, it may be true; when it's yelled, it can't," someone explained to me. Frankly, I didn't care what they thought I was doing, so long as they didn't know what I was really doing: being a literary scout, which sounds harmless enough, but could bring me into trouble if, some time later, it was discovered that I had been interested in Serge Saint-Fiacre—the story of whose murder we would be selling like mad—a few days or maybe a few hours before his demise. And I couldn't very well hide my interest in Saint-Fiacre, because I needed information about him for the book.

Olivia had done her homework well, but only so far as the official Saint-Fiacre was concerned. Here I got the gossip, and it was mainly the gossip I wanted. I was in luck. What I learned passed my wildest hopes.

I had just recognized an old acquaintance of mine, Helmut Trinkenbusch of *Die Zeit*, an enormous, bespectacled monster of a man whom I had nicknamed Herr Doktor—the nickname had stuck—and he had recognized me, and was pumping my hand and pommeling my back and complaining at the lack of beer—there was only whisky and champagne and neither was very good—

when somebody whom I had just met decided I'd better meet somebody else whom he had just met, and pulled me in the other direction. We laughed. The somebody else laughed. We were introduced all around. One more person joined us. Finally we stood in a circle, Herr Doktor towering over us, a short, thickset Frenchman called Lavedan on his right, a small, slim, very young, fairhaired American girl called Joyce, wearing octagonal glasses and a green dress, on his left, an elderly Swiss journalist, of indeterminate sex, beside me.

"Well, how have you been?" asked Herr Doktor.

"All right, I suppose," I said. "You never really know, do you? Tell me, when is your new Kanzler going to defect to the Chinese?"

Helmut laughed. He could stand a friendly dig.

"No, no," he said. "Our best people now are defecting to Europe."

That was my cue.

"You don't mean to the European Party?"

"Some of them, yes, yes."

"We've heard a little about it in the States. Mostly nonsense, I guess. Who is in charge of it?"

"Serge Saint-Fiacre," said Lavedan.

The Swiss person giggled. "Otherwise known as Bluebeard."

"Why?"

That, naturally, was the American girl speaking. She was pretty enough, in her undercooked way, and I turned toward her.

"My dear child, don't you know that in Europe you never ask why?"

"Why?" she insisted.

She had large, beautiful eyes, and a very large gaping mouth. I sighed.

"Because," I said patiently, "you are supposed to be either well-informed enough to know the answers or clever enough to guess them."

She thought I was making fun of her, and she wasn't going to play my game.

"Who was Bluebeard anyway?" she asked. "I seem to have heard of him."

"Bluebeard, young and beautiful lady," boomed Herr Doktor somewhere above, "was an abominable French aristocrat who married seven wives."

"But that's against the law!" she exclaimed. "That's polygamy!"

"Maybe," agreed our German friend, waving a cigar in the air. "Maybe. But imagine how deeply depraved the French are! The serious crime of polygamy they shrug off. The only reason he is considered a criminal is not that he married seven wives, but that he murdered them."

"Oh! That's better," said Joyce, who did have a sense of humor after all. He was not a polygamist, then; he was just a widower."

We all laughed. "And why," I asked—the habit was contagious— "do you call the President or Secretary-General, or Whatever of the European Party, Bluebeard?"

"I'd like to hear the answer to that one," said the girl.

She was obviously somewhat bewildered. She didn't know where she was. She wanted to learn as much as she could.

"Because of a slight confusion," said the Swiss in his voice which was neither male nor female but just in between. "As you may know, Bluebeard never existed, but his prototype was Gilles de Rais, or de Retz, one of the brothers-at-arms of the renowned Joan of Arc. And his greatest pleasure, as you may also know, was to do all sorts of unpleasant things to his peasants' children. Mainly boys, by the way. But in the absence of boys, he was content to torture little girls."

"What did he do to them?" asked Joyce.

She had grown a tinge paler, and her eyes had narrowed a little, and I'm not even sure she was really curious, but she craved culture, and culture she would get at any price.

The Swiss journalist smirked. "Well, he raped them, and killed them in different ways, all rather disgusting, the slower the better. You must understand, Miss . . . er . . ."

"I'm Joyce."

"Miss Joyce, that Gilles de Retz was an authentic sadist, whereas Bluebeard was just a . . . a . . ."

"A hedonist!" Herr Doktor supplied the word, but nobody understood it.

"He was the bravest and dullest of all men," I said.

"Why?" asked Joyce.

"Because," I said, "he was brave enough to do what most husbands just dream of, but then he had to do it seven times. How dull can you get?"

"And so they call Saint-Fiacre Bluebeard. That's funny!" observed Helmut Trinkenbusch, and his laughter shook the building.

"Why?" asked Joyce.

"Because it's true. Only true things can afford to be funny," remarked the Swiss.

"But I mean why do they call him that?"

"Oh! that's a long story," said Lavedan. "Do you remember the Ballets Roses?"

"Even if we do, we won't confess to it," said Trinkenbush. And laughed.

"Well, in the late forties or early fifties," began Lavedan, "it was discovered that several respectable politicians had organized a kind of club catering to their slightly peculiar tastes. Mind you, I'm not criticizing any one, but at that time the people were retrograds and pretended they were shocked."

"Were the politicians guillotined?" asked Joyce.

"Oh! no," answered Lavedan. "This is a free country. In fact, most of them stayed in office. But still there was a juicy little scandal, which the press baptized Le Scandale des Ballets Roses, because most of the privileged little girls honored by the politicians' attentions were young dancers from the Opera. *Des petits rats, vous savez.*" (In France, ballet students are unaccountably called little rats.) "As to *Roses,* pink is supposed to be the color of little girls. Now, that was by no means the only scandal of its kind in our blessed country. Blessed with scandals, I mean. Another one exploded in the seventies, and Saint-Fiacre was somehow involved. It was even said that he was involved in both the Ballets Roses and the more recent one, the Ballets Bleus."

"Bleu? Why?" said Joyce.

"Blue is to boys what pink is to girls," explained Lavedan patiently (Joyce was pretty enough in her way to deserve patience). "No one said though that Saint-Fiacre was a consumer of either

Ballets Bleus or Ballets Roses. Rather he procured for politicians, and this is how he would have started what looks like rather a promising career."

"All this is unconfirmed, I hope?" said Joyce sternly.

"You see," observed the Swiss, "the French are very clever. They never confirm that kind of rumor. If Saint-Fiacre displeases them, they want to be able to use all that against him. On the other hand, if he reveals himself to be a good politician, which he could, they don't want to spoil his career—and the use they can make of him—by completely irrelevant considerations."

"Disgusting," said Joyce.

"But true," agreed Lavedan. "I am not a member of his Party, but I may very well vote for him one of these days. What he says makes sense. A dozen or two of little girls or little boys who learned to enjoy themselves a bit early in life are a small matter compared to the future of the whole world. And then, what I like about him is that, although his name is Saint-Fiacre, he is really such an unpretentious fellow. A man of the people."

A voice, sharp, incisive, sardonic, cut in:

"And what is his name supposed to mean that he is?"

"Chantal!" I cried. "Darling! How are you?"

Chantal was a very close friend of mine, whom I had known for about two weeks about three years ago. She was handsome rather than beautiful, with an aquiline nose and a contemptuous manner. She was a P.R. woman and tremendously successful. There is nothing Europeans like better than to be snubbed, if it's done the right way.

She kissed me on both cheeks, but would not let her prey go.

"Well," she said, "what is his name supposed to mean?"

Lavedan seemed at a loss. It's always awkward to pretend you're a specialist in front of an expert.

"Saint-Fiacre is an aristocrat," he mumbled. "A liberal aristocrat."

She burst into a short, dry laugh.

"My poor Lavedan," she said. "I'd as soon believe you were an aristocrat yourself."

"Tell us about Saint-Fiacre, Chantal," urged the Swiss hermaphrodite.

"Saint-Fiacre is a bastard. I don't mean metaphorically but technically. The son of a printer's apprentice. . . ."

"Nothing wrong with that," said Joyce belligerently.

"Turned pimp," went on Chantal without paying attention to her, "and a streetwalker turned honest woman, meaning she made a living renting rooms to the dishonest women who worked for him. The father's father had had the same kind of occupation, only with him it was not rooms, it was hansom cabs: that is where the name Fiacre, hansom, comes from. Little Serge was even more brilliant. He started life by procuring *petits rats* for ministers of State, both radical and Catholic. He not only provided, he also gave a hand with the consuming. When the old Minister of Defense was in danger of capitulating, he would ask Little Serge to give him a flogging, and that would restore his spirits. The President of the Senate had no heart for the job unless his victim had been flogged under his eyes, and once again Little Serge would oblige. Finally the great man grew so fond of the little man that he decided to adopt him to replace a son he had lost in the war. By a wonderful coincidence, the Senator's patronym was Saint-Fiacre, whereas the young man's was simply Fiacre. By that time Monsieur Saint-Fiacre's appetites had dwindled to nil, and he had no more use for the technical assistance of his favorite. So he bought him a printing business, because the young man had some interest for that trade. That is what charitable people like myself say. Others maintain that Serge blackmailed the Senator into adopting him, which may be a little far-fetched."

"All that is a pack of lies," said Lavedan angrily. "Serge may have done some procuring, but he is the son of Saint-Fiacre, the one that had been given up as lost."

"Aren't the French funny?" asked Joyce from me. "They don't mind what their politicians do wrong so long as they are descended from the right people."

Lavedan turned to her: "There is no worse insult in the French language than whore's son. We don't want people to use it literally when addressing the man who may be the first president of a united Europe."

"But you don't mind his having been. . . ?"

"A mackerel?" (The French term for a pimp.) "Well, of course we would prefer him to have been a . . ."

"A general?" suggested Herr Doktor, and roared with laughter. The French have had quite a few military politicians in the past, but it hardly was what Lavedan had on his mind.

"On the contrary!" he replied with some heat. "A mackerel is a hundred times better than a general. The one deals in pleasure, the other in death. After all, he was young at the time," he added. "One must sow one's wild oats."

And he moved away. O Amarantha! What feminine or publishing intuition moved you when you suggested children as the underdogs rebelling against Saint-Fiacre? Now, we really had a case. With George Broker's Père Fouettard, we were in business. Les Enfants de Mai could only be applauded for disposing of such an abominable figure as the Master Flogger of les Ballets Bleus! It would now be possible to give a somewhat Freudian tinge to France's punishment lore. Every father spanking his child would appear as an accomplice in the odious sacrifices perpetrated by Serge Saint-Fiacre. I turned to Chantal.

"You seem to know a lot about all this," I said.

"I know everything. One of my uncles participated in the Ballets Bleus."

"On which side?" asked Joyce.

"On the side of the consumers, of course!" replied Chantal deeply shocked. "You are not insinuating, are you, that my uncle was a dancer?"

"But why not?" asked Joyce. She was hopeless.

"You'll have to tell me about it. Where were the headquarters?"

"On a large estate old Saint-Fiacre had at Moret near Fontainebleau."

"How did it finally come out?"

"The police put their long noses in it. Of course, all decent people did what they could to hush it up."

"Why?" asked Joyce. "If President Nixon had flogged little boys instead of taping in the Oval Office, we would have publicized it to all the world. Just the same."

"Well, there must be some difference between peoples, my dear," answered Chantal a trifle acidly. "If not, how would tourist agencies make a living?"

She moved on. I was left with the baby, I mean Joyce.

"I don't believe one word of what that haughty hussy said," she declared.

"I don't believe much of it either."

"Serge may very well have been Mr. Saint-Fiacre's son."

"That's what he says, and he should know."

"He was not arrested for participating in the Ballets Bleus. He was not tried. So he must be presumed innocent."

"I see no objection to that."

As a matter of fact, I did, but I was not going to tell her so. Besides, I wanted to get rid of her.

"I rather like Serge Saint-Fiacre," she went on, in the tone of someone talking about a special kind of candy or of toothpaste.

"Oh! What do you imagine he tastes like?"

She frowned at me.

"You must be half French: you talk nonsense half the time."

"You win. I am."

"I think I would like to meet that man. He appeals to me. I think he must be very brave to go on with his campaign in the face of such calumny. I'd like to tell him so. How does one meet that kind of people?"

"It shouldn't be too difficult. Who are you anyway?"

She told me the story of her life. She was an American student, majoring in French. She had made straight A's and received a scholarship to spend one year in France. She had decided to make the most of it. On arrival she had been picked up by a press photographer who had taught her the rudiments of French love-making 180 minutes after she had set foot on French soil. She was rather proud of herself for having been emancipated so fast, but on the whole she didn't think she would stay with the press photographer much longer: he never washed. On the other hand, he introduced her to lots of interesting people, so she wouldn't have to go through the ignominy and waste of opportunity of living in France without a lover.

This didn't tell me much about how she could get an interview from Saint-Fiacre.

"You could always pretend you were an American reporter."

"But that would be lying," she said.

So the Puritan background had not been completely washed away. At that moment Nénette happened to appear in my field of vision. In France, it is bad form for people arriving together to stay together at a party; and I had not seen her during the whole evening. She smiled at me:

"Philandering again, *darrlene?*"

I introduced the two girls to each other.

"Nénette, is there any way this child could meet that Saint-Fiacre character?"

"Oh! but of course," she said. "I just met somebody who was invited to a cocktail party at his place tomorrow. He knows Saint-Fiacre well. He'll give his cardboard" (which meant his invitation) "to the lady. Just a second."

She was nearly as good as her word. She ran away and five minutes later she was back, bringing the cardboard. Monsieur et Madame Maclou's name had been scrawled in. "But that doesn't matter," Nénette said. "Everyone knows them there and they can go in without cardboard." She left us.

Joyce looked at the card and then at me.

"Thank you very much," she said. "But he is such an important person, and the French are so snobbish . . . I'm afraid to go there alone."

"The card is for two," I said. "Take your photographer."

"Oh! no," she said quite seriously. "He does not use deodorants, if you know what I mean. Couldn't you come with me?"

I had not expected that. I had no particular wish to meet M. Saint-Fiacre. He sounded to me like some kind of mountebank whose acquaintance I could very well do without, and he was also a man whose murder I was, if not exactly arranging, at least condoning. But that set me thinking. I did not want to adopt the hypocritic attitude of people who like their steak rare but would faint in a slaughterhouse. What was I afraid of? Of changing my mind after I had seen the guy? Yes, that might happen, and it would make me lose lots of money and would be rather awkward as far as Amarantha was concerned, but I didn't think it very probable, and if it did happen, well, then it must. No use running away from it. On the contrary, it was much better to look the man in the face and tell him (making sure that he wouldn't hear): "Yes sir, I think I can do without you." Frankly, since the opportunity was offered, the only decent thing to do was to take it. So, a little rashly maybe, I told Joyce:

"All right. Give me your address. I'll take you there."

Although I am not afflicted with an over-fastidious conscience, this still bothers me a little. Of course, if Joyce had followed my advice throughout, she would have been safe, but on the other hand, if I had not provided that first piece of cardboard, she would have been still safer. She was what is known, in modern lingo, as a "nice kid," and I am sorry for her.

Do not frown at me, my dear. If you must read over my shoulder, do so, but at least do not misinterpret what I write. Joyce was nothing to me and my feelings for her were—would you believe?— quite disinterested. Well, *requiescat in pace,* which means: French scholarships are not good for everybody.

7

The next morning I got up early, had coffee and croissants in a nice little café and then visited three bookstores. In one I bought a calendar, for the word *May,* in the second one a children's book, for the word *children,* in the third one a dictionary, for all the other words. You see, I did not make the mistake of underestimating the police. I knew that any typewriter can finally be traced. I also didn't want any bookseller to remember selling that particular combination of books to a man with my appearance. In a dime-store (they call them "everything at one price stores," which is as untrue as our understatement about dimes) I bought note paper and envelopes. My readings hadn't told me how well fingerprints could be detected on paper, but that didn't worry me since in the street I always wore gloves. I would just have to go on wearing them.

Nénette was still asleep when I came back. I settled down in the living room and set to work.

We had spent the hours after the party at a café with a friend of hers, who was a journalist especially interested in murder cases, and I had made him tell me several, as yet unsolved. Two had struck my fancy, and I had made an effort to remember all the details. The first one, was the murder of an old maid, a retired schoolteacher, called Mlle. Pinchon. Her head had been laid open neatly, just in the middle, by an axe. The strange thing was that she was not known to have had any enemies, and all the same her house had not been robbed. The police had found some money in a drawer, where the killer couldn't have missed it. The obvious explanation was that the killer, frightened by a noise, or by the silence of night, or by the amount of blood that flew from poor Miss Pinchon's body, ran away before investigating, but it could be made to look like something else. The second case was more intriguing. A fourteen-year-old boy had been tried for shooting his father with a .22 long rifle pistol. He had pleaded not guilty, and the pistol had never been discovered. There was no proof of his guilt and so he was acquitted. But nobody could see any reason why anybody else would have wanted to murder M. Bradec; whereas, his only son had obvious reasons, since scarcely a day went by without his dad complimenting him with a sound thrashing. This again could be interesting.

First, I wrote my proclamation with a pen, then I began cutting out the words—sometimes syllables and even letters—from the three books I had bought, and pasting them on a sheet of paper. It was very boring. I had made the proclamation very short, on purpose. It read thus:

"The children of France have been mistreated for centuries. Time has come for them to organize and rebel against oppressive adult chauvinists.

"A network of young and very young people has been successfully organized in the past months. It has been called The Children of May *in honor of the glorious Revolution of May '68.*

"Violence calls for violence. We have already struck twice. Mlle. Pinchon, the tyrant schoolteacher who maintained discipline in the classroom by means of an iron ruler, has been liquidated by us. M. Bradec, who nearly killed his son, has also been executed by us.

"Soon we shall strike again. This time a public figure, a veritable incarnation of Father Flogger, who exercised his talent in particularly sordid conditions, will die.

"The other two murders were rehearsals for our killers. This one will mark the beginning of our campaign for the liberation of children.

"Children and young people of everywhere, the hunting season is open. All adults are your enemies unless they support us.

"Signed: LES ENFANTS DE MAI."

It was a brave, ridiculous, little piece, and I was rather pleased with it.

I burned what remained of the books in Nénette's fireplace. I also burned the written proclamation, keeping only the pasted version of it, which looked rather funny with its three different prints, but still would, I felt, do the job. It was time to leave for my appointment with Fifi. So I hid the proclamation in my shaving kit, and walked down the stairs: it was much faster than taking the elevator.

I met Fifi on the Esplanade des Invalides. The parking situation there is a little better than most anywhere else in Paris. He wore the same costume, had the same languid and supercilious look, the same rubber band circled his hair. We shook hands, French style.

"What I told you yesterday was incorrect," I said. "You are not supposed to follow the Third Secretary of the Polish Embassy and report on his movements. You are to accompany me to the Charles de Gaulle airport. There I shall point out to you a person whose shadow you are supposed to become, without being noticed by anybody but the person in question. He will probably be more or less a prisoner, although a willing one. If you have an opportunity to speak to him, here is your password." I gave it to him. "If not, you are to follow him around. He will be discarding cigarette packs after you have made a point of being noticed by him, not by his escorts. You will bring the cigarette packs to me."

"Yes, Mister Turner," he said with an ironical emphasis on the Mister.

"I have to warn you," I went on. "There will be messages in the cigarette packs. They will be written in English. You know the language. They will not be coded. You would understand them perfectly. So perhaps you'd better not read them."

We were standing by the two cars, my sumptuous azure blue Continental, and his decrepit, yellowish, 2 CV. He looked down at me through the narrow, slanting slits of his eyes.

"And what is that supposed to mean, *Mister* Turner?"

"Very simple. I have no way of preventing you from reading the messages. But if at any time you are caught doing what you are doing, it will be much better for you if you know nothing of what it is all about."

"I see."

He didn't tell me what he intended to do about it.

"As soon as you have made contact with the person, you will call me at this number which you will memorize now and never write down. If you have an oral message for me, you will give it to me by phone; if you have a cigarette pack, we will make an appointment for me to pick it up. You will dial the number, let it ring two times, hang up, dial again, let ring three times, dial again and wait for an answer. Got it?"

I gave him the number. He repeated it twice, and then a look of understanding appeared on his face.

"Oh!" he said, "so that's who told you how good I was."

I knew I was taking a risk by giving him Nénette's number, but I saw no other way out. You see, I was not a professional agent with safehouses galore; I was just a publisher's scout.

"Yes," I said, "that's who it is, and you'd better forget who it is and forget the number if anybody asks for it. We don't encourage tattlers, in my outfit."

I tried to sound as professional as I could.

"You mean the fuzz?" he asked.

"It might be the fuzz. It might be somebody else."

He scratched his head.

"In that case, I'd better make up another number. It's easier to talk nonsense than just to remain silent when they begin dipping you into the bathtub or giving you the electrical treatment." He seemed to have had some experience. "Any idea what number I could use?"

That in itself was a problem. No imaginary number would do. No obvious number like the American Embassy or the Communist Party would do either. It would have to be something that would keep the opposition running in circles. . . . In circles? I had it! I would give him Saint-Fiacre's own number, which I had noted down that very morning, because I wanted to call his home to ask what was the proper attire for that night's party. The cardboard had not mentioned it, so it was probably *tenue de ville*, more or less what we call semi-formal, but I wanted to make sure. I looked it up in my address book and gave it to Fifi.

"I thought we were not supposed to write anything down," he sneered.

"That was just a decoy number," I replied with dignity.

"Any other instructions, *Mister* Turner?"

"If you find it possible, call me every three hours. Even if you have nothing to say. Are you carrying any equipment with you?"

"A pair of binoculars. A flashlight. And this."

It was a nasty looking instrument made of four iron rings welded together through which you put your fingers; on top there were four sharp points.

"In France," said Fifi with a narrow smile, "we call that an American fist."

That sounded good, but I still had misgivings about the little car. In France, there are few speed limitations on the expressways, and those few seem to be treated as if they were for the birds. I didn't want to lose Chirpie just because Fifi was fond of his "poetic" car. Besides, I had read somewhere that two cars on a surveillance mission were more inconspicuous than one.

"Listen," I said, "we don't know if my, or I should say your, client will be coming to Paris, or if he's going to take the expressway to go somewhere else. Maybe we'd better rent you a less poetic car. We would leave this one at the airport."

"If you say so, *Mister* Turner," he agreed. "If he drives a Jag, obviously I'm not going to race him in this bathtub."

He affectionately patted the 2 CV on the hood.

"We could leave it here," he added. "This is a pretty central location. In time I'll get a few tickets, I guess, but I'll put them on expenses, O.K.?"

He obviously had more experience than I and I made up my mind to use it without bothering too much about my reputation as a case officer. We got into the Continental and drove off.

Once again a word of explanation may be in order. By hiring a legman and confiding in him, be it ever so little, I was partly endangering myself. He could sell me to the opposition or to the police. He knew Nénette's number. They could come after me. Why did I hire him in the first place? There were three reasons. One was probably cowardice. I felt that some conflicts might arise along the way: you must remember I was not a black belt in anything, and I knew perfectly well any professional hood would knock me about as he pleased and maybe forever spoil my physique, to which I have the weakness to be attached. The second one was cautiousness. I wanted to stay as far away as I could from the murder. If Fifi were caught he might sell me out and again he might not, but if I were caught, that was final, and one of the least evils that would result from it would be the unavoidable merger of the Bopkins and the Munchin and Munchin companies. The third reason was my lack of expertise. I was afraid to lose my quarry at the first traffic light. Although I didn't exactly know how good my legman would prove to be, I was pretty sure he couldn't be worse than I. At least I would then have someone to blame. On the other hand, I didn't think that employing him was taking too great a risk. He had named his own fee and would receive it regularly. If he asked politely for some kind of bonus, I wouldn't refuse it. He would be rather foolish to sell out, and he didn't look foolish to me. Besides, I had some confidence in Nénette's judgment of men. He could be caught, but if it were by the opposition, he was better off lying for me than betraying me. If it were by the police, he might decide to make a clean breast of it. Let us suppose he would even quote Nénette by name, it would be the worst he could do. She would be called in. She would tell the exact truth, with one reservation: my identity. Nobody, not even the police, would be surprised at learning that Nénette had met a handsome fellow at a party or in a café, had brought him home and agreed to help him by providing a phone number and Fifi's help. She would talk thirteen to the dozen about the C.I.A. and how I worked for it, and that, I hoped, would be the end of it. I had every confidence in Nénette. Maybe that was a little optimistic of me. After three days and nights of the French version of third degree, she might blurt out my name. Or the police could learn from an informer that at the time she was supposed to "help" Mike Turner, she was seen at such and such a party with Walter de Walter. True. But I estimated that these risks were to be preferred to the other ones. Whence Fifi.

We arrived at the airport with ample time for renting a Citroën GS, one of the best cars in the world, and still very inconspicuous on the roads of France. After that, we sat down to wait. I must confess I felt pretty nervous, but I held myself well in hand. Fifi seemed perfectly calm. Only he chain-smoked his villainous Gitanes cigarettes. We must have made a rather strange couple, he, dressed like some kind of Apache, and I with my immaculate white turtleneck sweater and sky blue pants, the best Muse's ever sold.

Chirpie's flight was announced to have arrived. We could not see the landing, so we just went on waiting. I imagined Chirpie and

his escorts going through police control, then through customs. . . . Would Chirpie be nervous too? I wondered. Or would
he consider it all as a big lark?

A door opened and passengers began to trickle into the hall. The
trickle became a flow. Above the flow towered a mass of human
flesh surmounted by a rotund, unintelligent face: I recognized Mr.
Boudin. He pushed and shoved right and left and pretty soon
extricated from the crowd the dry, thin Mr. Snipe—who looked
like a stick figure made of matches—and the stocky, broad-
shouldered, hairy Mr. Chirpwood. So far so good.

"Here they are," I whispered into Fifi's ear. "Your client's the
one in the middle. If he books into any hotel under his own name,
which I doubt, it will be Charles W. Chirpwood. Got that?"

"Who is that Fatso character?"

"Mr. Boudin, partner of Mr. Snipe, private dick."

"Boudin? That's a French name."

"We have quite a few in the States. Never heard of Huguenots?
Or, of the French Revolution?"

I was talking with my back to them. I had been disguised at the
time of my encounter with Mr. Snipe, but I didn't know how good
my disguise had been or how bad a detective Mr. Snipe was.

"If you want my opinion," said Fifi, "Fatso doesn't look like an
exiled nobleman, nor like a runaway watchmaker. But that
doesn't matter. They are walking toward the exit. Shall I follow
them?"

"Yes. Good luck."

He nodded and walked off at a leisurely pace. I don't know
what I wanted to sound clever for at such a time, but I shouted at
his receding back:

"*Fortuna audaces juvat!* Which means: give'em hell, buddy!"

He looked at me over his shoulder.

"Thank you very much," he said. "I teach Latin myself. And
what it really means is: backseat drivers, shut up!"

I never quoted Latin to him any more.

*

I drove home, I mean to Nénette's. Strangely enough she was

already up and out. So I went to a little restaurant called *Chez Bobonne*, which served delicious home-type cooking to a dozen *habitués*. I had an artichoke and a calf's kidney with mustard sauce and some Brie and a cup of excellent coffee and a bottle of very reasonable straightforward Morgon. Oh! and I forgot: a wonderful plate of fresh watercress in olive oil and vinegar after the kidney.

To solace my loneliness, I had picked up *Le Figaro*, which is the most conservative French morning daily. Not that I think of myself as a conservative person. Conservative, preservative, all these words sound rather silly to me. I, may it be stated here, have no political opinions whatsover, and I cannot help feeling that if more people were like me, this world would be a nicer place to live. Of course, this may just be conceit on my part and I'm not pressing the point in any way. I just wanted to mention that I was not conservative so that you wouldn't stop reading here and now. *Le Figaro* is printed on whiter paper than most dailies, it is written without too many misspellings, and it is not more misinformed than most papers. That's why I occasionally read it. Period.

By what at the time seemed a rather startling—and very lucky—coincidence, *Le Figaro* was full of Serge Saint-Fiacre. There was to be, a few days hence, a convention of the European Party at the Palais de la Mutualité. I couldn't have wished for anything better. There were articles about Saint-Fiacre, there were articles against Saint-Fiacre, there was mild gossip concerning Saint-Fiacre, and there even was an open letter by Saint-Fiacre. That open letter was the only bit of print I found distinctly favorable to Saint-Fiacre, but obviously the situation would soon change: the leader of the European party announced *urbi et orbi* (which means: to all and sundry) that he would very soon launch a weekly paper, called *Le Haut-Parleur* (The Loud Speaker) which would defend European truth against anyone who didn't like it, either on this or on that side of the Atlantic. He didn't specify that the printing would be done by his printing establishment, but that was fairly obvious. What he did specify was that he counted on "the friendly and sportsmanlike rivalry" of his competitors this side of the Atlantic, and that the attitude of the press on the other side of the Atlantic would be a final test of its trustworthiness (so he hoped) or of its hypocrisy (so he had good reasons of fearing). Anyway, with *Le*

Haut-Parleur, the conspiracy of silence that had been plotted against him would come to an inglorious end. So long as Serge Saint-Fiacre lived, the voice of truth would resound from it and couldn't be stifled.

I was bound to be disappointed on one point. Not one word Saint-Fiacre said could in any way be distorted as to sound directed against the younger generations. Neither did the gossip column—*Le Figaro*'s gossip column, is, I think, composed by an Areopagus of old ladies—mention M. Saint-Fiacre's career in flogging. It was mentioned somewhere that he was the son of the Senator, but whether adopted, natural or unnatural, was not indicated. Obviously *Le Figaro* felt which direction the wind was blowing and wanted no unpleasantness with a possible future president of a united Europe. Still, all that was very good, as far as Munchin and Munchin was concerned. As for the gossip, there is always *Minute.* I walked back to Nénette's flat with *Minute* in my hands. Rather unsensational news was clad there in very sensational terms. At least, I found the nickname Bluebeard mentioned several times. There were some very broad hints at Saint-Fiacre's present dissolute life, and a short paper about *Bluebeard's Unkilled Wives.* Several starlets, who probably had paid the reporter to have their names mentioned, were supposed to have enjoyed the favors of "Barbe-bleue." Just as in the tale, he had entrusted them with a little golden key which opened a certain closet in which they were forbidden to have the smallest peep. Of course, not one resisted the temptation to open the closet and they found themselves not in a slaughter-house full of dead wives, but in a kindergarten full of very much alive little boys! That was the kind of humor of *Minute,* and I didn't know if we could do very much with it "on the other side of the Atlantic Ocean." Still it could serve when the book was being written. I stopped at a kiosque and bought *Le Canard Enchaîné,* the leftist gossip publication, and found no more factual information there. There never is any. The insinuations were broader and the puns as atrocious as usual. Still, although the grossest jokes were made about S.F.'s antecedents, I sensed no real animosity, which was rather remarkable, since S.F. seemed to have no friends among the traditional left. This should have set me thinking. I must confess it didn't.

Nénette was still out. Nothing surprising about that. I got myself a Chartreuse Verte from the liquor cabinet—Nénette had nothing dryer than that: it would have to make do—and, after a look at the telephone—a message from Fifi could come any time now—I sat down to work. First, I stuck stamps on fifty envelopes. Then I cut to pieces Nénette's phone book, and stuck fifty addresses on the same. One thing was done, and still the telephone kept silent. Suddenly it rang. Uncoded call: I didn't answer.

Then I began to work with my scissors on the French papers I had bought. The most important American newspapers have Paris correspondents, of course, but they tend to play up what *they* think is important and we did not necessarily see eye-to-eye concerning the importance of the European Party. They would judge by American standards: since no one as yet had voted for the new party, it was to be treated as one more European whim. I knew Europe better, since I was at least partly part of it, and also I had special interests in the matter. So clip-clip went the scissors, and soon a bulging envelope with Olivia's address on it was ready. Second thing done. The telephone rang, and my heart began doing things inside my chest. Two rings. Silence. I jumped up and ran to the instrument. One ring. Silence. It was one of the coded ones, but not Fifi.

I remembered then that I had to call Saint-Fiacre, which I did. It was *tenue de ville,* as I expected. Nobody ever dresses up in white tie in France; I hadn't even bothered to bring my frock-coat, but I had brought my dinner-jacket, so curiously known to the French as *un smoking.* But since the party was not to be "*habillé*," I thought my charcoal gray suit would do perfectly. Incidentally, if you are invited to a French party and told it is not going to be *habillé,* and if you look up the word in your pocket dictionary and find it means *dressed,* do not jump to conclusions: you are not being invited to a streaking party.

"Mademoiselle," I said to the beautiful, low-keyed, feminine voice which had answered, "may I allow myself to inquire if I have the honor of speaking to a member of M. Saint-Fiacre's family or his household?"

It's not really difficult to talk like that if you've been bred to it. She sounded startled. "Why do you ask?"

"Just because I happen to think your voice is perfectly charming."

It's bad form to thank for a compliment in France, and she didn't. Instead she laughed. For a second she was at a loss. Then:

"Both, I suppose," she said. And hung up.

Three things were done and still no phone message for me. At that time I began to do some swearing at myself, and from that standpoint I can tell you I'm fairly fluent in quite a number of languages. "What will you do, you * &/§ + %!, if Fifi has lost track of Chirpie and his escort? Who is going to repay Munchin and Munchin for all the money you have invested in this crazy venture? And who is going to prevent Mr. Billy B. Bopkins III from merging with Miss Amarantha Munchin? Don't you know, from dire though not extensive experience that there is nothing easier than losing a car in traffic? Don't you understand that you should have hired several people to do the job, or been there yourself, to intervene in case of need? Now you've made a mess of it!" I even added some Arabic insults at the end, but that didn't help. I tried some more Chartreuse. It did. (Probably because it was Chartreuse Verte: the Jaune wouldn't have.) If, so I reasoned, Fifi had lost track of the car, that didn't yet mean a complete fiasco. Maybe he had jotted down the number, and we could start from there. If he had not, we still had a chance to find Chirpie by sticking as close as we could to Saint-Fiacre. I didn't know the exact range of those rifle-scope combinations, but it could not exceed 300 yards. So, at some time or other, Chirpie would have to come to that distance, or a shorter one, from Saint-Fiacre. . . . That last consideration did not sound too hopeful, but one consoles oneself as best one can. The telephone rang. One ring. Another ring. Silence. Ring, ring, ring. I picked it up.

"Hello?"

"*Mister* Turner?"

"Fifi?"

I made an effort and controlled myself. Calmly I said:

"Let's have your report."

"The client and his two friends had a car ready. A van. Grey. No windows. Made by Renault. The number is as follows." He gave it to me. "The client was asked to step into the rear part of the van. From there he could see nothing, if, as I believe, the little window between the front and the back had been sealed. The two escorts got together in front. I nearly lost them because I had to run get the GS, but I caught up with them at the exit."

"So you didn't lose them?"

He did not bother to answer.

"They took the South Expressway. They didn't seem to suspect I was following them, I or anyone else, for that matter. It was an easy job. We got off at the Fontainebleau exit. I'll show you on the map what we did after that. We finally came to an iron gate. I had to drive by while the fat fellow was fooling around with a key. The lock seemed rusty. I took ten minutes and then drove back. The van was not in sight any more. I presume it had entered the driveway. I am calling you from a service station, about three kilometers from that place."

"Describe the place."

"Rather lonely. Narrow road. Woods all around. Stone wall, about two and a half meters high." (Nearly eight feet to you.) "Iron gate. Winding driveway. Big trees. No house in view, but at a guess it looks like the entrance to a château. I've talked to the service station attendant. He doesn't know whom the place belongs to. What do you want me to do?"

I reflected.

"Try and follow the wall," I said, "and find if there is any other entrance."

"Can do," he said, and hung up.

I was relieved. Things were certainly looking better now than five minutes ago. With his long hair and languid looks Fifi seemed to be doing his job with competence. Unless—unless he had lost Chirpie and made up the whole story? That was a possibility, but not a probability, I decided.

There was something I could do now. Two things, in fact.

Once again I went out. I found a place where there was a coin-operated photocopying machine. I put my proclamation face downwards on the glass, closed the rubber flap over it, and operated the machine fifty times in a row. I hoped nothing would go wrong with it. My eye never left the "Call key operator" sign. The storekeeper—he sold photographic equipment—came up to me about half way through.

"Wonderful machine, isn't it, Monsieur?"

The French are not usually so chatty with people whom they don't know, but I couldn't afford to take advantage of such an exceptional friendliness. Next thing he would be asking me was what sort of a document I was copying.

"Yes," I said glumly.

"Everybody is buying them nowadays," he went on. "I take it you don't have one in your office."

"No."

The machine indicated it had already made thirty-five prints. Fifteen more to go.

"Does your material come out well, Monsieur? Not too light?"

He made as if he would check. I had to move in front of him.

"My material comes out fine, thank you," I said. "Could you show me a Nikon camera?"

"But certainly, Monsieur."

I lost three minutes looking at a Nikon camera I didn't buy, but I had got him out of the way. I discovered now that I didn't know where to put the fifty sheets. I would just have to carry them like that, which was a little awkward. I thought I could buy a large envelope in a stationery store, but the man very obligingly provided one. I thanked him briefly, to stay in character, and walked out.

I didn't know this part of Paris too well. It was not even exactly Nénette's part of town, for I had made a point of photostating the proclamation some distance from her home. I stopped a passer-by and asked for the nearest post office. I didn't have far to go, it appeared, and I was already on my way, having thanked the lovely informer with my most Parisian smile, when suddenly the blood seemed to stop flowing in my arteries. I nearly fainted there and then, on the sunny sidewalk. I remembered that I had left the master copy of the proclamation in the machine, under the very eyes of the inquisitive storekeeper. Maybe it was the Chartreuse Verte's fault, maybe not: what did it matter? And what was I to do now?

I turned back. The lovely passer-by said, with a smile:

"It's the other way, Monsieur."

I rushed past her. I never was a great runner, but this time I must have beaten the world record. People began staring at me while I sprinted along the Avenue Marceau.

The store was still there; the storekeeper was still there; the machine was still there; but was my proclamation still there?

There was a funny look on the storekeeper's face and the two tufts of hair above his forehead had a distinctly diabolic appearance.

"Did you have second thoughts about the camera, Monsieur?"

I hastened to the machine and with beating heart and choking lungs opened the rubber flap. The mastercopy was there.

The storekeeper smiled knowingly.

"Oh! yes, Monsieur, that happens very often. People forget master copies. That is a trend of human nature."

I looked furiously at him. Had he read it? Surely not. He would have called the police. Not necessarily, though. The French distrust the police.

"Human nature be damned!" I said. "And you ought to have told me instead of gaping at me, species of fool!"

In French, if you add the phrase "species of" to any insult, it is as if you had multiplied it by itself. *Espèce d'imbécile* is something like, in mathematical terms, *imbécile* squared.

I rushed out again. I saw clearly that the real *species of fool* was yours truly. Whereas I had hoped to make fifty copies of the proclamation in the most discreet way available, I had now, on the contrary, attracted the storekeeper's attention, and he would be sure to give my description to the police if they began looking all around Paris for a suspicious character having used a photocopying machine. The only professional way out, I suppose, was to resort to another method of copying and to throw these sheets away. But I decided I would do no such thing. There were thousands of photocopying machines in Paris, and no reason to suppose that the police would come and question this particular store-keeper. If he read about the proclamation in his daily paper, or saw a copy of it on TV, he might remember our little altercation, but if he had not read the proclamation, he would probably see no connection between the two facts: on the contrary, he would think that anyone arrogant enough to call him *species of fool* was definitely not trying to remain inconspicuous, and consequently had a clear conscience. Add to that the ordinary French reluctance wherever the police are involved and I thought I was more or less safe from the man. On the other hand, if he *had* read the proclamation, there was nothing I could do about it. The only precaution I decided to take was to mail the proclamations from a post office located in a different part of Paris.

So I walked back to my car, and drove all the way to the post office of the rue Danton, in the Sixth Arrondissement. The fifty envelopes were in my pocket. I shoved the fifty copies of the proclamations into the envelopes and sealed them. I hoped I had chosen the fifty addresses judiciously enough. About ten were obvious people like the Minister of the Interior, the Préfet de Police, and the President. About ten were decoys: high school principals, directors of penitentiaries for young people, the Minister of Education, the Planned Parenthood Association, the Cardinal. The rest were the really important ones: journalists, TV personalities, foreign correspondents (all the American ones, of course, but also others: I hoped the book would sell well in translation). I could not resist the temptation to address one to M. Saint-Fiacre himself. I didn't think it would put him on his guard, since threatening letters are a very usual thing, but I thought it would look nice in the dossier, if, by any chance, he didn't throw it into the wastepaper basket as soon as he received it.

Having completed my task, I walked to the mailbox, holding the fifty envelopes in my hand, and feeling, if I must tell the truth, somewhat ill at ease. In a few seconds I would have anonymously declared war on a certain number of people, very powerful and known to be rather vindictive, such as the Minister of the Interior, for instance. There was still time to forget about the whole business and to start looking for a rich widow, or a pretty divorcee with a prettier alimony pension. As soon as my fingers would have opened, it would be too late: I would have become a "public enemy" and more or less accomplice to a murder. What is it in us that tells us that it is more honorable to murder men than to live off women? It's a ridiculous idea, of course, and I am not trying to say that my decision was motivated by a particular desire to feel honorable. It was motivated by an old gentleman who was stand-ing by me and waiting to mail his letter.

"Make up your mind!" he growled. "I don't have all day."

I turned on him: "Don't mail it," I said. "It's no use. She couldn't be faithful to you anyway, *species of cuckold*!"

Just a normal exchange of courtesies on the streets of Paris, but in the meantime my fingers had opened and the fifty envelopes were inside the post office, waiting to be sorted and sent on to their respective addresses.

"*Alea jacta est,*" I murmured. Which means: this is the point of no return.

8

From that same post office—French post offices are conveniently equipped with telephone booths—I called Joyce. Since Nénette was out, I thought it would be fun to have dinner with the girl before taking her to the party. Only I didn't know how the unclean press photographer would like it.

Apparently it was the unclean press photographer himself who answered.

"Hello," I said. "My name is Walter de Walter. I'm sorry to trouble you. May I speak to Miss. . . ."

I realized I didn't know her last name, which, in French at least, makes it rather awkward to ask for a girl. The press photographer interrupted.

"Just a minute, she's taking a shower. Eh, Joyce," he yelled, "It's for you. Listen," he went on, lowering his voice, "are you by any chance that American chap who smells so good and who is going to take her to a party tonight?"

"Well, I am American, and I use *Moustache,* by Rochas. And, yes, we are going to a party tonight, I mean if you don't mind."

"Me? Mind?" He laughed. "Why don't you keep her? I have no use for that kind of girl. She takes eight showers a day, and would like me to do the same. There is only one shower here. So, if we're busy showering all day, when are we going to have a little fun? Maybe you at least have two bathrooms in your apartment."

"I'm afraid I can't oblige you. I live with friends."

"Well, too bad. I'll look for someone else. I had set my hopes on you, but I suppose somebody will come along. She is really a nice girl and all that, and if I had time to form her, she wouldn't be bad at all, but with all that showering. . . . And then she doesn't want me to eat any garlic! What would life be without garlic? Not

103

worth living, eh? And yesterday I sneezed, so she didn't want me to kiss her. Afraid of germs, she was. Well, that beats me! If a good kiss isn't worth a few germs. . . . Ah! here she comes."

Joyce then took the receiver and we arranged for me to pick her up at seven o'clock.

"I will have had dinner," she said. "You won't have to bother about that."

"You've got it all wrong," I said. "No one who is anyone dreams of dining before eight o'clock in this country, and the whole point of my invitation was dinner anyway. So don't you dare have dinner without me. So long."

One more thing remained to be done. I drove to another post office and sent a cable to Olivia. The telegraph is dependent on the Post in France. It was a very long and expensive cable. I wrote about the convention of the European Party and about the new weekly, *Le Haut-Parleur*. I did not say one word about pimping and flogging. If everything went well, she would find out soon enough. And I hoped at least one of the American correspondents would express some interest concerning "Les Enfants de Mai." That would send George Broker raving about guerillas wars, because he would feel that my unconfirmed piece of information had suddenly been confirmed. Yes, everything looked rather rosy at that point.

I drove home and changed into my light charcoal grey suit, with an eye on Nénette's white telephone. It rang one uncoded, two coded rings, but nothing from Fifi. Too bad. Pleasure before duty, always. I used plenty of *Moustache* and sauntered down to my car.

*

Joyce and her press photographer lived on the fifth floor of a dirty old building which had seen France switch from a monarchy to a republic, to an empire, back to monarchy, back to an empire, back to monarchy, then to constitutional monarchy, then back to republic, then back to empire, then back to republic, then to dictatorship, then back to republic, then back to mitigated dictatorship, then to a republic again, all that in much less than 200 years.

The old stones would have lived to see France become part of a United Europe under Serge Saint-Fiacre as president, if Fate and I hadn't had different designs on the said Serge Saint-Fiacre.

I didn't get the opportunity to smell the press photographer, but Joyce smelled quite nice, thank you, and she looked very pretty and innocent in her proper green dress. At least it was very proper from the front. It was also sleeveless and practically backless, but it is a well-known fact among travelers that different nations have different ideas about the relative sinlessness of the various parts of the body: American girls show their navels but hide their bosoms; French girls think it a charity to expose their breasts but, until lately, have been a little reluctant about exhibiting their stomachs; it is said that Arab women will show you *anything* before they show you their face. I didn't complain about either the front or the back, the ensemble being rather pretty to look at in a guileless way. The make-up, on the other hand, was heavier than I like. Joyce had tried to give herself the looks of a *femme fatale* and had only succeeded in looking like a provincial girl at her first ball in the great city, but that mattered very little to me. If she enjoyed blue and green paint, let her put on as much as she liked.

As a general rule, I am not overfond of freckled young idiots with starry eyes, but for a change I didn't mind. I watched her with amusement express satisfaction at being driven in an American car and even did all the running around and opening of doors that keeps American boys in such trim shape. Joyce took all that as her due: Nénette would have laughed in my face; Chantal would have said "You're not a flunky to do that."

I took little Joyce to *L'Oenothèque* which, to anyone who loves wine, is the best place to go to, and to anyone who doesn't also, because he will learn to.

We had a little scuffle at the entrance. Joyce had visibly made up her mind that I was the perfect gentleman and expected me to let her enter first. But, since I had devoted my evening to the young lady's education, I did it the French way. No decent Frenchman would let a lady enter first into a public place, because she might find herself at a loss there, or have to witness an unseemly sight. If I had opened the door of a restaurant for Nénette, she would have shoved me in; if I had done it for Chantal, she would probably have turned her back upon me and walked away. Joyce obviously thought I had forgotten my manners and tried to elbow her way in first. I caught her arm.

"I'll give you an F for conduct, college Miss," I said. "This side of the Atlantic, as Saint-Fiacre says, gentlemen face dangers first."

"Is there a danger?" she asked.

As I mentioned earlier, she was hopeless.

It pains me a little to remember that at first she was not too pleased with the place. It was not dark, as a fashionable American place would have been, and it was small, and the waiters had no fancy frock coats on. There were no candles on the tables, no flowers in vases, no trimmings. The service was efficient, but with no flourish to it. The cuisine was good but without fancy names on the menu. It was only the wines, and at the start she didn't give a damn about wines. At the start, yes. At the end, I had converted her, and I was perfectly sure that from now on she would study wines as seriously as she had studied French grammar and pass her exams, if any, with an A +. Poor child, she never came to do that after all.

We began with a half-bottle of Taittinger champagne, just to stimulate our taste buds.

"D'you mean we are not going to have a highball?" said Joyce.

The poor girl who was the daughter of a Baptist minister had just finished unlearning everything she had been taught from childhood, had just finished learning the great highball doctrine, and now she had to unlearn that.

"No, my dear," I answered sternly. "Hard liquor dulls your taste buds instead of sharpening them. No hard liquor before good wines."

I was really pedantic about it. I explained how champagne is made and taught her never to touch the glass itself but only the stem, so as not to warm the wine up. Joyce was interested, but she didn't like the Taittinger too much. It was too dry for her. She was glad to learn though that when speaking of champagne dry really means sweet, but sweet does not mean dry. She gravely thanked me for the lesson.

With the smoked salmon, we had half-a-bottle of Puligny-Montrachet, Clos de la Pucelle 1966. I explained the difference between white wines and red wines, and tried to impress upon her that the difference being real, it was a question of greater enjoyment, not of better etiquette, to drink these with one sort of food and those with another one. Joyce understood what I meant, but she was half-incredulous, half-disappointed. Enjoyment was a difficult word for her. She much preferred to be able to memorize a chart than to have to use her own judgment. She was still thinking in college terms and she liked it. She didn't mind spoiling a meal; what she really hated was flunking a course.

Still I could see she rather liked the Pucelle. She left me less.

With the entrecôte, we had a memorable 1959 Pommard. A half-bottle again. A wonderful way of sampling several wines and still be able to enjoy them. The *patron*—as you may know, in France it is the owner, not the client, who is called the patron—was a little shocked at my choice. Purists—and he was a purist—tend to prefer bordeaux to burgundy, and *patrons* also, because the great ones are even more expensive. But I rather like to shock a purist, and on the other hand I felt myself responsible for Joyce's education. Now burgundy is easier to enjoy than the more delicate bordeaux, and pedagogically I thought it better to start my student with a really pleasant impression. Joyce was indeed a good student. She gasped with pleasure at the superb full-bodied Pommard, and left me even less of it. Still I was drinking about two thirds of the bottle, while explaining the difference between the two kinds of perfume that you find in a wine, *bouquet* and *arôme*.

Joyce didn't want any cheese, but I wanted her to taste something more full-bodied than Pommard, and so we had cheese with a half-bottle of an excellent Nuits-Saint-Georges, which she liked even better than the Pommard. Such progress deserved a reward, and although I personally detest sweet wines, I ordered some dessert and a 1955 Haut-Peyraguey. This she loved and I felt a nearly fatherly pleasure to see her drink it in little, sensual sips.

"Like it?"

"There is nothing better on earth," she said firmly—well, as firmly as she could. "And to think that people drink whisky!"

We had a cup of coffee, no brandy, and, after that, felt ready for Saint-Fiacre's party.

Saint-Fiacre lived in one of the most charming parts of Paris, known as le Palais-Royal. Let me give you a brief description of the place. It will come handy a little later.

The Square du Palais-Royal is a public, formal French garden, with sanded walks, geometrical lawns, fountains and statues, lots of flowers, of course, forming intricate designs. Children come to play here and old gentlemen feed the pigeons. The square is surrounded on all sides by noble eighteenth century buildings, all in the same style, so that the garden appears to belong to them. Expensive apartments are to be found in those buildings. Many famous people live in them. The great writer Colette had her flat here. The ensemble has a great look of dignity and of charm at the same time: nothing stilted and nothing over-relaxed, a typical French atmosphere.

The beautiful old buildings stand back to back with other buildings, much less beautiful, separated from them by small courtyards, narrow as wells and about as clean as sewers. But these squalid neighbors cannot be seen from the glorious square; and that also may be typically French. Some passageways, though, connect the sumptuous square and the surrounding world. Through one of these, Joyce and I entered the gardens. The fountains whispered and gurgled. The world, which smelled of gasoline just a few meters away, here smelled of spring flowers. The streetlights shone dimly in the trees.

We had no trouble finding the house where M. Saint-Fiacre lived. The entrance hall to the whole building had been transformed into a checkroom. If you had brought a coat, you gave it to the concierge who hung it on a hanger and gave you a number. When you wanted the coat back, you would be expected to come up with a generous tip. France is definitely tipping country.

We walked up the broad staircase to the first floor, where Saint-Fiacre's apartment was located. The landing was full of people leaning on the marble balustrade, talking, gesticulating, drinking champagne or Scotch and eating *petits fours*.

"Where is the receiving line?" whispered Joyce, who felt shy, up to a point, but not altogether: she knew she was a good student and would learn to perfection whatever she was taught.

"You're in France, my child," I said. "No receiving line here. You have to go and look for your hostess yourself. Your host, in this case, since I gather Saint-Fiacre is unmarried."

Two strongly-built guys in white dinner jackets stood on each side of the door that led into the apartment. They were dressed up like waiters, but they looked what they were: bodyguards. You gave your cardboard to them.

"Monsieur et Madame Maclou?" said one of them looking at Joyce and me with a distrustful expression on his pink face. He was reading the card at the same time and comparing it with our appearance as if it were a photograph.

I shook my head. "No. This is a young lady from the United States and my name is Walter de Walter. M. Maclou let me have his invitation since it was too late to ask for a personal one."

"Irregular! Highly irregular!" commented the waiter.

"My good man," I said "I should encourage you to keep your comments to yourself. Neither the lady nor I are interested in hearing them. Let us pass or be so kind as to ask for instructions from your superiors."

He scowled at me, and Joyce gaped at me. I remained calm. I despise musclemen, and if they want to go disguised as flunkies, let them suffer the consequences.

The fellow winked at his partner and retreated a few steps into the apartment. There I saw him stop a very small young girl—she was even shorter than Joyce—dressed in an exquisite black long gown. The gown was obviously Haute Couture, the delicate body it half-hid, half-exhibited, came from an even better couturier. The whole impression was of something supple, soft, silky, yet strong: a Siamese cat, I thought. The eyes fitted: they were dark blue although the hair was light brown. She walked toward us and eyed my companion and her outrageous make-up with some amusement.

"What is the problem?" she asked.

Immediately I recognized the voice. It was the one I had heard on the phone: low-pitched, which was a little funny because the lady was so small, very soft, *velvety* I would say if I were a sentimental writer.

I introduced myself, explained the whole business and ended by asking to whom I had the honor of speaking. She looked at me with some irony, as if my question had been somehow rather ridiculous.

"I am M. Saint-Fiacre's bodyguard-in-chief," she said with some dignity.

"What?" cried Joyce.

It was not a very tactful way of putting it, but it is true that such a declaration coming from that diminutive figure was a little startling. I contained my surprise, though.

"Oh! indeed," I said. "And are you good at your job?"

She looked at me very gravely. I could read nothing in the mysterious dark eyes.

"Very," she said. And then, adopting a less serious tone, "Also I am sometimes his social secretary. The two fit rather well together. I think you may come in," she concluded. "And if you'll follow me, I'll try to introduce you to M. Saint-Fiacre."

So we walked past the two phony waiters. Joyce gasped with admiration at the sight of the apartment. It did look pretty rich, I must say, with its vast rooms, its beautiful inlaid floors, its high ceilings and massive ponderous rows of moldings, its tall windows draped in heavy, dark green curtains, its sparkling chandeliers, its inestimable Oriental rugs, its tenebrous mirrors and gilt bronzes everywhere. The furniture was Empire, much too majestic for my taste, but authentic and valuable.

The party was like most Parisian parties. A solid bourgeois entrée, salted with intellectuals, peppered with remnants of nobility. This one was a little under-peppered and much over-salted. It was not, by any standards, a political reunion, but the press was represented a little too heavily for the party to be really distinguished. I yawned. I hate that kind of party. I thought about the telephone I had left at Nénette's. Maybe it was ringing. I should have stayed by it. My only consolation was the bodyguard-social secretary's exquisite nape right there, under my nose.

"You haven't told me your name," I said, thinking that a mild flirtation with her would help the evening go by.

"Everyone calls me Mistigri," she replied, without turning her head.

Mistigri, in France, is a name for a cat, and I thought it was perfectly appropriate.

I recognized Saint-Fiacre from a distance. He was talking volubly to several men who stood listening with tall glasses of whisky or flat glasses of champagne in their hands. He was short and thin although he had fairly broad shoulders. His head, as I had seen on his photographs, was triangular in shape, with a narrow pointed chin and high, wide, receding forehead. The ears were incredibly long and narrow, which somehow didn't him make look like an ass at all, but like a very sardonic Mephistopheles. I noticed that he had a way of smiling at the end of nearly each sentence, not because it was in any way funny, but because it was his way of emphasizing what he said. It was an unpleasant smile, devoid of mirth and full of big sharp teeth.

"Our first responsibility," Saint-Fiacre was saying, gesticulating with his *coupe* of champagne, "is to the poor of all countries. Yes, I am not afraid of using this outdated word *poor*, because if the word is outdated, the disgraceful reality that hides behind it is not." (He smiled, as if he had said: See?) "The Christians among you must concur with me in that, because it is a tenet of the Christian faith that the last must be made first, and so we, at the European Party, are making the last people of all our countries our first preoccupation." (He smiled as if he had proved something to his own satisfaction and hoped to convince people by forcing them to mimic him.) "We may not be Marxists in the strict sense of the word, but are Marxists in this: we believe that progress cannot be obtained without revolution. We believe that the word *revolution*, which is *thought* to have two meanings, rotation and uprising, has only *one* meaning, which is the essence of revolution itself. We believe that humanity must revolve precisely as the earth revolves around itself and around the sun." And he smiled cunningly, as if to say: Well, what do you think of it? Aren't we clever, you and I, I just a little more than you? At that point Mistigri intervened:

"Excuse me, Monsieur Serge," (it was a very strange way of addressing him, this Monsieur plus the first name) "may I introduce two American guests, Miss. . . ?"

I thought Joyce would say "Call me Joyce" but she was not that dumb.

"Price," she said, "Joyce Price."

"Miss Price, and Mr. de Walter? They particularly wanted to meet you."

I did not particularly want to meet him. I did not not like his face, I had not liked his speech (which had reminded me of Hamlet's "Words, words, words"), I had caught a *coupe* of champagne from a passing tray and I didn't even like the champagne. I didn't like the party either, mainly because there were no American correspondents to be seen. But I bowed and said I was honored.

Saint-Fiacre, interrupted by his social secretary, was looking at us with a curious air. He might have been wondering what sauce he would eat us with. That supposition, by the way, was not far from the mark. Only, as will be seen, Joyce and I were not elected for the same sauce. Maybe it was my fault.

"Sir," I said, "I was very much interested by the point you developed just now. You were speaking about the essence of revolution which sounded like a synthesis of rotation and violence. Wouldn't you say that the word *revolver* then would contain both these notions and could be used as a symbol of what you wanted to express?" And I smiled as naïvely as I could.

He looked at me with his colorless eyes and I could sense that the sauce had been chosen and that it was going to be a spicy one.

"Mr. de Walter," he said with a dangerous suaveness, "I understand you are an American?"

"Yes, Monsieur."

"I believe you were not invited to this party?"

"I was not."

"But just decided to do me the honor to drop by?"

"And myself the pleasure, Monsieur."

"Well, since you seem to like symbols, don't you think that your very flattering decision could be used as a symbol of your country's attitude in world politics?"

There was some tittering around.

Saint-Fiacre smiled. I am not a violent man but at that moment I would have enjoyed smashing all those ugly teeth of his.

"Don't you think," he went on, "that quite a few nations have been put by your countrymen in exactly the same position as I find myself in tonight? In a position, shall I say, of reluctant hospitality? Do the names Chile, Iran, Congo, Spain, Greece, Turkey, ring a bell, Mr. de Walter? Does the name Vietnam ring a bell?"

He smiled. He had raised his voice so that people would surround us. He was writing aloud his next article for *Le Haut-Parleur*.

"Wouldn't you say," he went on, "symbolically, of course, that it has become something of a habit with Americans to crash parties all around the world?"

"Well, yes," I said. "I seem to recall a fellow named Hitler having a ball. We crashed it all right."

There was a dead silence. Suddenly I heard a very low gurgle at my elbow. I could have sworn it was Mistigri's voice, but when I looked at her she seemed serious as ever.

I should have stopped there. But I wanted to mark one point more.

"I also seem to recall a guy named Marshall," I said. "Personally, I don't believe in gratitude for nations, but still I don't think we ought to forget how indiscreet and tactless he was with this plan of his, which reconstructed all Europe."

"The Marshall Plan was an investment," said Saint-Fiacre dryly.

"Oh, I realize that," I replied. "The only thing I wonder about is why you didn't take Mr. Marshall by the collar and throw him out the window."

I turned to Mistigri.

"Don't worry, Miss Bodyguard, you won't have to do that to me. I have better manners than Mr. Eisenhower and Mr. Marshall: I know when I am not welcome." I turned to Joyce. "Miss Price, I apologize for having put you into such a position. Being partly French I also have to apologize for my countrymen's rudeness. I seem to be related to boors on both sides. Let's go."

At that point the other sauce came into play.

"My dear Miss Price," said Saint-Fiacre looking at her with the expression of a cannibal confronted with an appetizing human steak, "I would hate for you to take this personally. For one thing, a pretty woman is always welcome in France wherever she wants to go. And also we have nothing against Americans as such. They are a wonderful people who have taught us to love freedom. What we object to is some of their politics, but as soon as they get rid of the people who insist on making themselves obnoxious to all the world, we shall be ready to embrace them as our brothers . . . and sisters," he added with a brilliant smile.

Joyce should have turned her back on him and walked out with me. Instead she said:

"Oh! you see, Walter, it was just a misunderstanding. Monsieur Saint-Fiacre is really very nice."

"Yes," he said laughing, "very nice, I assure you."

He looked like the wolf disguised as the grandmother in Little

Red Riding Hood. I didn't know at this point if he was considering using Joyce for personal pleasure purposes, or if he was only campaigning, or both, but I didn't think he was very nice either way. Of course the poor girl didn't want to give up this party, which must have seemed very brilliant to her; still I thought she ought to sacrifice her pleasure to our dignity.

"The point is not whether he's nice or not," I said, "but he's made it very plain that he does not want us here. We were wrong in the first place in overestimating his manners. Let's remove ourselves as gracefully as we can."

"Oh! but I want you to stay," he said lightly. "Politics shouldn't spoil our personal delightful relationship."

He was looking ironically at me, with head cocked and one eye half-closed. It was strange to think that I was arranging this man's murder. If I had known at that time how much more intimate than that we were to become, I wouldn't have believed it. But I did think that he would make a charming cadaver.

"So you see," insisted Joyce with tears in her eyes. "Let's stay. We are invited now. And everything is so wonderful here. . . ."

I suppose I should have known better than to leave her there. But I couldn't stay and she didn't want to go. What could I do? Besides, I was angry with her for letting me down and also for not resenting a little more his slighting remarks about America. I am not very patriotic myself, but in that kind of a situation give me Chirpie any day! I bowed very formally to her.

"My dear Miss Price," I said, "I don't know who taught whom to love freedom, but I will certainly respect yours and leave you here. Kindly consider mine and get a taxi when you are ready to go home. As to everything being wonderful here, that is a matter of opinion. I find the champagne a little cheap for my taste."

I bowed as formally to M. Saint-Fiacre, even more formally to Mistigri who was biting her lip—yes, yes, I remember it, in vexation or amusement I couldn't tell, and walked out with as much dignity as I could muster past Pink-Cheeks whose eyes bulged as if they were going to snap out of orbits.

When I got home, Nénette was back and holding the phone.

"It's Fifi," she said. "It's for you."

9

"Where the bloody hell were you?" It was Fifi's voice.

"Who the bloody hell do you think you are speaking to? This is your case officer."

Fifi was not abashed. "Well, my case officer could bloody well have stayed by his phone to tell me what to do when I lost the client."

My heart missed a beat.

"What do you mean: lost him?"

"Just lost. Like a needle in a haystack, or a little girl her virtue."

This was a major catastrophe. But I was the officer in charge of the case. I had to remain calm. Anyway I was so flabbergasted I couldn't think of one swear word. With what, I hope, sounded like *sang-froid,* I managed to ask:

"How did it happen?"

Very simply indeed. To obey my orders, Fifi had begun circling the park. He had no trouble following the stone wall. He found one secondary gate. At one time he heard some shots.

"About twelve or thirteen," he said. "Pretty heavy caliber. It did not sound like a fight: it was the same weapon firing all the time."

Chirpie was sighting his rifle in, I thought.

It took Fifi about an hour to get back to his starting place. He had never left the woods. He evaluated the perimeter of the park at about three kilometers, which made a pretty sizable estate. He had just reached the road when he saw the back of the Renault van disappearing around the corner. Naturally he had had to have left his own GS some distance from there, not to make his surveillance too conspicuous. He ran to it as as fast as he could and then rushed in pursuit of the Renault. It could have taken any of the many roads that forked off right and left.

"What did you do then?"

"I found a service station and called you, *Mister* Turner, to tell you that we should have been at least two on the job."

That was true, of course. Well, one learns.

"And then?"

"Then I drove back to the park, left my car under some trees, took my flashlight and walked back to the gate."

"And then?"

"I climbed the gate, got on the other side of it, and had a look around. There is a house there, Napoleon III style, very ornate, in bad taste if you ask me."

"I don't. What next."

Somehow I felt that he still had something to tell me.

"Well, the house seemed empty and in disuse. I nosed a little around and guess what I found?"

"What? A dagger with its handle toward you? Of course I can't guess! Speak up, man."

"Oh, you know Macbeth too; that is gratifying. No, what I found was an old crumpled pack of Gauloises."

"Fifi! What was in it?"

"According to your instructions, I shouldn't have looked, but I did. Some child seemed to have scribbled on the lining of the package the two words *Hôtel Cardinal.*"

Yes, Chirpie's handwriting was not exactly that of a genius.

"Next?"

"Next, I pocketed the package, got out of the park, into my car, drove to the service station and called you again, *Mister* Turner. Still no answer. I could have waited. I decided against it. I called Information and discovered there was an Hôtel Cardinal in Paris. Of course, there are hundreds of Hôtel Cardinals in other cities, but I thought it was worth a gamble. I drove to Paris."

"Well?"

"I investigated the Hôtel Cardinal. It is a rather shabby place on the rue de Montpensier. I went in and talked some to the clerk. I asked him if it would be all right to bring a broad. He said yes, provided that I demonstrate good manners, which meant tipping him. I got to talking with him and had no trouble learning that he did have a chubby long-haired American on the third floor. His room had been reserved for him quite some time ago. His name was Mr. Chirpwood. Mr. Chirpwood had arrived a few hours ago. He had brought a very big trunk which they had had trouble hoisting up the stairs."

That made sense: it would have been the Ruger, all sighted in, and not to be disassembled.

"Next?"

"Next I decided the Hôtel Cardinal would be a snug place to stay in. I told the clerk I would be back. I found a phone booth and called you. Nénette said she hadn't seen you all day long. You were probably busy with the C.I.A. So I walked a little around the streets and found a broad to bring back to the hotel. She is with me now, drinking Suze by the bottle. I have to warn you they all go on my expense account: the hotel, the Suze and the broad."

"Next?"

"That's for you to tell me, *Mister* Turner."

Now I had to make a difficult decision.

"Are you under the impression that the client is watched?" I asked.

"I don't think so. The two men who brought him, that Laurel and Hardy team, drove away. I didn't see anyone else. Of course, I can't be sure."

It seemed possible to go and make contact with Chirpie without attracting too much attention. The night clerk would be sleepy, and it didn't seem to be the kind of hotel where they are over-mindful of their guests' morals. It would be very efficient to get straight from Chirpie whatever information he had. On the other hand, I was the case officer and had nothing to do in the field. Fifi seemed good at his job and he spoke English. I had quarreled with Saint-Fiacre that very evening, and, although nobody would suspect me of having him murdered because he had been rude, it would still be better to stay as far away from the murderer as I could. Besides, don't forget that the rue de Montpensier runs alongside the Palais-Royal square; the party was still not at an end; I could meet someone who had noticed me, which could prove awkward in the end. I was not particularly fond of the idea of confiding entirely in Fifi, but . . . I closed the telephone with my hand and looked at Nénette who had just appeared in the doorway, clad in the most interesting nightie.

"Nénette," I said, "how much would you trust Fifi?"

"All the way," she said simply. And by way of explanation she added: "He hates everybody. So. . . ."

"Fifi?"

"Sir?"

I heartily disliked his ironical manner, but I made up my mind to stand it a little longer. It seemed safer, in the long run.

"Fifi, check into that hotel, and make contact with Chirpie. I don't know what cafés are open at that time in that part of town, and anyway I don't want to go there now. Meet me at half-past two where the statue of Musset used to stand."

I once had a special tenderness for that statue which stands practically at the corner of the Palais-Royal: it had been the meeting place of my first love, or, as the French poetically put in the plural, of my first loves. Not having the same recollections, André Malraux, when he was Minister of the Beaux-Arts, had my pet statue taken away.

"Half past two!" cried Nénette. "But then when are we going to. . . ." She pouted.

"Before and after, my dear," I reassured her. To Fifi who had just acknowledged my instructions, I said:

"Keep up the good work, and you might get a bonus in the end." Then I tried to hang up as fast as I could, but he beat me to it.

It was about midnight then and what I did to keep me awake is, as I mentioned once before, none of your business. At ten past two, I walked down the stairs, as silently as I could, out of consideration for Nénette's neighbors: the French will forgive you anything except being deprived of sleep.

The night was cool and sweet, one of those inimitable May Paris nights. Just to drink Parisian air in that season and at that hour is to feel young and strong and in love. Strangely enough, as I walked to the place where I had parked the Continental, it was not Amarantha's or Nénette's image which swam before my eyes. It was not Joyce's either, I must confess: I had forgotten all about the little fool. It was the tantalizing, mysterious, ambiguous picture of that little Siamese cat; Mistigri. I gave her little thought at the time, but obviously my subconscious was quicker than I.

It was pleasant to drive fast through those streets through which one had had to crawl in the daytime and in the evening. Most windows were dark, but from some, still lit up, came the joyful sound of music and laughter. Cats investigated garbage cans. Policemen walked their beats. And I had left Nénette's bed to plot murder.

Fifi was waiting for me.

"Come," he said.

We walked up the rue de Montpensier which runs alongside the Palais-Royal square and is separated from it by a double row of houses standing back to back: the beautiful ones, as I have described, opening on the square; the shabby ones, opening on the right side of the rue de Montpensier. The iron curtains of all the stores were down. There seemed to be not one window lit up in the whole street. On the right, Fifi showed me a closed door, with the half-erased words HÔTEL CARDINAL painted above it in a half-circle.

"Fourth floor, second window from the left," he commented.

As there were only three windows to a floor, it was not hard to find.

"Come on, I want to show you something else."

We went further up the street. Suddenly two mini-miniskirted redheads emerged from a doorway.

"Hello, darlings," said redhead number one.

"Come up with us?" offered redhead number two.

"Thank you, ladies, not tonight," I courteously replied.

"We'll show you things," insisted number one.

"Four is a nice figure," added number two.

"Go to hell or I'll smash your heads together!" said Fifi.

"Is that all you can do?" asked number one with a heavy irony.

"Well, it's not much!" concluded number two in the tone of a gross insult.

They walked on down the street, and we walked on up the street.

"Fancy paying to get a woman!" I exclaimed. "I'd as soon be paid myself."

"Doesn't surprise me, coming from you," growled Fifi.

About one hundred meters—three hundred feet to you—from the Hôtel Cardinal, Fifi stopped and showed me a building on the left, i.e., on the other side of the street. It was an old, grey house, which in former days must have looked opulent: the house-in-town of some wealthy bourgeois at the turn of the century, or a little before that. Now, it was somewhat run down; it was used partly for offices, partly as a printing shop. Above the huge door which had been built to let carriages enter into the courtyard, you could read IMPRIMERIE SAINT-FIACRE (Saint-Fiacre Printing Company) and at eye-level, on the side of the door, there was a large brand new brass plate, which had been engraved to read thus: LE HAUT-PARLEUR, PORTE-PAROLE DU PARTI IN-TERNATIONAL EUROPEEN (The Loud-Speaker, Voice of the International European Party). So this then was Serge Saint-Fiacre's office, located less than a quarter of a mile from his apart-ment in the Square du Palais-Royal.

"Very convenient to come home to lunch," I commented.

There was no point in trying to hide from Fifi what he already obviously knew: that Chirpie was after Saint-Fiacre.

"That's exactly the point," he answered a little mysteriously. "Come, there is a café open in a side-street."

"Not too close by?"

He just shrugged his shoulders as if my remark had been very silly indeed. We walked for about ten minutes before we reached his café. We sat down and ordered some coffee and Calvados (apple brandy). When the waiter had left us in our corner, Fifi looked at me thoughtfully and finally said:

"Well?"

"Well?" I repeated.

He smiled his languid smile.

"Well, it's for tomorrow. 12.05 approximately. Bluebeard leaves his office regularly at 12 noon. As a matter of fact, it's the last time he's going to do it for some time, since the Convention of the International European Party is opening the day after tomor-row. He walks down the rue de Montpensier on the left side of the street, till he reaches a crossing which I can show you. He always crosses there, because on the right side of the street there is a *café-tabac* where he buys his cigars and usually has a small *apéritif* with some of his workers. Very democratic, as you see. After the apéritif, he comes out of the café and goes down on to the end of the street, passing before the HÔTEL CARDINAL. At the corner, he makes a left and enters the Square du Palais-Royal where his apartment is located, but I guess you know all about that. Well, here's what's scheduled. At 12.02, your intellectual friend Mr. Chirpie gets into position at his window and waits. The fat guy, Boudin, stays with him to point out Bluebeard as soon as he shows up on the right side of the street. After that, Boudin leaves to check that nothing will interfere with the escape plan and Chirpwood is on his own. He seems to know his job well as far as shooting is concerned and he certainly has a very nice rifle. He waits for Bluebeard to reach the crossing: that's what the rifle has been sighted in for: 100 meters. Of course, there will be some traffic, but Bluebeard is known not to jaywalk and never to cross between cars. So it should be pretty smooth-going. Bluebeard stands there, or, at worst, he is walking at a normal pace. Chirpwood has all the time in the world to aim and press the trigger. That's it."

"What about the escape plan?"

"Yes, I guessed you would be interested in that. Chirpwood shoots. One shot should be enough. After that, he runs down the stairs. Nobody is expected to try and stop him, because the shot won't have been heard because of the traffic. If they do, Boudin is to dispose of that problem. Now, the hotel has a small back-courtyard, which communicates with the back-courtyard of a house that gives on to the square. Chirpwood and Boudin slip away into courtyard one, then into courtyard two, then into the house on the square, then into the square itself. They cross the square and exit at the other end. There, Snipe will be waiting with a car. Chirpwood is booked on a flight to London and from there to the U.S. They've timed the escape. From Chirpwood's room to the groundfloor, 30 seconds. From the groundfloor of the hotel to the square, 20 seconds. To cross the square without running, 50 seconds. To get into the car: 20 seconds. In under two minutes they should be on their way."

"Did Chirpie do all the timing himself?"

"No. It was done before he came."

"Does he have his passport with him?"

"I thought about that. It seems Snipe has confiscated the passport."

"Do you know what car they will use?"

"Chirpwood didn't say. I don't think he knows."

"What flight is he booked on?"

"Air France at 13.09. They're cutting it pretty thin but they can manage. It's from Orly, you know. Even if they miss it, they probably could get him on another one, unless somebody finds out immediately who fired the shot. Usually the police are good, but they don't work so fast as that."

"The way it's set-up, it seems France will be able to extradite him from the U.S.?"

He smiled at me.

"That's not the way I've got it figured out," he said, "but in principle you are right."

"Let's hear your theory, Fifi."

"My theory? Well, you see, I was very much impressed with Mr. Chirpwood's intellectual capabilities. Of course, it could be a coincidence, and you, Americans, chose him only for his shooting performance, but I think you must also have given some consideration to the fact that, in a pinch, he would get completely confused and could never realize that he had been set up for it all. My theory, *Mister* Turner, is this, and you can put it in your pipe or anywhere else, I don't care. Some U.S. outfit or other feels the need to butter up the French. A fairly prominent political figure is chosen, one which is supposed to be displeasing to the Americans, but about which, in reality, they couldn't care less. Part of the outfit is designated to play the role of Bad Americans. They plan and prepare the assassination of said political figure. Part of the outfit is designated to play the role of Good Americans. *Mister* Turner is a prominent member of that part. Of course, he possesses all the information he needs in advance, but he has to make it look good, so he hires a French—how do you say? thighman?— to run a few errands. The exact time of the assassination is determined, also the escape plan. After that, the American Ambassador, or C.I.A. resident, or, whoever, calls the French and says: 'Bad Americans are going to assassinate Frenchman at such and such a place and at such and such a time. That Frenchman, by the way, did make himself obnoxious to us, but we love you so much, we couldn't help telling you all the same. Your move.' Well, the

French tell Saint-Fiacre to stay in his office, and a battalion of armed gendarmes come to arrest poor Mr. Chirpwood. The only thing I haven't figured out is whether Snipe and Boudin play a part—in that case they will disappear from the scene in time—or whether they are being deliberately sacrificed just as Chirpwood, in which case they are going to be arrested too, and the plan, then, must have some ramifications in the United States."

"Meaning?"

"Meaning that they really think they are preparing for Saint-Fiacre's assassination, and that the person who recruited them and gave them their orders is being framed by some good friends of his. Just a supposition. The C.I.A. really want to dispose of Saint-Fiacre. They have to discuss the plan with the intelligence community before they go ahead. Some other outfit, let's say the D.I.A. for instance, encourages them to do it, and then denounces them to the French. Chirpwood is caught; he knows nothing; but Snipe is caught: he knows something. The French extradite him to the Americans. The Americans give him the third degree. He denounces his C.I.A. boss. 'See what the C.I.A. has been doing!' yells the D.I.A. 'Destroy the C.I.A. and give us all their money. We are nice guys, we do not assassinate people.' Something like that."

I looked at him with some curiosity. It all sounded very probable, only I knew I had not been sent by the D.I.A. or by any Good Americans' gang.

"The pity of it all," he concluded, "is that Saint-Fiacre is going to go on living and stinking. Couldn't you have the French move in after he's dead? If you would, I'd willingly give up my salary."

"What do you have against him?" I asked. I was deeply surprised.

"It wouldn't interest you," he said.

"It would."

"I'd have to tell you the story of my life to make you understand."

"Go ahead. And by the way, I didn't mail any money to you. Since we seem to be meeting more often than I expected, just tell me how much you want now."

"Ninety, plus expenses. Shall we say two hundred? Gas is expensive in this country."

I slid him the money under the table as I had seen it done in films.

"Now, why do you hate Bluebeard, as you call him? Were you one of the little boys he used to flog?"

"Oh! you've heard of that? No, it's much more simple than that. I was born in Algeria. Ever heard of it?"

"A French colony."

"Yes, maybe a colony. Although my family had lived there for more than one hundred years. Quite a few Americans, I think, would feel that America is their country even if they were not fourth generation Americans. . . . Well, that's neither here nor there. As you know, some of the local people rebelled. I'm not saying it was entirely unjustified. I'm not saying we had done nothing but good to that country, although I think that we had done mainly good: agriculture, school, hospitals. . . . Anyway, there was a war, and the French won it in the field. But while they were winning it with the help of half-a-million locals, natives, whatever you want to call them, there were people sitting in France and yacking about the sacred right of peoples to choose their own destiny, and so on. For some reason, it's always the other peoples who have that right: never you. We also were a people, and we wanted to stay in what was our country. But we didn't have the right to choose our own destiny. We had the right to leave our houses and our churches and our cemeteries and to pack one bag and to be 'repatriated' as they called it. We were not repatriated: we were exiled."

"Why did you go?"

"Who, me?"

He gulped down his Calvados and signalled for more.

"Everyone has got to die," he said, "but I would prefer not to die with my balls in my mouth. Thank you."

He was deeply moved about what he had just told me, and I was too, in a way.

"And Saint-Fiacre?" I prompted.

"Oh! Saint-Fiacre was one of those who kept busy waving the flag very high. The enemy's flag, of course. Men love flags, you know. But it has become ridiculous to wave your own: so you wave the opposition's."

He was bitter. I could understand that.

"There are quite a few people in France whom you must wish dead," I said.

"Oh! yes," he responded cheerfully. "Quite a few."

I tried very hard to think. The last twenty hours or so had not been very conducive to creative thought, but I knew I had to reach a decision. Would I go on from there alone, or would I take Fifi even more into my confidence? I felt some sympathy for him, in spite of his undisciplined manners, and he had been very good so far. When he had lost Chirpie, it had been my fault, not his. There was another point which might be worth taking into consideration: I mean Fifi's reconstruction of the case. He was wrong concerning me, but the rest sounded plausible enough. Indeed, it was the only explanation that I could see of the fact that Chirpie's identity had not been protected. Well, there was another explanation, of course: my readings had taught me that there were quite a few American tycoons playing not Kriegspiel but Spionspiel around the world and they were bound to be amateurish in some of their methods. Imagine a rich, patriotic American annoyed by Saint-Fiacre's attitude and deciding to do a good deed by ridding the world of the impudent frog-eater. Would he have thought about extradition and the like? He might even have figured that the U.S. would not extradite such a patriotic murderer. I wouldn't have put that kind of reasoning past quite a few magnates whom I happened to know. And one thing more. Maybe the U.S. government didn't deal in assassinations. But provided that one had been committed which was not altogether displeasing to the Establishment, wouldn't the Establishment maybe consider denying all knowledge of the assassin? . . .

I acted on an impulse. I felt somehow responsible for Chirpie's safety.

"You spoke of false passports. Could you provide one?"

"What nationality? How soon? How good a fake? Mind you: a good one would take several days."

I was impressed by such professionalism.

"And what about an entry visa on a real passport?"

"No problem at all. Two hours time. Fifty bucks. Forty-five for you."

He smiled ironically at me. I knew now that I would use him again. But I would make the most of it.

"Fifi," I said, "you got it all wrong. That comes from thinking too much when you are in a subordinate position. You think that I want Saint-Fiacre alive and Chirpwood in the jug? I want the opposite. I want Chirpie free and Saint-Fiacre as dead as can be."

I did. An attempt at murder never sells as well as the real thing.

"You do?" said Fifi. He tried to betray as little surprise as he could but I saw him try. "Well, good for you."

"Can you tackle Boudin?"

"What do you mean: tackle? Wrestle with him? No, I cannot."

"Just incapacitate him for a while."

He thought for a second.

"Will a broken kneecap do?"

"It would be splendid."

"Then I'm your man. I'm not really very good at beating people up, but I'm good at kneecaps. Nobody ever thinks of protecting his kneecap. And with a piece of heavy pipe, it's really very easy if you know in which direction to hit. Of course, I'll want a bonus. I'm committed to legwork, not to armwork."

"Thirty more a day," I promised, "and it's only fair since, after all, you are becoming accessory to murder after the fact, you realize that?"

"Oh! that doesn't frighten me. I have been that already. Once before the fact, and another time during the fact, if you know what I mean."

I looked at him. With his long hair held together by a rubber band, his pale skin, his blue eyes, his nearly feminine features, he did not look the part of a tough. But in those cool eyes of his I could detect now a certain wariness and a certain cruelty which were difficult to notice at first sight.

"All right," I said. Under the table, I gave him Chirpie's original passport. "I'll need an entry stamp on this before tomorrow eleven a.m."

"Date of entry?"

"I don't care. A few days ago."

"Can do." He pocketed the passport deftly.

"Tomorrow, I want you in the hall of the Hôtel Cardinal at

noon. When Chirpie comes down after firing his shot, I want you to knock Boudin out. I will be cruising on the Place du Palais-Royal with the Continental. Chirpie will come and join me there."

"Does he know that already?"

"No, you will have to tell him tonight."

"And he will obey you instead of the Boudin-Snipe team?"

"Yes. He knows about the plan but he does not know how it's going to come off. How did he receive you when you talked to him?"

"Oh! he received me very well, after I had gone through the password rigmarole. I say! Maybe he is a fake moron?"

"Stop trying to be clever. Just go and tell him what the plan is. After you've knocked Boudin down, disappear. I want nothing else from you. Report in the evening at Nénette's. Don't try to help me in any way. Just get the hell out of there."

"Understood."

"Under what name did you check in in the hotel?"

"A false one, of course."

"How about your bedfellow? Did you throw her out? She must be wondering at seeing you gone for such a long time."

"Oh! no, she isn't wondering."

"Why not?"

"I told her I wanted no wondering. And if there were any, I would cut her."

"Is it that simple?"

I didn't see him move and suddenly there was a switchblade in his hand, pointed at me.

"Yes," he said languidly, "it's simple."

He folded the knife and put it in his pocket. Suddenly he laughed.

"What are you laughing at?"

"It makes me feel good to think that tomorrow night the worms will begin on old Bluebeard," he said. "Thank you, *Mister* Turner. I didn't think I would enjoy our relationship as much as I do."

10

It was nearly four when I crept back home.

"Coming to bed?" asked Nénette.

"Not yet."

"It's hard work, working for the C.I.A.," she mumbled in a sleepy voice.

I sat by the phone and called Gerhard Cromlinckx. I had to let the phone ring quite some time before he bothered to pick it up.

"Who is the damned fool . . . ," he began.

"Did I wake you up?"

"No, you didn't, and that's the worst part of it. Who are you?"

"It's Walter, Gerhard."

"Walter?" He gave a joyful yell. "I'm glad to hear your voice, old chap, but I shan't hide from you that if you had called a few minutes later it would have been more diplomatic."

"Is she pretty?"

"Gorgeous, my dear fellow, simply gorgeous. A real Rubens! I can't circle her waist with my two arms. Where are you calling me from? New York?"

"No, no. Paris. Very close to your place, in fact."

"Won't you drop in for a drink? We need a rest anyway."

"No, thanks. I was just going to ask a favor of you."

"Fire away."

"Are you using this hunting lodge of yours, where we had such a nice time with Anny and Fanny?"

"No! I can't be in two places at the same time. For when do you need it?"

"Tomorrow."

"A *partie fine*?"

"A square party, which, as you know, is not a party for squares!"

He guffawed. "Well, of course, my dear chap, whatever you like. You know where the key is, don't you? And there must be some booze in the cabinet. And the refrigerator should be full. You'll need it!" He roared with laughter.

"Thank you, Gerhard. Everything all right with you?"

"No, but I hope it will be soon."

He roared again. I thanked him and hung up. Gerhard is the enormous son of enormously rich Flemish parents. In spite of that, he is very fond of things French, including French women, although as a rule he finds them too slim for his taste. He has all the qualities of his Belgian compatriots: he is warm, hospitable, lusty and lustful, and he has a somewhat robust sense of humor. His hunting lodge is used very often, as much by his friends as by himself, and, I must confess, not always in hunting season.

Now, I had finally earned the little sleep I could get, and I fell into bed as if I had been shot. Yes, sleep, I mean it. It had been a long day, I hope everybody has already understood that I am not James Bond, and Nénette can be quite humane when she has to. I never slept better in my life than on the night before the proposed murder of Bluebeard.

∗

The next morning I was a new man. At least that was Nénette's opinion. She even wanted to serve me breakfast in bed, but I am a classicist at heart and hate this *mélange des genres*: whatever gratitude I deserved, if it were presented in an edible form, I would consume it comfortably seated at a table and not reclining as a sick man.

"The C.I.A. seems to be feeling better this morning," said Nénette brightly.

She had a white déshabillé on, and the sun was shining, and she had already been to the bakery for fresh croissants. The coffee smelled delicious.

We had a charming little breakfast together, and then I went out. I did feel a little sleepy and had the shadow of a headache, but nothing that a quarter of an hour's walk would not take care of. I went to the post office and bought seven *pneumatiques. Pneumatiques*, or *pneus*, as they are called for short, are the fastest way of communication in the good city of Paris, where some people still don't have a telephone. You drop the thing in a special box, and a flow of compressed air takes it, in a matter of minutes, to the post office nearest to your addressee's residence. Then a young boy on a bicycle completes the way, gets a tip, and drives back to the post office where he waits for the next *pneu*.

I borrowed Nénette's typewriter—she never uses it, but M. Gillet thought that such an intellectual young lady as she is couldn't live without one, so he gave her this expensive Hermès instead of a dress from Courrèges—and typed six times (the seventh *pneu* was in case I made a mistake: I hate erasing) the following text:

After 12.30 inquire after Serge Saint-Fiacre's health. If the reply sounds interesting to you, you'll find it worth while to be around 18.00 at Saint Hu. Consider this as confidential. Only five other reporters, all of your caliber, are being asked. You may bring cameras but not photographers. We pledge not to use you as hostages if you do not make contact with the police. Signed: LES ENFANTS DE MAI.

Detailed explanations of how to get to the hunting lodge followed in a postscriptum. The great advantage of this place ridiculously nicknamed Pavillon Saint-Hu was that it stood just on the other side of the Belgian frontier, which would make it much cosier for Chirpie's press conference.

The six people to whom the *pneus* went were reporters with a certain standing in the profession; moreover, they were people whom I either knew personally, or about whom I knew enough. I was sure they would not betray the confidence of anybody who was willing to give them an interesting and exclusive piece of information. The hostage bit was mainly to keep in character with my Enfants de Mai organization: the journalists knew perfectly well that they would not be taken as hostages: no one wants to antagonize the press. So I didn't worry too much about the typewriter: yes, the police could trace it, but the police would never know about the message. The first thing these six responsible people would do would be to destroy the *pneu,* whether they planned to attend the conference or not. As to the message itself, I would have liked to make it longer, more picturesque, still more in character, but, to tell you the truth, I despise typing, and typing the same thing several times in a row is really too much of a bore. Don't tell me I could have used a carbon: it is discourteous, and journalists don't like to be treated that way. Not that they seriously object to the carbon, but they wonder who got the master copy, and that makes them furious.

I addressed the *pneus* with the same typewriter. One went to my friend, Herr Doktor; two to French journalists; two to American correspondents; one to a very lovely Italian newspaperwoman, of whom I had the most pleasant recollections.

I kissed Nénette: "*Darrlene,* are your going out again?" she asked.

"Soon, my dear. But if all goes well, we can have supper together tonight. Where do you want to go?"

For all her intellectualism, Nénette was not above liking a floor show.

"*Le Camp du Drap d'Or?*"

"All right. I'll call to make reservations."

I had just finished calling when the telephone rang. It was coded. It was for me.

"*Mister* Turner," said Fifi's voice, "I've got it."

"What?"

"The pipe."

"What else?"

"The visa."

"Good. Where are you?"

"On the Esplanade des Invalides. Busy throwing to the winds the tickets I found under the wipers of my 2 CV."

"I'll meet you there in ten minutes."

Nénette looked at me with some anxiety.

"Walter *darrlene,* are you sure that you are doing the right thing?"

"What do you mean?"

"The right thing for you. You look so serious. You have that awfully earnest expression on your face that men get when they are trying to make money. You were not born to make money. You were born to spend it. It's always a great mistake to rebel against one's fate," she added with a wise air.

What could I say? She was right, of course. But the illusion that before spending money you have to make it is so widely received in our times that it is sometimes impossible to revert to the sensible, healthy approach of past centuries, when there were people born to make money, and people made to spend it, and they were never the same. So much more efficient, really, so much more specialized and modern, but it just doesn't work that way any more.

"Yes, Nénette. Would you have an old pair of black stockings?"

"Of what?"

"You heard right, my dear, and I'm not going to earn money by making female impersonations."

She looked at me to check whether I was completely crazy or just half.

"Does it matter if they have holes?"

It didn't, so she brought me a pair and I drove off to Les Invalides.

Fifi reported that Chirpie had been elated upon hearing about my plan. Snipe and Boudin had been giving him a hard time since the arrival. When he was doing the sighting in, they kept hissing: "If you miss S.F., we won't miss you." So he had no objections whatsoever to that piece of pipe colliding with Boudin's knee cap, although I must say it looked vicious enough. I winced on seeing it. Fifi looked ironically at me.

"What do you care? It's not your knee cap, not your pipe even. By the way, you are not curious to know what will become of the rifle?"

"I was going to ask you," I lied.

He grinned. "Chirpie is to abandon it in the courtyard, hidden behind the garbage cans, so the police waste some time wondering which window the shot was fired from. Snipe's instructions were for Chirpie to close his window after shooting, but I took the liberty to change them. The weather is nice and many windows will be open: it is better not to risk attracting attention by closing it. I told Chirpie the orders came from you. Was that all right, *Mister* Turner?"

I decided to try some irony myself. "Fifi, what would I do without you?"

"I'm beginning to wonder," he replied immediately.

"I have changed my mind about the car," I said. "A light blue American car would be very conspicuous. Why don't you let me borrow your 2 CV? I would leave the Continental here and later change cars. The only trouble is someone could note the 2 CV's license plate number, and that would put you in a fix."

He smiled his superior smile, led me to the 2 CV, opened the door and extracted something from under the seat. It was a bundle of six or seven license plates.

"Where did you get them from?"

"When I have nothing to do at night, I walk along lonely streets with a screwdriver in my pocket," he explained. "The plate which is on now is not the real one. Just leave the 2 CV around here somewhere and I'll pick it up and change the plate."

He gave me the keys and checked his watch. I did the same. It was ten past eleven. His usually dispassionate eyes twinkled.

"Till we meet again," he said, and got into the rented GS. I don't know why, I had some trouble swallowing. After all, there was still ample time to call everything off and to let Serge Saint-Fiacre go on living. I got angry getting used to the preposterous gearshift system of the 2 CV and drove off with a disgraceful lot of racket.

I arrived at Place du Palais-Royal much too early, so I found a nook to park the little 2 CV and walked over to the Café du Louvre to have a drink. Not that I needed it: it's so vulgar to *need* a drink, but I *wanted* it very much. I had a Scotch Perrier. I don't usually spoil the good Scotches that I drink, but somehow the discreet bubbling of the Perrier water seemed to fit in with my mood. The weather was great. Even the Parisians smiled. I tried not to look incessantly at my watch but apparently I didn't succeed, for the bald sympathetic old waiter smiled to me in a fatherly way and said:

"Don't worry, sir. She'll come. They always come in the end. She's just a little late. They always are."

He obviously spoke from experience. Well, the Café du Louvre is a fairly popular place for appointments and rendezvous of all sorts.

At ten to twelve, I made up my mind to begin cruising. But at five to twelve I decided this would just be a way to attract the attention of the policeman who was standing on that corner, and who already seemed to look at me with a ferocious glint in his eye. So I sat five minutes more in the car. It was a harrowing experience. Not so much because a murder was going to take place that I still could prevent, but because it was the first time in my life I was sitting in a car with borrowed license plates. At twelve exactly I finally allowed my hands and feet to start working. I was supposed to back out from my little nook; instead, I charged forward and nearly squashed Fifi's 2 CV into the back of a Rolls Royce. I slammed the brake down and somehow extricated myself from that ridiculous position. Passers-by had already begun to stop and laugh at me. They always laugh at you in Paris if you make the smallest mistake in driving, and they make nasty remarks to you like "Did you get your license through a correspondence course?" or "Where did you leave your wooden shoes?", wooden shoes being the distinctive mark of a peasant and peasants being supposed not to know how to drive.

I began cruising around. There was no clock in the car so I had to look at my watch all the time. It all seemed somehow very ordinary and tame. Now Saint-Fiacre was leaving his office. Now, with his usual demagoguery he was inviting some of his workmen to have a drink with him. Now he was leaving the building. Now he was walking down the street, talking to the men at his side; they listened to him very respectfully and thought about what they would order at his expense in the *café-tabac*. Now Boudin had seen him and was poking Chirpie in the ribs. . . . I had a temptation to turn into the rue de Montpensier but, of course, I resisted it. At the very idea my intestines began to curl and uncurl in my belly like a couple of cobras. Somewhere on the other side of the Palais-Royal Snipe was waiting too, maybe as nervous as I.

Now, surely, Saint-Fiacre was reaching the crossing. Chirpie was squinting, his eye very close to the scope. . . . Very foolishly I began listening for the shot, although I knew I couldn't hear it with all the din all those cars were making. I visualized Chirpie's hand slowly closing over the trigger, "like pressing a sponge" they tell you, when they teach you how to shoot. I knew. I also had been a decent shot in my time. Now Chirpie was running down the stairs, while Saint-Fiacre—Bluebeard, they called him—with a neat little hole in the forehead, was falling on the pavement. I could see it. I could see it as if in slow, very slow motion: the arms spreading out, the head collapsing on the chest, a little to one side, the feet leaving the ground and falling back with a thud, and Chirpie breathlessly running down the stairs.

"Wally! Wally! Stop!"

I had passed him without seeing him. He was standing there, in front of the Palais-Royal, for everyone to see, gesticulating and shouting frantically. And he held a long bundle in his right hand, a bundle wrapped up in a sheet. I could guess what it was. My heart sank. I wanted to drive away at full speed: it seemed like the only chance of saving myself. But however lax my upbringing, it didn't include abandoning a chum at the time of danger.

I braked, stopped, backed. About three hundred drivers began hooting at me, and I seemed to hear some discourteous remarks about correspondence courses and wooden shoes. But I managed to throw the door open for Chirpie, and to drive off in the right direction while he still had one foot on the sidewalk. It was not exactly a discreet disappearance. Still all would have gone off tolerably well if it were not for that bundle.

"Hi, Wally, I'm sure glad to see you again," remarked Chirpie, happily unconscious of the situation.

I forced myself to drive slowly. I mean slowly for a Parisian driver.

"What the hell did you bring that damned thing here for?"

"I wasn't going to leave it with those bastards," he replied indignantly. "It's a good rifle, Wally. Really."

"Don't you realize that about one thousand people must have seen you with it?"

"It is wrapped."

"You mean they couldn't guess what it was by the length?"

"It's not the right length for a Ruger any more. I disassembled it."

"You took the time to disassemble it?"

"Sure. It was worth it."

Another idea struck me.

"And the sheet, Chirpie! As soon as they find a sheet missing, they'll know it was you!"

He had a very sly look on his face. "Ah! but I didn't take one of my sheets. The next door room wasn't locked. I took somebody else's sheet."

He was very pleased with himself. I was looking into the rear view window. So far, we were not pursued.

"So," I said, "how did it go. Is it. . . ? Is he. . . ?"

Chirpie nodded complacently.

"Saw him fall, the damned anti-American bastard. Fell backwards. Like this." He tried to show me how Saint-Fiacre had fallen. Then he patted the bundle: "Good girl," he said.

I couldn't describe my feelings at this point. I don't know what they were. I probably should say that I was utterly disgusted, and I was, but not utterly. I also was deeply relieved that all seemed to have gone reasonably well. "Ah! Mr. Bopkins," I thought. "You didn't know with whom you were dealing, did you?"

"What about Boudin?" I asked.

"When I came down," said Chirpie, "Boudin was lying on the floor, bawling like hell. And the clerk was lying next to him."

"Bawling too?"

"No, silent like."

"And then?"

"Nothing. I went into the back-courtyard, and through the other house and through the gardens. No problem. I ran a little to make up for lost time."

My heart sank. Chirpie's long-haired figure running through the gardens of the Palais-Royal, waving a sheet-wrapped bundle, couldn't have remained unobserved. Then the scene on the Place. . . . I was glad to have reached les Invalides without being stopped by any of the policemen who were directing the traffic. We changed cars. Chirpie brought his infernal Ruger with him. I was glad to feel all the power of the Continental at my disposal now. We made straight for the Belgian frontier.

*

I didn't know at what time the radio would announce Saint-Fiacre's assassination. It was bound to create a sensation, since the Convention of the International European Party was beginning on the morrow, so I just put the radio on and left it. Meantime, I made Chirpie tell me the whole story again and again. He was in a talkative mood. He described the trip, the arrival, the sighting in in the old park—he hadn't the slightest idea of where it was located since he had travelled in the back of the closed van all the time. He described a meal he had had in a restaurant with Snipe and Boudin. "They were treating me buddy-like, you know. But now and then, they would bark at me: 'If you miss him, son-of-a-bitch, we won't miss you.' And the wine we drank. Wally, I respect you very much, but I'm sure you never tasted the like. It was white, and sweet and it bubbled like Coca-Cola." I was pretty sure Chirpie was right and I had never tasted the like. He asked me for the name of it and I told him it must have been some kind of *vin mousseux*. He repeated the name several times, and although his pronunciation was anything but perfect, he managed to get out sounds like *vahn-moo-sur* which didn't sound altogether impossible to understand.

We had a big quarrel, Chirpie and I, on the road. I wanted to throw the Ruger into any of the rivers we crossed. He wanted to take it with him to Belgium. I tried to explain that the European feeling about firearms is completely different from the American one, that trying to cross a frontier with any kind of weapon is sheer madness, unless you are equipped for it, that it was just as simple, if he insisted on being arrested, to go up to the first gendarme we saw and to tell him: "Pardon, Monsieur, I just bumped off M. Saint-Fiacre." "Yes," replied Chirpie with a child's logic, "but I want my Ruger. I'm going to make a notch on it to show I've already done for one anti-American bastard."

"You mean you're going to do it again?"

"Huh?"

"You mean you're going to do it again?"

A smile of anticipation appeared on his face, the kind of smile you see lighting up children's countenances when you pronounce the word ice cream.

"I'll sure try," he said, modestly enough.

We finally compromised. As we were driving through a wood, I took a little road on the right and allowed Chirpie to bury the Ruger under a chestnut tree. He dug the hole with his knife, marked all the neighboring trees, and came back to the car perfectly happy. I didn't tell him that I didn't expect him to come back to get the rifle; it was enough that he was pacified for the time being.

I don't like to cross frontiers. When I get there, I always seem to remember something not quite right I did on this side of it, and to wonder what the customs officials, and the police officials, and all the other officials would have to say about me if they knew what kind of man I really am. Sometimes I imagine that dying must be exactly like that. They will ask what you have to declare, and look for your name in big yellow books, and all that nonsense. This time, I was perfectly in order, but Chirpie had just killed a man and had a fake entry visa stamped on his passport. The visa worried me more than the murder. Anyway, I felt responsible for both. It was without the least bit of pleasure that I stopped my car on the French side and waited for the uniformed people to come up and salute me. I would have been much better off without their salute. The idea had crept into my mind to send Chirpie on alone, and to follow him a few minutes later, but I was so unprofessional as to resent the idea itself. We would die together if die we must, or, rather, he would go to the guillotine and I would spend a few months in complete leisure at the taxpayers' expense, but no matter: I wouldn't be the one to have shunned my responsibilities.

The officials were very polite. They didn't even ask us if we carried firearms, just if we were not exporting more French money than we were allowed to. We said no, and were signalled to drive on. At the other end of the no man's land, the uniforms were different and the language heavier and heartier, there were no questions asked at all, and we entered the Kingdom of Belgium with the wholehearted approval of the frontier authorities. The faked stamp looked very well, and now there was a new one on the passport, so nobody would ever think of looking at it again. On one point at least Chirpie was safe.

Belgium is the dearest country in the world. Of course, they have their own racial problem: *Wallons* against *Flamands* (in other words, French-speaking population against Dutch-speaking population) and they are so sensitive to the fact that whatever they write has to be written twice: one time in French, one time in Dutch, so that even *Coca-Cola* is written two times on the ads: it is spelled Coca-Cola in French . . . and Coca-Cola in Dutch too. But to foreigners all the Belgians are equally hospitable, and I have spent some very pleasant hours, even days, in that last haven of good humor, unpretentiousness and sheer *joie de vivre.* I was happy to be there again, and I felt safer after having crossed that frontier, not only because I was in France no more, but also because I was in Belgium. The Belgians are nice people: they wouldn't think of arresting Chirpie or me, when I am so fond of them: such was my unconscious way of reasoning.

It took us about one hour from the frontier to the Pavillon Saint Hu, as Gerhard's lodge was irreverently named after Saint Hubert, the hunter's holy patron. The lodge, a wooden structure in the German style on the outside, stood on a hill surrounded by deep woods, where wild boars were plentiful. I showed the pointed roof to Chirpie and said:

"Here is where you make your press conference."

I parked the car some distance from the house, so that the journalists wouldn't see it when they came, and found the key in the hollow tree in which it is always kept. Some of Gerhard's friends are not so delicate as I: they go to his place even without asking his permission, and the key is there for them to use.

Inside, everything was comfortable and cosy. Downstairs, a hall, a dining room and a kitchen, with a staircase leading straight from the hall to the two bedrooms and bathrooms upstairs. The walls were natural, warm, blond, fruitwood. The furniture was natural wood and tapestry or natural wood and leather. The fireplace worked but there was also a central heating system which was most welcome at that time of the year. Heads of different animals, mainly deer, stags and boar decorated the walls. There were also a few funny prints representing well-endowed females seen from the rear: Gerhard's Teutonic taste, definitely not mine. We had not lunched, and so we had a go at the cans. Chirpie inquired if there were no *vahn-moo-sur.* Of course, there wasn't and I was not going to spoil on him the dozen odd bottles of champagne that were kept on ice. So we drank beer instead, good Belgian beer, the best in the world.

And we listened to the radio both Belgian and French. Still no one mentioned Saint-Fiacre's death. Chirpie couldn't understand what was said, of course, so he was all the time after me, asking me to translate what they were saying and to change the channel. I took some time realizing that he was waiting for the dawn of his international, anonymous fame, and getting impatient with it.

The cuckoo cuckooed five times. It was five o'clock and not one of the journalists I had written had thought fit to come. Something must have delayed them, since journalists arrive early or not at all.

We went several times over the *mise en scène* of the conference. Of course, Chirpie was not to say anything, since he had no French. I would do all the talking and sound as young as I could, but at least he would be there for me to point at, and they could put questions to him: he would whisper the answers in my ear, and I would then relay them to them. This would be easy to justify: after all, he was a murderer, and he didn't want to be recognized by his voice any more than his face. Several times we thought we heard a car and hastily pulled our black stockings on our heads . . . that was wishful thinking. In the mirrors we looked absolutely frightening, but there was no one else to see us besides ourselves. When Chirpie finally said: "Wally, I'm beginning to be afraid of you," I hastily took the stocking off and asked him to do the same. As the evening grew darker and darker, I began to feel a little afraid of him too. After all, he had killed a man for lunch and seemed none the worse for it. Unprincipled as I am myself, still I was a little irked by his utter lack of sensitivity.

Half-past five: no journalists. Six o'clock: no journalists. Belgium is just a few hours' drive from Paris, and exclusive details concerning Saint-Fiacre's death were well worth that to any newspaperman; I knew that. Something must have happened. An awful doubt crept into my mind, but I dared not express it. Chirpie, who looked more and more sullen and offended, began fiddling with the TV which had come on at 6, and suddenly I heard him cry:

"That's him."

I was looking through the window, hoping against hope that a car would appear on that particular bend I could see from where I stood. I turned back. Saint-Fiacre's triangular face was grinning at me from the little screen.

"What's he saying?" Chirpie wanted to know. "What's he saying?"

He guessed the truth already but he didn't want to believe it.

"They must be showing the story of his life," he said. "They always do before a guy's funeral, if he's important enough."

Chirpie could go on fooling himself for a few minutes if he wanted to. I couldn't. It was not a video tape replay as I also had hoped for a few seconds. It was a live picture. And Serge Saint-Fiacre, known as Bluebeard, appeared on it just as alive as you and me.

"Yes," he was saying, his triangular head half-cocked, "*Le Haut-Parleur* will be printed simultaneously in French, German and Italian. Later, I hope, in all the other languages of the European community. We are starting with French for practical reasons, because I happen to be a printer and happen to be French."

He smiled as if he had proved something. The camera turned toward the handsome and earnest young lady who was interrogating Saint-Fiacre.

"And now," she said, "since we have a few minutes left, may I ask you a personal question? What was all this to-do this afternoon about an attempt at assassination of which you would have been the victim?"

Saint-Fiacre laughed, showing his hideous teeth.

"I felt that question coming," he remarked. "Unfortunately I think there was nothing of the kind. I do have enemies, but not that sort. Rather, I have enemies in the Establishment, who try to make me ridiculous by putting me in that kind of situation. They have not forgotten that in France 'ridicule kills,' as the saying goes, and they are trying their best, but they won't succeed, I can promise you that."

"What happened?"

"I was going home from work. It was lunch time, and I was going to have a little *apéritif* in a little *café-tabac* with three of my workmen, when I slipped on a banana peel that some fool had left on the pavement. At the same time a car backfired somewhere, I guess. My workmen, who are very nice guys and, I think, rather fond of me, because they know I know I am just the same kind of man they are, jumped to conclusions. They thought I had been shot at. Of course, there were lots of windows open all around: May is so beautiful in Paris, and they had no definite suspicion as to where the shot had come from. They ran a little to and fro, and came back looking rather sheepish. So we went to the bistro, and had a little drink, and I went to lunch, and they went to lunch, and then we went back to work, and worked hand in hand the rest of the afternoon, as we usually do, and that was it. I'm sorry to disappoint you, my dear child, but that's all that happened."

He smiled as if he had made a point. The picture changed. A very formal looking young man appeared on the screen.

"Ladies and gentlemen, you have just seen an interview of M. Serge Saint-Fiacre, President of the International European Party, whose convention. . . ."

I turned him off. For a full minute Chirpie and I looked at each other.

Finally, he began to cry like a child. Tears fell from his eyes. Sobs shook his powerful frame. He was trying to say something I couldn't make out. At last I caught the words:

"I've lost face, Wally, I've lost face!"

Strange that he should use the oriental phrase to express it, but I could sympathize with his feelings. On the other hand, I had lost lots of money, and more than that, Amarantha Munchin. To me it seemed a greater loss than Chirpie's face, which had never amounted to much in the first place.

"How did you manage to miss him?" I asked. "He was not very far from you, was he?"

He shook his head.

"Maybe he was too close. I had sighted the rifle in for one hundred yards. He was closer than that. And then it was pretty windy."

It didn't sound very convincing to me, but I am no specialist. There was another consideration which I didn't mention to Chirpie because there was no point offending him but which to me seemed much more important than the difference in distance and the presence of some wind. Chirpie had never before shot at a live target. He might hate all anti-American bastards, he might be sure of his own right in bumping them off, to use his vocabulary, but still there had to be a difference between shooting at a piece of cardboard and a man's head.

"Chirpie," I said, "did you ever go hunting?"

He shook his head. So he had never even killed a quail or a rabbit or a squirrel or a deer. No wonder if his hand had trembled.

"Wally!" he cried. "You always were my special buddy and I let you down! There will be no book now with nice pictures in it! Wally, why don't you beat me up? I'd feel so much better."

I walked to the fireplace and back.

"Chirpie," I said, "we're both going to feel very much better as soon as you stop blubbering and begin thinking how we are going to bump off Saint-Fiacre for good."

He looked at me through his tears.

"You mean . . . you mean you're going to let me try again?"

Solemnly I nodded.

"You bet!" I said.

Mr. Bopkins hadn't won yet.

11

I drove Chirpie to the railway station. Pitiful as he might be, the fool had bungled up the operation; I was angry with him and if he got himself arrested at the frontier, I preferred to be as far from him as I could. After all, he didn't have so many talents that he could afford to treat negligently any of them. It was all very nice to feel compassion for a fellow-creature, but then what was the use of being a marksman? I had no more patience with a compassionate marksman than I would have had with a chaste prostitute.

I explained to him where he would have to change trains. "See, everything is written twice: it should make it easier to understand. You get to the Gare du Nord and wait for me there, at the buffet."

After that, I sent off a telegram to Amarantha: "Surgery unsuccessful. Uncle still alive. Will try again." On rereading, it seemed a rather heartless way to put it, but I didn't think Amarantha would mind. I asked for a reply by general delivery at the main post office in Paris.

That done, I took to the road again. I still listened to the radio. I wasn't sure whether Saint-Fiacre was telling the whole truth or whether he was minimizing the whole business on the instructions of the police. On the whole, I didn't think that very likely: he was rather a man to do the opposite from what the police would ask him to do. Maybe the police hadn't even been called in. At any rate there was no gigantic manhunt organized on a national scale, with all our descriptions given to the public every five minutes on the radio, as I had vaguely feared there would be. One always tends to exaggerate one's own importance. Saint-Fiacre had a point in saying that there had been a number of open windows on that street, and if no one had seen Chirpie at his, there was no way of knowing from which the shot had been fired. So far, nobody seemed to have noticed Chirpie running in the square and in the Place du Palais-Royal. Was that likely? No. But it was possible. Parisians are generally rather egotistic people, preoccupied mainly with themselves, and if they notice anything on the streets, it is only pretty girls. There being quite a few of those in Paris, Parisians keep pretty busy "rinsing their eyes" as they call it. There was a big risk involved in going back, of course, but if I wanted to succeed in the end, there was a bigger one in not going: if Chirpie disappeared without his luggage, there was bound to be an investigation. Anyway I was not connected with the case: there was no risk for *me*.

At this point in my thoughts, I realized that the situation had changed considerably from what it had been a few hours earlier. At that time, some unknown organization had planned to murder Saint-Fiacre and I had only planned to reap the benefits of the operation. It was *their* murder. But that organization had failed, and I, by deciding to make Chirpie try again, had made it *my* murder. Not entirely: *they* had provided the idea and the weapon, and I still could argue to myself that *they* did have some responsibility in the case. It was even possible that *they* would try again, but that would take time: they would have to find another murderer in the first place, since there was no plausible way in which Chirpie could offer them his services, and if there were, *they* would probably not accept them. After all, Boudin had a broken kneecap, and Chirpie had not shown up at the appointed time and place, besides bungling the job. But, however that might be, from now on *I* was the mind behind Chirpie's finger on the trigger, and that was worth examining from at least two points of view. First, from the official one: instead of being just a sharp capitalizing on somebody else's efforts, I seemed to have become a killer by proxy: that meant a completely different kind of punishment in case of detection. Second, from the moral standpoint: instead of condoning Saint-Fiacre's assassination, I was ordering it, and what for? You may think it was for the money, if you like. I was not tough-hearted enough to put it that way. It was much more pleasant to believe that I was killing Saint-Fiacre for love's rather than for money's sake: the ignoble Bluebeard was to perish so that my beautiful Amarantha should not merge with the repulsive Mr. Bopkins. Here you may want to observe that a simpler way to arrange that was to assassinate Mr. Bopkins himself, but who wants simple ways? And it did seem safer to dispose of M. Saint-Fiacre, since nobody could guess my motive at this end, whereas it would have been pretty obvious at the other one. Besides Mr. Bopkins's death would not attract any attention at all, since Mr. Bopkins was, or so I thought, an honest fellow; whereas M. Saint-Fiacre was a scoundrel, etc., etc., etc. To make a long story short, I had very few qualms indeed about nipping Saint-Fiacre's European stink in the bud, if the metaphor makes sense.

The crossing of the frontier was unpleasant as usual, but nothing happened and I went on driving, listening to the radio and thinking my thoughts. On one point I had no information whatsoever, and that annoyed me very much. What had happened with Boudin? And with the unconscious hotel clerk? Had the police—who must have been called in at least to look into that incident—established any connection between it and the Saint-Fiacre business? They might have, they should have, but it was not certain that they had yet done so. On the other hand, if they managed to extract some part of the truth from Boudin, who was probably lying in some hospital, at their mercy, they could very well deduce the whole set-up. I ought not to have allowed Fifi to break the fellow's kneecap: that was the moral of the story. I was reduced to hoping that Boudin had been able to think up some logical story to explain why he was lying on the first floor of the Hôtel Cardinal with an injured limb exactly at the time when a well-known politician was slipping on a banana peel.

It was night when I reached the place where Chirpie had buried his rifle. The idiot had been right after all not to throw it away. I had some trouble finding the exact spot of the entombment, but at last I succeeded, broke two nails trying to dig it out, and carried it to the car, where I hid it under the rug. It was not a very good hiding place, but I could think of no better one.

I reached Nénette's at about eleven. She was gorgeously attired in a golden lamé long dress. Happily, although there was lots of it below, there was not too much on top.

"Have you made heaps of money?" she asked. "*Darrlene,* you look tired! Maybe we shouldn't go out after all. I'll put you to bed with a warm bottle."

You see, she is really a good girl.

"No, my dear, I wouldn't dream of going to bed with a warm bottle. We are going to the *Drap d'Or* to empty a few ice-cold bottles."

"Fifi called. He said he would call again."

He did.

"Sorry," he said as soon as I had identified myself. "I missed it too."

"What do you mean?"

"Well, Chirpie missed Bluebeard, didn't he? But at least he had an excuse. I didn't. Boudin didn't slip on a banana peel."

"What are you talking about?"

"Don't *you* know, *Mister* Turner?"

"What's all that about a banana peel?"

"I thought you might have heard on TV that Bluebeard slipped and it must have been exactly at the time when Chirpwood pressed the trigger. Tough luck."

Of course! That was the explanation of Chirpie's clumsiness. Why didn't I think about it before? Chirpie wasn't so sensitive after all. That sounded like a much better explanation. I mean: much more hopeful for the future. On the whole, there is more sensitiveness around than banana peels.

"And what's that about Boudin?"

"Yes, you couldn't know that. When I arrived, Boudin was already there, and talking to the clerk. Only Boudin was talking English (or what you call English in the slums of the deep South) and the clerk was talking French, the Parisian variety, i.e., the worst one. The clerk was saying: 'What the bloody hell are you doing here?' and Boudin was saying 'I'm waiting for a pal and don't you dare interfere with me' or something to that effect. When finally Boudin saw that he could not make himself understood, he just raised his fist and smashed it down on the clerk's skull. That must have made his meaning pretty clear, because the clerk shut up immediately. Then I heard Chirpwood clattering down the stairs. So I brought my pipe into action and slammed it hard across Boudin's leg. After that, instead of running away as you had advised, I stayed around. I wanted to see what would happen. By staying around, I mean I went to have a look at what I hoped would be Saint-Fiacre's cadaver. When I caught a glimpse of the cadaver standing at the bar in the café-tabac and drinking Cinzano, I rushed back to the hotel, and found the clerk rubbing his head and Boudin gone. He must have hopped away by the back door, but he couldn't have done that with a broken kneecap: he would have fainted from pain. So, my apologies."

I thought it was rather lucky that Fifi had missed but I didn't tell him so. Instead I asked:

"What about the clerk? Did he call in the police?"

"Oh! no, *Mister* Turner, not that kind of clerk. You see, the nice thing about associating with establishments like the Hôtel Cardinal is that they never call in the police. They are much too busy trying to keep the police off the premises, not to call them in, if you see what I mean."

"So you think it wouldn't be dangerous for Chirpie to go back there?"

"Well . . . they are bound to find the rifle, sooner or later."

"No. Chirpie brought it with him."

"Poor fellow! Couldn't bear the idea of leaving it behind, eh?— Well, there's no danger then."

"You're positive the police didn't set up a trap in his room?"

"I am. I've been hanging around all day. Everything's been quiet, besides the clerk using tons of aspirin."

"All right. Then you go and get Chirpie at the buffet of the Gare du Nord. Let him sleep the night at the Cardinal, check out tomorrow morning, and check in at some other place where they don't ask for identification. Find him a false name that he can remember. I don't think that he should use his own any more for some time at least."

"No problem. May I ask a question, *Mister* Turner?"

"You may."

"What are we going to do next?"

"A man of your abilities, *Mister* Fifi," I retorted "should have no trouble deducing that."

And this time I managed to hang up first.

*

When I awoke the next morning, my first thought was not for the show of the Drap d'Or, which had been good, nor for its menu, which had been quite acceptable. My first thought was to wonder that I, hitherto a perfectly inoffensive character, should be, in fact, masterminding a political murder. For one second I may even have felt half a conscience pang. But you see, it was really made very easy for me: I was not planning to murder a man who would have been left to live up to a hundred if I had not been there—I distinctly felt I was murdering a man already dead. I could also have looked for extenuating circumstances in the fact that I wasn't going to press the trigger myself, but I was clear-sighted enough to know that that would have been sheer hypocrisy. I didn't mince matters to myself: yesterday, a mysterious Mr. X would have been Saint-Fiacre's murderer; tomorrow, it would be me; Chirpie was just our instrument.

I patted Nénette affectionately on that part of the body which was created for patting. She murmured sleepily "Oh! Lulu! I love you!" I got out of bed, with a sigh: that was life. Sometime maybe I would pat a girl who wouldn't take me for somebody else. I had breakfast at a café and went on sitting there and reading newspapers. There were several points on which I wanted to be up-to-date.

Point number one. The proclamation of Les Enfants de Mai was nowhere quoted or even mentioned. Newspaper editors are always afraid of practical jokes which would make them look ridiculous. I had expected that. But there were quite a few allusions to possible disturbances caused by teenagers, expected for the near future; there were a few bad jokes about the effect of spring on teenage emotions; the two mysterious crimes I had used were mentioned again, and the journalist—without quoting his sources—remarked that one possibility had not been so far given consideration: organized revenge. I cut all those paragraphs out, put them into an envelope and mailed them off to George Broker.

Point number two. Saint-Fiacre was everywhere. That was in itself good. The Convention had begun at the Palais de la Mutualité. Serious politicians were still pooh-poohing it, but at least they could not afford to disregard it entirely. Saint-Fiacre must be pleased and I was as pleased as he. The whole program of the Convention was given in *Le Figaro*. *Le Haut-Parleur* was expected to appear three days hence, after the Convention had concluded its work. I gave some thought to the program—the reason can easily be guessed; although nothing too brilliant sprang into my mind, there was one obvious solution which would have to be investigated later.

Point number three. The attempt against Saint-Fiacre was mentioned only once and with some humor. Saint-Fiacre was such a wonderful boss to work for that his workmen imagined assassins where there were only banana peels and backfiring engines.

On the whole, the press was good, very good. I went home. Nénette was still asleep. I typed six new *pneus* to the people to whom I had mailed the first ones. Now that murder had been in question, they might feel it their duty to take the things to the police. I had somehow to quiet their consciences. Yes, some journalists have one. I wrote:

"No one can foresee every possible accident. A banana peel saved S.F. For the time being, we shall skip him and go on to the next adult chauvinist on our list.

"The youth of France will not allow crimes against it to go unpunished. We shall succeed this time and one of the worst monsters of our time will die.

"When it is time for us to speak to you, we shall make contact.

"Death to all adult chauvinists!

"Signed: LES ENFANTS DE MAI."

I put in a few spelling mistakes to make it look even better and went to rue du Louvre to mail everything off. There was nothing for me on general delivery. I drove back home and had a very pleasant lunch with Nénette. We were sipping that damned Chartreuse Verte when Fifi called in. He had found Chirpie at the Gare du Nord with a bottle of *vahn-moo-sur* to keep him company. He was becoming addicted to the stuff. Fifi had found him a small hotel near the railway station, the Hôtel des Grands-Ducs, the kind of place where the police might drop in on its own accord but would not be called. Chirpie's name was Charles W. Watergate.

"For heaven's sake, why Watergate?"

"It's easy to remember."

"But it will make him so conspicuous."

"Don't count on it. The French were not very much interested in that farce. You have to have cuckolds in a farce for the French to find it funny."

Mr. Watergate had breakfasted and lunched with Fifi. What was he to do now?

"Get him back into his room, find him some American comics and don't let him out."

"Oh, he won't go out alone."

"Why not?"

"He's afraid Snipe and Boudin will find him and break every bone in his body."

"Excellent. Encourage him in that direction."

"Encourage him to be afraid, *Mister* Turner?"

"Precisely. And Fifi. . . ."

"Yes, *Mister* Turner?"

"You've seen the papers?"

"Yes."

"The program of the Convention?"

"Yes."

"D'you think there is anything to be done before its conclusion?"

"No."

"But on the last day?"

"Yes."

"The marble plaque?"

"Yes."

"Why don't we meet there?"

"Now? Certainly."

We hung up simultaneously. Nénette was shaking her head with a reproving air. Suddenly the telephone rang again. I picked it up, ready to give it to Nénette. But no: the low gurgling, very feminine voice at the other end—surely I had heard it before—asked very clearly to speak to me. Now no one was supposed to know I was living at Nénette's. But when that kind of voice asks very gently for Mr. Walter de Walter, and when you happen to be he, what do you do? Still I decided I'd get some information first.

"Just a second," I said. "I'll see if he is in. Who is speaking please?"

"The social secretary of M. Serge Saint-Fiacre."

Of course! It was the little Siamese cat of the other night.

"Mistigri!" I cried. "I don't remember giving you my phone number."

"Well, it didn't take long."

"What?"

"Seeing if you were there."

I laughed. "I'm never quite sure," I said. "I pay so very little attention to myself!"

"That I don't believe. Mr. de Walter, I'm instructed by my employer to extend to you his apologies for his bad manners the other night. He was very tired, preparing the Convention and the *Haut-Parleur* at the same time and he is very sorry he got carried away. He tried to run after you but you had already left."

For once I was completely taken by surprise. I didn't know what to say.

"Are you still there, Mr. de Walter?"

"Yes, yes. I'm just . . . a trifle surprised. After all, I had somewhat crashed the party—with your help, I must say."

"Yes. And I also would have apologized to you, if you had not knocked the champagne. I happen to have chosen it."

"Then let me apologize to you."

"Not at all. You were probably right. You see, Mr. de Walter . . ." here her voice gave a quaint, pitiful little break "I never had the opportunity of learning much about champagne."

The way she said it, she made me feel like an awful brute.

"I had another message to communicate," she went on in her official tone. "If you feel you can accept M. Saint-Fiacre's apologies, he would very much like you to come over and have dinner with him tomorrow night."

Dinner? No! I would not eat my future victim's bread if I could help it. On the other hand, I was curious to see what Saint-Fiacre had to tell me. Obviously he was not inviting me for the pleasure of my company.

"Sorry, I'm committed for dinner."

"I know! This is such short notice."

"It is."

The usual delay in France is three weeks.

"Before dinner maybe?"

I was curious. "Well, yes, before dinner . . . why not?"

"The Convention adjourns at five. Can you make it by five-thirty?"

"I'll be delighted."

"But not at the Palais-Royal apartment. That will be besieged by Convention members, and M. Saint-Fiacre especially wants to relax. So he is coming to his house in Le Vésinet, very secretly, so to speak. Only the dinner guests will know where to find him."

"Then I'm more than delighted: I'm flattered."

She gave me the address.

"We'll try to have some decent champagne for you this time," she said in a much less official tone. She added, "I'm looking forward to seeing you." And hung up rather hurriedly, I thought.

"My dear," I told Nénette, "I'm going to have a drink in Bluebeard's castle tomorrow."

"Well, you're not a wife," she said. "It's probably safe."

12

The Boulevard Saint-Germain and the Boulevard Saint-Michel, affectionately known as Boul' Mich', cross at right angles in the heart of the Latin Quarter and about a quarter of an hour's walk from the Palais de la Mutualité, where the more explosive political meetings usually take place. The crossing itself has traditionally been one of the hot spots in Paris: it is here that students indulge most often in their favorite sport, baiting the police, and the police in theirs, knocking the students on their heads, mainly with sticks and capes. These fights belong to the Parisian folklore, and the merriest capital on this earth would not be its own cheerful self without them. But there was a time when more deadly fights raged exactly at the same place: that was during the Liberation of Paris, in 1944, and men died on those stones which now witness only the occasional sparring of the Schools of Law against the Forces of Order.

If from that point you follow the Boulevard Saint-Germain toward the Seine (away from the Palais de la Mutualité), you come very soon to the triangular Carrefour de l'Odéon, a rather ugly place decorated with a statue of the scoundrel Danton and a Métro station. Several streets meet here, on which rebellious students often confronted, and sometimes even con-behinded, the police during the mini-revolution of May '68. There are no plaques on the walls to inform posterity about these epic clashes, when a rain of screws and stones obscured the sun and clouds of tear gas transformed day into night, but there are some that tell us about the Frenchmen, mainly policemen too by the way, who died in '44, fighting against those it is now deemed polite to call Nazis, but who, at the time, were simply German soldiers, like any other soldiers in the world, doing their job. One of these marble plaques is—or maybe I should say was: it may very well have been taken down after the events which will be told hereafter—attached to the wrought iron fence surrounding Danton's ugly monument. It was a fairly small plaque, about one by one and a half feet, stating in letters of gold that Jean Durand, aged 20, had fallen on that very spot for the freedom of Paris. Two tricolor flags punctuated the story. So far so good.

Now The International European Party had discovered—or pretended to have discovered—that a German soldier, also aged 20 and called Hans Schmidt (which is exactly as common in Germany as Jean Durand is in France) had died exactly on the same spot. Maybe he had killed Jean Durand, maybe Jean Durand had killed him, maybe Jean Durand was killed by mistake and by the French, maybe Hans Schmidt was killed by mistake and by the Germans: all that was completely immaterial. The question that was being asked, and pretty loudly, was why didn't Hans Schmidt get a plaque. The fact that he, at least, did not die for the freedom of Paris was somehow disregarded. Both the young men were to be considered not as warriors earning their daily bread making war, but as victims of two opposed nationalisms, just as bad the one as the other. Symbolically, the Delegates of the Convention were to hang a plaque to the memory of Hans Schmidt beside the plaque to the memory of Jean Durand. This profound ceremony was to take place at five-thirty, the day after tomorrow: it would be the crowning achievement of the Convention which was now in full swing.

So far so good, once again. It even grew better and better. For, whereas during the Convention it was practically impossible to come close enough to Saint-Fiacre to be able to shoot him and at the same time keep a way of retreat open, here on the contrary was an occasion when he would appear in public, at a very precise place, at a sufficiently precise time, would single himself out from the crowd (since he was going to attach the plaque himself) and would have created enough interest by what he was doing, to redouble the interest people would take in his death. The fact that the Carrefour is surrounded by houses was a great tactical advantage: there were lots of windows there from which to shoot, and there were plenty of streets to retreat to after the shot had been fired. There was only one objection to the plan: although the plaque business offended the more patriotic French (a counter-manifestation organized by the right was already announced), most people would probably feel sympathy for a man who was burying a very old tomahawk. Well, I would have to write a special paragraph showing how unworthy Bluebeard had been of the noble cause he had pretended to serve.

Fifi and I met, as arranged, at the foot of Danton's monument. We could both imagine Saint-Fiacre's speech and all the famous quotations he would make from the great trickster's speeches: "We need boldness and boldness and yet again boldness. . . . Your fatherland does not stick to the soles of your shoes" and the like.

"Seems appropriate," quipped Fifi. "One big stinker at the feet of another."

We examined the terrain. The procession carrying the plaque would be coming from the Mutualité. The people would mass on the sidewalks of the Boulevard Saint-Germain, and, if there were enough, would fill the whole triangle of the Carrefour. The traffic might well be diverted by policemen into different directions. Saint-Fiacre would stand exactly where we were standing and harangue the populace with his back to Danton and the plaque. Then he would turn and hang the second plaque beside the first. In other words, the best position to shoot from would be either one of the houses on the right side of the Boulevard Saint-Germain or the School of Medicine at the corner of the Boulevard and the Carrefour. But the School is a relatively low building; we didn't know how close the crowd would come to Saint-Fiacre: it might be that the angle wouldn't be right. That left us with the apartment houses, and preferably with the one facing the statue. It was a question now of checking a possible way of retreat.

I know my Paris fairly well, and I remembered that behind this row of houses (not behind the one facing the statue, but a little further down the Boulevard, still close enough to shoot) lay the Cour de Rohan, a little labyrinth of absolutely delightful old alleys, running between seventeenth and eighteenth century houses, and communicating with at least three other streets. I won't say that the picturesqueness of the idea didn't appeal to me, but what appealed most was this threefold possibility of escape. It would be practically impossible for the police to seal off the whole block in a matter of minutes, and it would be an easy job for the killer, once he had reached the Cour de Rohan, to take a leisurely air and saunter down to the Rue Saint-André-des-Arts, where a car could wait for him, motor running.

"*La Cour de Rohan?*" asked Fifi.

I saw that his thoughts were running parallel to mine and nodded.

So we turned our gazes toward the only house which would serve our purpose, being at the same time close enough to the statue and having its back toward the Cour. "Let's go and see," I decided.

We began by entering the labyrinth and having a look around. The wonderful old houses, a few years ago grey with age and soot, had been completely renovated and the heavy rectangular stones, cut at right angles with the precision of a razor, shone in all their beauty: a lovely grey with a touch of orange in it. Some of the walls were covered with ivy. You could have thought yourself not in Paris, but in some old provincial town or even in the courtyard of a château. Iron rings sealed into the walls reminded you of a time when horses would be tied to them, and one wrought iron structure, a *montoir,* of a time when ladies didn't jump into the saddle but climbed into it with the help of that instrument. There were very few people there. A couple of students necking in a doorway. An old gentleman lost in nostalgic contemplation of the old stones. He looked in particular at one high, noble window surrounded with ivy. I imagined that once he had loved someone who lived here. . . . Strange fancies for a murderer by proxy.

The houses in the Cour de Rohan were lower than the house on the Boulevard: they had from three to four floors; it had six, plus the attic, where the servants used to live and which now was probably converted into rooms for students and poorer people. We didn't know if the backyards of these houses communicated in any way, so I had thought in terms of roofs. I had done some Alpine climbing in my time, and it seemed to me that it was not impossible to descend from some roofs to some other ones, but that solved only part of the problem. First, it would be necessary to reach the right roof on the Cour de Rohan side and, last, to reach the ground from another one, which lay three floors above the ground.

"What about a ladder?" suggested Fifi. "No one pays attention to a ladder."

Yes, a very long ladder could maybe stand in the corner under the poetic window the old gentleman was still contemplating. Nobody would think of moving it, because everybody would take for granted that it was being used for repairs. The other end would give us more trouble. There probably was a way to get from inside the Boulevard house onto its roof, but what did we do from there? In a detective story, the hero slides down waterspouts, jumps from gutter to window sill, all the time carrying the heroine in his arms, but I couldn't visualize Chirpie in the part.

"A rope?" suggested Fifi.

I had just thought of it. A rope tied to a chimney-stack would make it fairly easy to descend from the roof of the Boulevard house to the first roof on the Cour de Rohan side. From there it wouldn't be too hard to follow on until one reached the ladder. I could do it. The question was whether I could do it fast enough and whether Chirpie could do it at all. It would be so much easier if the backyards communicated.

We went back to the Boulevard.

"Let's investigate," I said.

"You stay here: I go."

I had been very careful so far never to come too close to the scene of the murder. And in theory nothing had changed. I knew Fifi could investigate as well as I and I could leave it all to him. But for some reason I wanted to have a look myself. Maybe because it had become *my* murder.

We walked into the house which was arranged like most apartment buildings in Paris are. A first hall, with false marble walls. A glass door. A second hall with another glass door giving into the concierge's den, an ordinary door giving into the backyard, and the stairwell. The delicate point was the second hall. Traditionally, as soon as you enter it, the concierge jumps at you and barks: "Who do you want?" There are more and less honest ways of pacifying her. But we didn't have to use any of them: the concierge was sitting with her back to us looking at TV. I don't know who invented TV but I do know he's made things much easier for us burglars.

The door leading to the backyard wasn't locked. Fifi pushed it and we found ourselves in yet a third hall, but this one was narrow and filthy. A door on our right led to the cellars. I did have the romatic idea that maybe the cellars would communicate with the neighboring cellars and that Chirpie could worm his way under the ground until he reached some exit point at the other end of Paris, but this door was locked and we couldn't try any means of persuasion against the lock with the concierge sitting three yards from us. Another door led into the backyard. We went out. It was the usual scene. Trash cans in a row. A water faucet. Brooms and brushes. And four walls, seven floors high. Windows, of course, to light up kitchen, bathrooms and children's rooms, but not one door besides the one we had just used. It would have to be the roof.

We went back into the house. The problem now was: how to get on the roof? Without saying one word to each other, we took the stairs and not the elevator. We didn't want any noise and French elevators tend to make a lot.

There were two apartments to each floor, with heavy polished doors and shining brass handles on them. On the last floor, there was a third door, smaller and not polished. It would be leading to the last staircase, the small, ignoble, uncarpeted one which ascends to the former servants' quarters. We took it. Silence reigned here as everywhere. Only some radio played somewhere, behind very thick walls. In France, in a bourgeois house, there is one thing that is held to be sacred: silence.

Now we found ourselves in a long hall, twisting and turning around the building. There were doors on both sides, some polished, some unpolished, some with visiting cards on them, some without. At the very end of the hall, there was another door of yet a different size. We thought it led to the roof.

Fifi tried to push it, and I tried to push it, and it was locked. Fifi looked at me with surprise.

"Why do you look at me like that?"

"Can't you pick a lock?" he asked, genuinely astonished.

"No," I said with as much dignity as I could manage. "I'm not in that branch."

He smiled languidly, and extracted a folding knife from his pocket. There were at least twenty different instruments on that knife: what with scissors, a turnscrew, a corkscrew, a tool to clean horses' hoofs. . . . Anyway the lock didn't resist very long. We had still a few stairs to ascend and here we were, on the roofs of Paris.

In the middle, the roof was nearly flat. You could lie on it and shoulder your rifle very easily. If you crept down to the ledge, you had a nice view of Danton's statue. A decent shot would kill a man from here even without using a scope, if he knew his rifle, of course. Chimney-stacks stood out everywhere and it would be easy to tie a rope to one of them. We crawled on all fours to the other side. Although people generally don't look up, we were afraid of being seen from the street. The drop to the first Cour de Rohan roof was about four meters: twelve feet to you. No great problem there if you weren't afraid of heights. I hoped Chirpie wasn't.

We left the roof and went down. Fifi slid a match into the lock, so it wouldn't close again. Now we stood in the long tortuous hall.

"We can have him shoot from the roof, right?" I said.

I had come to rely very much on Fifi's advice.

He shrugged his shoulders. "There might be helicopters."

He was right. The police would want to check on the ceremony and the best way would be from a helicopter. So we would need a room. But this was not a hotel. We pondered this question for some time.

"I can come back tonight," said Fifi, "and try to rent one from the person who occupies it now. Just for the time of the ceremony. I would say that a foreigner wants very much to watch the plaque business. A German family, I would say. These people are not rich. They would jump at the chance of earning some money for nothing."

I hestitated. It sounded right. On the other hand, wouldn't the person guess what we were renting the room for? No, he probably wouldn't. And the time was good: five-thirty is half an hour before most Parisians end their day's work. So the tenant wouldn't come and interrupt us at the most interesting time.

"All right," I said. "And you get the rope and the ladder. There is still one point though."

"Time?"

He guessed everything.

"Yes, time. It will take Chirpie at least five minutes to get from the roof to the ground. And one minute to go from the room to the roof. The police are not very fast, but still they will have thought of the Cour de Rohan before six minutes."

That seemed an insuperable difficulty and I was not willing to sacrifice Chirpie. Besides, if he were caught, what became of the book? Nobody would take Chirpie for a French Enfant de Mai.

We left the house without trouble (the TV show was still on) and went back to the Cour de Rohan. As we entered it I noticed that there was, under the arch that led to it, a wrought iron gate, which was at the present time open, but which obviously could be closed. Fifi and I exchanged glances. It was the same thing at the other end. If these gates could be closed, with only the one on the Rue Saint-André-des-Arts remaining open, there was a good chance that the police wouldn't find their way into the Cour before Chirpie had finished his descent.

"A good padlock," I murmured.

"By police order, in case anybody objects," added Fifi. "Yes, it can be done. I'll do it, for three hundred more, because that's really running a risk."

I acquiesced. It was either doing it or forgetting about the whole thing.

*

Le Vésinet is French suburbia in all its glory. Silent streets between high stone walls or higher iron fences. Trees and flowers everywhere. The smells and blossoms of May were everywhere when the Continental began winding its way among the charmingly old-fashioned abodes of the French bourgeoisie. For some reason this visit to the enemy's camp amused me very much. I was wearing a typical American light grey suit and a light blue shirt with a buttoned-down collar. I thought about Mistigri and found myself humming a little song.

M. Saint-Fiacre's villa was surrounded by a huge park, and the park in turn by a white stone wall. A semicircled wrought iron gate, adorned with the initials S and F, also cast in wrought iron, was opened for me by my old friend Pink-Cheeks. I drove up to an imposing Napoleon III façade. The ground was neatly sanded and several cars had already been parked before the double stairs: one Mercedes, one Jaguar, one Alfa Romeo (bigger than mine but much less pretty), two Pallas's. I parked my Continental in that noble company and was about to ring when the door—a majestic double door chiselled from top to bottom—flew open. A butler in a white coat and striped vest begged me to follow him. We crossed a panelled hall and went out by another door which led to a beautiful terrace on which the company was gathered. Seen from here, the park was very beautiful, with its formal French gardens next to the terrace and a more picturesque landscaped English panorama surrounding it.

"Whom shall I announce?" asked the butler.

"Mr. de Walter."

He did, with a grand air, and I walked toward my host who was lounging on a garden chair and talking with animation to his guests. I counted four of them: one swarthy Italian whom I didn't know, one journalist with whom I was not acquainted although I knew him by sight, an English Countess who was widely known for being, politically speaking, on the left of everybody who happened to be present, so that she appeared to be mildly liberal in a conservative setting, but was a fierce Maoist among communists and a *gauchiste* among Maoists, and finally my old friend Herr Doktor. Also, in the background I caught sight of my little Siamese cat, Mistigri. Only today she was sitting some distance from the company on a stone balustrade, dressed in a sweater and blue-jeans, and, fondling a rifle in her lap.

M. Saint-Fiacre rose as soon as I had been announced and walked toward me. He took me by the hand and shook it at some length. The Italian snapped a picture. I saw the print later, in rather different circumstances. A fairly tall young man with black hair, blue eyes and a haughty look on his face has his right hand pumped by a gent with a receding forehead, narrow ears pointing skyward, a sharp chin, a mouthful of carnivorous teeth and colorless, wary eyes. Yes, Saint-Fiacre smiled broadly, but I could see he didn't feel affectionate toward me. I think he recalled with some sadness his bygone flogging days and would have given much to have me in short pants and a good bundle of pickled rods in his hand.

"Mr. de Walter," he said, "I'm so glad you could come. I'm so glad you forgave me my grumpy reception of the other night. I do not enjoy the honor of knowing you very well, and so you must pardon me if I address you more as a representative of the American people than as an individual. I sincerely welcome this opportunity of telling an authentic American that, whatever is ascribed to me by ill-wishers, I have no bad feelings at all toward that great people. On the contrary, I am sure that as soon as Europe has seen reason and overthrown her *elected betrayers,* as soon as we are all united into one great whole, we shall be able to deal with your country on a basis of equality, sound understanding and deep friendship. I know good and sensible people live on both sides of the Atlantic, and I gladly entrust our future to them. My dear Mr. de Walter, let's drink together to all the underprivileged people of this earth, in your country and in ours. I hope this time the champagne will be to your taste."

He had made a speech and forgotten to introduce me to the company. I suspected the Italian, or maybe the unknown fellow, of taping the declaration. What was the point? I couldn't see it. There was no reason why I should be treated as an outsider anyway, and so I asked M. Saint-Fiacre to introduce me to his guests.

"Oh! certainly, certainly," he said. "I forgot about it: I was in such a hurry to express my feelings to you."

It sounded as if he wanted me also to make a speech. But I wouldn't be drawn.

"Your feelings do you credit, sir," I answered. "And your champagne does too," I added.

The second part at least was true: the Dom Pérignon was excellent.

I was introduced to the company only after I had drunk M. Saint-Fiacre's toast with him and the Italian had snapped a second picture. Then I went the rounds and shook hands with everybody.

"Fancy meeting you here!" said Herr Doktor.

"Oh! I'm an American. I run no risk of being compromised. It's much stranger to meet *you* here, Herr Doktor."

Saint-Fiacre hastened to explain:

"This is just a dinner party, Mr. de Walter. The point is to relax from politics, not to make them. Herr Doktor in no way belongs to our Party."

"Yes," assented the big German. "I represent the press. That's the only reason I was invited." He guffawed.

I had the very special feeling all this was a play, expertly staged by some internationally known director. The only thing I couldn't see clearly was who were the actors and who the audience.

"If Monsieur Saint-Fiacre will excuse me, I have a friend there, that I have not greeted yet," I said.

I went up to Mistigri and kissed her hand.

"I'm not a married woman," she said, taking her hand back, not with exaggerated haste.

"Oh! I'm sorry. I forgot you were Miss Tigri."

"How is the champagne today?"

"Did you choose it?"

She shook her head.

"I regret to say it's much better. Now tell me, what are you toting this thing for?"

I indicated what I had taken for a rifle. It was an automatic carbine, .22 long rifle, I thought.

"Didn't I tell you I was M. Saint-Fiacre's bodyguard?"

She looked up at me and her dark eyes seemed to mock me. A voice spoke at my elbow.

"Mistigri is very good with that thing, really. Would you like a demonstration?"

It was Saint-Fiacre breathing down my neck. Up my neck, I should say, for he was definitely not a tall man. I didn't know what to answer. I'm not usually awkward in society, but this was not society. It was a play, and everyone seemed to know his part by heart, except me.

"Well, yes, certainly," I replied, feebly enough. "I would be interested in seeing a display of any of Mademoiselle's talents."

I didn't want it to sound like a challenge, but it did.

The English lady made a diversion.

"Young man," she asked me, "what are your political opinions?"

"I'm afraid I have none, Madam."

"That shows you're a damned reactionary."

"Does it? I'm terribly sorry, Madam. What should I do about it?"

"Humph! Go to the people."

"Which people, Madam?"

She was awfully thin, aristocratic and arrogant. They said she had tried all kinds of drugs and finally taken up Marxism as the most hypnotic of them all. Her old shrivelled hand was heavily bejeweled and her drooping lids filtered the most exclusive glance you could think of.

"The only people who count, sir," she said. "The poor."

She was a countess and I couldn't resist the opportunity.

"There was a time," I said, "when the poor counted the little money they had, and counts counted, period. Now it seems the poor count, period. And the counts count only the few poor left around."

A low gurgle on my left showed that Mistigri had understood my weak pun.

"No, really," Saint-Fiacre was at it again "would you like a demonstration?" He didn't seem to enjoy our debate with the Countess. "Come now, Mistigri, show Mr. de Walter what you can do."

Herr Doktor came nearer, while the Countess was still counting the counts.

"Sure," he said, "let's have a demonstration. I'm interested. Once upon a time I could shoot straight enough myself."

"Anybody can shoot himself straight enough," quipped I.

"If he has the guts," said the Countess. "And the intelligence. Some people are so damned stupid that they can't even see they are too stupid to live."

She walked back to the table and began stuffing herself with sweets.

Saint-Fiacre took the cork of one of the champagne bottles.

"For instance," he said, "someone of us could position this cork on his head, and Mistigri would knock it down at a distance of . . . how much, Mistigri?"

I looked at him as he looked at her. His gaze was cold, transparent, utterly inexpressive. I turned to her. Her gaze also was cold, but it seemed to express something deep and I would say 'pathetic' if the word had not become corny through being used too much.

"I could do it easily at fifty meters," she said, "but the light is not so good. Let's say thirty meters."

"Thirty meters, then. Does any one want to try? If no one will, I shall not hesitate to entrust my life into Mistigri's hands," said Saint-Fiacre very lightly. And again this cold look was exchangd between them. I wondered if they were lovers.

I don't know what came over me. Maybe it was Mistigri's ironic look roaming over the company and dwelling on me with some more insistence than on the others. Maybe it was this idea that she and the odious Saint-Fiacre were lovers. Maybe it was the fact that I intended to have the man murdered the day after next and that I felt it would be decent also to undergo some danger myself. I don't know. Anyway I smiled rather foolishly I guess, and said:

"I'll do it."

Maybe they should have given me the script after all. As soon as I said it (and it obviously was not in the script), Saint-Fiacre cried out that I was a special guest and that he wouldn't dream of asking me to participate in a demonstration which had been his own idea all along. That was all right, but he couldn't resist the temptation to make a little fun of the other people present. I could see the sadistic glint in his eye as he turned toward the journalist whom I knew by sight and said:

"What about you, Tonio? Are you just a playboy or could you look a .22 in the barrel at the same time as you look a pretty girl in the eye?"

"I think this is a silly joke," replied Tonio. "Firearms are not toys. I scarcely believe that you need all those bodyguards of yours and I am certainly not going to play that kind of game with them."

Saint-Fiacre smiled as if he had proved something. He turned to the Italian photographer, and held out the cork to him:

"Would you like to try, Vittorini?"

Vittorini laughed uneasily. "I like to do the shooting, not the being shot at."

"Herr Doktor?"

A man always feels silly when presented with an idiotic challenge to his physical courage. Tonio had had the decency to refuse flatly, but Herr Doktor had to squirm a little.

"I have had so little opportunity to acquaint myself with the charming young lady's markmanship . . ." he began.

A shot answered him. Mistigri had just broken the neck of another champagne bottle which scarcely emerged from the ice bucket. And she had practically not taken any aim.

"Well?" insisted Saint-Fiacre.

A bead of pleasurable perspiration appeared on his forehead. His ears looked positively like horns. I could imagine him tempting and terrorizing little children just for gratification.

"No, thank you. Some other time perhaps," finally said Herr Doktor, and somehow faded into the landscape.

Saint-Fiacre approached the communist Countess with the cork in his hand. She looked at him indignantly, then at the cork, then at him again, and very loudly said:

"Up yours!"

Saint-Fiacre blinked. For some reason commoners always think of aristocrats as being mealy-mouthed.

"I'll do it myself," he said.

I wouldn't let him. I snatched the thing from him, rather rudely, stood at the end of the terrace and balanced the little cork mushroom on my head. Saint-Fiacre bit his lip. There was nothing more he could do about it. I had spoiled his game. Too bad. He smiled graciously at me and refilled my glass with Dom Pérignon.

I felt awfully stupid with the cork on my head. Of course, I knew this was not a trap, Mistigri would not kill me, Saint-Fiacre had not invited me to have me executed in front of his guests. But accidents do happen. Chirpie was probably as good a marksman as Mistigri, and he had missed. What if she missed too? I smiled bravely and drank a gulp of champagne, carefully, not to unbalance the cork.

"Shoot, Miss Tell!" I commanded. "On the whole, I think I prefer a champagne cork to an apple. Men have been known to get in trouble because of apples."

It was strange to stand there, glass in hand, and to look at that little black hole that seemed to be looking at me. I guess I'm a fatalist. Some thought of an ulterior Judgment crossed my mind. I don't remember it all very clearly, but it seems that I did reason out something like this: "If she kills me now, it means it would have been bad for me to kill him the day after tomorrow." At the same time, I knew it was all a joke, and still at the same time I decided that since it was unpleasant to look at the gun, I would look at the girl. The girl, in spite of her viciously squinting eye, was nicer. Her sweater bulged where it was supposed to, and I was longing for a rearview when the shot rang. The cork fell into the grass. I drank another gulp of champagne.

"Well, yes," I said, "I distinctly prefer this to the one you had the other night."

Saint-Fiacre smiled very sourly, as if I, not he, had made a point. I walked over to Mistigri.

"The bodyguard is very efficient. And the guard's body is very lovely. Good-night."

I kissed her hand again, although she had told me she was unmarried. Somehow the old, noble gesture fitted in with what had just happened.

"I hope you are not leaving us," said Saint-Fiacre in the tone of someone who would have said: "I hope you are."

"I hope I have to," I answered. "I mean: I am afraid I have to."

I bowed, and he bowed, and I bowed again, and he bowed again, and I thought he was thinking "If only I could kill you" (but that's not what he was thinking at all) and I also thought, "Day after tomorrow I'm going to kill you," and we bowed once more, and we hated each other's guts. I then went and took leave of all the other guests. They looked at me in stern disapproval. They all thought what the Countess was alone to voice: "Damned young fool, that's what you are. Don't know the value of life."

"I'm sure I'll appreciate it more fully when I am seventy," I replied. It was a little rude, but she had asked for it. Herr Doktor poked me in the ribs. "I'm glad you're still among us," he said. "Not so glad as I," I said lightly. And still not understanding the whole scene very well, I walked toward the door which led into the house.

I was halfway down the heavily panelled hall when the blue-jeaned Siamese cat caught up with me.

"I'll walk with you to your car," she said.

It was not a very long way to go, but better than nothing.

"You'll do it much better than the butler," I replied.

And we said no more until we were standing at the top of the steps which led into the front courtyard.

The sun was setting. There was a great quiet all over the place. The shiny beautiful cars lay at our feet like a row of coffins. Birds flirted in the trees.

"I wanted to tell you something," said Mistigri.

"I wanted to ask you something," I retorted.

A new idea had crept into my mind, not the kind of ideas I usually harbour there. If Mistigri and Saint-Fiacre were lovers, it threw a new and not altogether pleasant light on my murderous intentions. It is never pleasant when a pretty girl likes another fellow; it is worse when you happen to like her and she happens to love him; and still worse if you are conspiring to kill him, not for reasons of jealousy but for a completely irrelevant motive. Also, I had never thought of Saint-Fiacre as of a man whom anybody would weep for. I didn't want Mistigri to weep for Saint-Fiacre.

"What did you want to ask?"

I dared not answer the truth.

"What did you want to say?"

"Foreigners go first."

"I'm half French. Besides, ladies go before foreigners."

"Oh! ladies," she said with a wistful air. "I am no lady. I'm a bodyguard."

She laughed.

"Mistigri, what's your real name?"

"I have no real name."

"Who were your parents?"

"I come from the Assistance Publique."

That sounded like a pretty grim story. Unwanted children, foundlings, sons and daughters of criminals usually end up there. Then they are rented out to people who are supposed to educate them and usually make them work. A chapter on the Assistance Publique would do very well in the books that Les Enfants De Mai would publish with Munchin and Munchin.

We were standing side by side and looking at the beautiful park sinking into darkness. Why did I feel so close to this girl? Because she had shot at me? I didn't know anything about her, she didn't

know anything about me. Wait, though. She knew my phone number. How did she get hold of that?

"Mistigri?"

"Mr. de Walter?"

"Just Walter, please."

"Sounds like calling you by your last name. All right. What do
you want, Walter?"

She threw a mischievous glance at me, sideways.

". . . I want to know how you found my phone number."

"Is that what you were going to ask me? I thought it would be
something interesting."

"It was to be something interesting."

"Then ask it."

"First, tell me how you got my phone number."

She sighed deeply.

"Walter," she said, "you are allowed one question, not two. I
promise to answer truthfully whatever you ask, but it has to be
only one question. If you want to know about your silly phone
number, I can tell you. If you want to ask me that interesting
question of yours, I can answer it too. But I won't answer both."

"What a cruel dilemma!"

"I'm a cruel woman. Or 'lady' as you say."

"Well, let's see. One answer could be useful, the other could be
pleasant."

"I wouldn't hesitate."

"But it also could be very unpleasant. One question is rather
ordinary, the other one rather insolent."

"I'd rather answer the insolent one."

"Here goes then. Are you Saint-Fiacre's mistress?"

She gasped. For a long time she said nothing at all and her gaze
was completely lost in the dusk. At last she said:

"I'm his servant."

"That was not what I asked."

"But that's what I'm answering!"

So far the tone of our conversation had been mildly flirtatious,
but this last sentence she threw at me with a kind of savage
earnestness which I was obtuse enough to disregard. I went on in
the former style:

"You shoot straighter than you talk, Mistigri."

Suddenly she turned on me with an extraordinary violence. She was still the Siamese cat, but hissing, scratching and biting.

"And why would my love life be any of your damned business? Monsieur Serge is right: Americans are overbearing and thick-headed. How does it concern you if a girl of ten is taken from the Assistance Publique to serve the pleasures of fat old men who fortunately can do little damage, but will torture her to their hearts' content? How does it concern you if a girl of ten gets paid for being beaten? If she has to look up to her torturer to find just a little bit of tenderness in the whole world? If the same man flogs her for the pleasure of others and caresses her for his own? And when she reaches the uninteresting age of thirteen—there are not so many Humbert Humberts in this world—if she is sent away to a convent, where she is systematically bullied with hell and brimstone, how does it concern you, 'Walter'? And if, when she is eighteen, she discovers she can stand no more hell and brimstone and runs away and the torturer who gave her candy from time to time decides she doesn't look too bad and, since, by some strange quirk of fate, she happens to be a good shot, she can be turned into a cute little bodyguard, makes up his mind to employ her as such, how does it concern you, 'Walter'? And if she is loyal to him although she doesn't love him, what do you think about that, 'Walter'? And generally speaking, why don't you just go to hell, 'Walter'?"

I looked at her with a compassion I had never felt in my life. Here then was one of the victims of Les Ballets Roses, and she was faithfully serving her "master's" designs. That didn't surprise me: women are like that—really. And she had nowhere else to turn. My heart felt for her. She had answered my question after all: she didn't love him, although he probably had made use of her in former times and perhaps even more recently. What did it matter? If she would cry for his death, she would be easily consoled. I would gladly console her myself, for that matter, and here she was, sending me to hell.

"You obviously know the address," I said dryly.

She didn't misunderstand me. She guessed this was as simple an expression of compassion as I could manage. She sighed deeply:

"Go away. I've made a fool of myself."

I didn't reply. I went down the stairs. I was getting into my car when she called me back. She was leaning on the railing and I stood at her feet.

"Walter", she said, "are you fond of that little thing you brought to the party the other night?"

"Fond? Not particularly. Why?"

"Tell her to stay away from Saint-Fiacre."

Something seemed to bite at my heart.

"Why? Are you jealous?"

She winced. "He's not exactly what you'd call a nice man," she said, and, turning on her heel, entered the house.

13

I had not been driving for more than a quarter of a mile when I found out I had practically no brakes. Fortunately, I am a pretty careful driver and I stick to manual transmissions. I got into low gear and managed to stop without having to ram into anything. I asked a passer-by where I could phone from; he indicated a café; I called the rental company and they promised to deliver another car in an hour's time. Having nothing to do, I decided to call Joyce and pass on the warning to her. I probably wouldn't have done it if I hadn't had this free time: for one thing it sounded either silly or melodramatic; for another, I still bore Joyce a grudge for the way she had let me down. It was the press photographer who answered.

"May I speak to Joyce?"

"I'm sorry. She's taking a shower. You are the American, aren't you?"

"I'm not *the* American. I'm an American, yes."

"Well, I mean Joyce's American."

"I am not Joyce's by any means."

"Yes, I know you had a little problem together. Too bad. I was hoping. . . . Well, no matter. I'll tell her you called to apologize."

"What do you mean: to apologize?"

"She told me you had behaved very rudely to her. Left her alone at a party. 'And I thought he was such a gentleman,' she said."

That was a new way to look at things.

"My dear man, I wouldn't dream of apologizing to Joyce. She has got it all wrong. *She* treated *me* very rudely indeed, but she probably didn't realize it. So let's just forget about it. Will you tell her I called to relay a message from a lady? The lady says: 'Keep away from Saint-Fiacre. *He is not a very nice man.*' Got that?"

"Got it. She'll call you back."

"She can't. She doesn't have my number."

"She does too. I do too. In fact, I gave it to a woman who called yesterday."

"Where did you get it from?"

"Oh! somebody told me you had arrived at that party with Nénette. So I guess you must be one of hers."

"One of her what?"

"You know what I mean."

"Well, I'll thank you not to give my phone number to anyone. We may do it in America, but let me tell you I'm about one-third French and in France it's considered indiscreet. Don't you know *anything*?"

"Yes, if you had given it to me. But you didn't. I figured it out myself. It was my property."

"Don't talk nonsense. If I give you something, it still belongs to me; and if you steal it, it belongs to you? Is that what you're saying?"

"Monsieur! I shall not allow you to. . . . Oh! Here comes Joyce. It's your American, Joyce."

Joyce picked up the phone and said very distinctly:

"I don't want to speak to you." And hung up.

There was nothing more I could do besides drinking a Kir or two, and waiting for my car. It arrived punctually and that same night I had a very charming dinner with Nénette at a small restaurant in Montmartre, where performers from neighboring night clubs would drop in between acts and talk to the fat *patronne* and do a magic trick or sing a song or take some clothes off between the tables. Having had a champagne cork knocked from the top of my head a few hours earlier, I felt somehow resurrected and very jolly. Nénette didn't complain of the way I showed my jolliness, and it was about ten the next morning when the phone woke me up. I began swearing because I thought it would be, as the press photographer put it, one of Nénette's, but it was Fifi reporting from the field.

It had not been easy to find a room in the Boulevard Saint-Germain house. One tenant, a patriotic old lady who hated all Germans, had practically thrown him out: she said she would gladly have assassinated S.F. herself if she had had a gun. Since she didn't have one, we still were in business. Another tenant, a German student, had a different attitude: she invited Fifi and his friends to come and join her at her window: she would be sure to watch such a touching ceremony from beginning to end. Finally, he had found a Negro student from Black Africa, who let him have his room for an exorbitant fee, but warned him that all his beautiful tailored suits would be under lock and no one should try and touch them, or else! . . .

Also Fifi had acquired a ladder, a rope, chains and padlocks, and could acquire a police card, if I were willing to pay for it. It was one hundred dollars and I said go ahead.

I told him I would have to take Chirpie for a trip to the country this afternoon, and the infernal fellow said yes, he had been expecting that; if I didn't want to come to the hotel, he would take Chirpie to the Gare du Nord, where we could meet. I said I would meet them there at two. Funny how I had come to depend on Fifi whom I had tried so hard to subdue in the beginning.

"Who is Fifi?" I asked Nénette who was beginning to stir.

"A Trotskiite," she answered sleepily.

"He's as much of a Trotskiite as I!"

"Somebody told me he also belonged to the Delta Commandos."

I whistled.

The Delta Commandos were the toughest part of that tough subversive organization called O.A.S. which had tried to keep Algeria French by hook or by crook. That explained a few things.

After that, I called Crommlinckx, to thank him for the use of Pavillon Saint-Hu.

"Were they big? Did you have fun?"

"We had a spot of bad luck. Neither of the ladies showed up."

"What happened? Some damned husband came home unexpectedly, I suppose?"

"Something of the kind. But we are going to try again this weekend. May I again presume on your old friendship and. . . ?"

"You may, my dear fellow, you may. And now if you'll excuse me, I have to go back to work."

"Work? Gerhard!"

"Oh! not that kind of work. I mean this one happens to be a little frigid. But such a size, my dear fellow! Such a size!"

I laughed and went to the post office on the rue du Louvre. There was nothing to laugh at there. Amarantha's telegram read thus:

"*In view of uncle's prolonged good health merger inevitable. Come back. Good job guaranteed in joint company. I make this condition of merger. Love. Amarantha.*"

Standing there in the middle of the post office, I began swearing in Arabic. A few startled heads turned my way. Those who didn't understand were surprised. Those who understood were shocked. Good job guaranteed! Condition of merger! Love, Amarantha! What the. . . . Did she think I would serve under Billy B. Bopkins III, that tycoon of cartoons, good for a cartoon himself? She might have some excuses but not I, thank you very much. Oh! I could imagine how he had made use of my absence to work on her, not in Gerhard Crommlinckx's sense, she didn't need it, but to persuade her that he represented the only chance of salvation for Munchin and Munchin. Merger inevitable! Inevitable indeed! I would show her how inevitable it was. I scribbled the answer and cabled it off.

"*Uncle entered last phase agony. Tell Bopkins keep cotton picking hands off. Walter.*"

I had lunch alone. It was pretentious, expensive and mediocre. I had the *patron* called in and asked him to recommend a good restaurant. Only the newspapers were good: the Convention of the International European Party made everybody very angry, and they said it. Even the American press began expressing some interest.

I drove to the Gare du Nord. There a surprise awaited me. I found Fifi sitting on a bench beside a kind of interplanetary monster, with all his hair shaved off.

"Chirpie!" I cried. "What did you do to yourself?"

"It's a disguise," he replied. "You ought not to have recognized me, Wally."

"He is afraid Boudin and Snipe will find him," explained Fifi.

"If they find him, they are sure to run away," I muttered.

I didn't think it was a particularly good idea to have Chirpie, with his already distinctive physique, look like a kind of unhappy medium between Kojac and Brynner, but, short of getting him a wig, there was nothing that could be done. I bought him a sun hat, though, which would hide both his head and part of his face. He was very pleased with it. He had never worn a hat except his professional peaked cap.

First, we took him to the Cour de Rohan and showed him his escape route. It would probably have been more sensible to let Fifi do it and not show myself there again, but I felt more and more responsible for *my* murder and also for Chirpie's safety. So I couldn't stay away. Besides, I thought Chirpie might panic at the sight of the steep roofs, and I wanted to keep his morale up. Chirpie did not panic. He seemed in a very good mood. He cracked jokes at all the passers-by. "I'll show all them frogs what an American country lad can do!" That was his attitude. Fifi and I had to calm him down. I did not at the time pay enough attention to this newborn sprightliness in him. I had cause to regret it later.

Then we drove out into the country. All the way Fifi kept reminding Chirpie of the escape route. "From Mr. Bobo-Diulasso's room, you follow the hall to the left, open the door, climb the stairs, get on the roof. I will have attached the rope while you are in the room. It will be around one of the chimneys. You have nothing to do but slide down the rope. You will find yourself on another roof, follow it down, slide to a third one and to a fourth one. All very easy. No problem. There is no rain. The slate won't be slippery. If by any chance you slip, the gutters are sturdy: they will hold your weight. From the fourth roof, just drop onto the ladder and climb down."

"I'll slide down," said Chirpie.

"Good idea. You will be wearing gloves, so why not? It will make it faster. Then you take the passageway on your right, you remember?"

"Sure I remember. Who do you take me for? A moron?"

"And Wally will be waiting for you in his car. All right?"

"Sure, it's all right. There's nothing that could go wrong!"

There were quite a few things which could go wrong. Chirpie

could miss again. Also, he could break his neck or panic when he actually had to come down from that roof. Finally, he could be caught. At times I thought I was completely crazy to make him try and do it. What if the poor fellow died in the attempt? What if he didn't die and was captured and made to talk? Where would I be then? But then I reflected that "due to uncle's health the merger was considered inevitable" and concluded once again that any operation was better than no operation at all. Good job guaranteed! I would see Chirpie dead first!

*

Since Chirpie's rifle had been disassembled, had traveled back and forth, had even been buried in the damp earth, it probably needed sighting in again.

To sight a rifle in you need a few things: first, the rifle and the scope; we had those; I had transported them from the blue Continental to the silvery grey they had given me to replace it; the attendant had been surprised to see me carrying "golf clubs" wrapped in a sheet but he had made no objections. Second, you need a quiet place in the country, and this is more easily said than found when you happen to live in Paris. Finally, we found a little valley in the Rambouillet forest, that seemed discreet enough; we hoped that no hidden lovers were busy under the bushes, but, of course, we couldn't tell. Still there were no tire marks on the little dirt road that had taken us there, so we felt sufficiently safe. Third and last, but definitely not least, you need ammunition, and there was the rub.

The Ruger held five shells. One had already been shot. Four remained. I asked Fifi if he couldn't find some 308 shells somewhere, but he said no: police cards could be found for the right amount of dollars but rifle shells of a caliber seldom used in France couldn't be found for gold. Chirpie was confident that with three shots he could do the sighting in to a T. One would be left. I didn't like that. You don't find rotten shells often, but you do sometimes. Besides, I thought Chirpie would have time enough for two shots if he missed the first one. I didn't want to rub it in, but he had missed once: why not twice? Of course, there would probably be no banana peels in front of Danton's statue. Still. . .

"O.K.," said Chirpie, "I'll do the sighting in in two shots."

"Can you do that?" asked Fifi.

"I can do anything!"

I had never seen him in that kind of mood. We drew a very crude target on a square piece of paper: two diagonals and the bull's-eye: it ought to suffice. Fifi thumbtacked the paper to a tree. We made calculations to find out the distance at which the rifle should be sighted in.

"There was a guy named Pythagoras who invented something quite appropriate," remarked Fifi. With the help of Fifi and Pythagoras, we figured out that the shooting distance would be about 25 meters, 75 feet to you. 30 meters (90 feet) should be considered as a maximum.

"At that distance, I don't need a scope," boasted Chirpie.

That was true, he didn't. But he would have to sight in the rifle anyway, so why not use the scope? Chirpie himself reassembled the weapon. Fifi measured thirty meters, and we stood aside, while Chirpie was inspiring and expiring, all by the book.

The first shot was about an inch from the bull's-eye, at 14.00 hours.

Chirpie fiddled a little with the scope, took aim, inspired, expired, inspired again, expired halfway. . . .

Bang!

We ran to the target. The second impact was in the bull's eye, at 19.00 hours. We had a good rifle, a good scope and a good man to operate them. That much was clear. If we kept away from banana peels, we could publish that book yet.

"D'you want a third shot?" asked Chirpie.

There was no point to a third shot. The second one had been good enough: at such a short distance there was no doubt whatsoever that Saint-Fiacre's brain would be shot through and through.

"No," I said. "Let's keep one shell in reserve."

It had taken us nearly two hours' drive to get to that place, and about three minutes to do the job.

Of course, we couldn't disassemble the rifle now. It was laid in the trunk of the Continental in a bed of moss that Chirpie insisted it needed.

"My goodness, he must be in love with that damned rifle!" I said.

"Let's hope it will be faithful to him," answered Fifi.

And "Amen!" I rejoined.

I locked the trunk and we drove back to Paris. D-Day was tomorrow. Of course I should have stayed with Chirpie and kept him company like a good case officer, but I was a lousy case officer: it was my first mission, and I underestimated the effects of loneliness . . . and thirst. I asked Fifi to keep an eye on Chirpie and imagined that would be enough. Fool that I was! I drove back to Nénette's and invited her out.

"Where shall we go?" she asked.

"Wherever you will."

"I don't know. You choose."

"No, you choose."

We made quite a night of it. I thought it would be my last night in Paris, as indeed it was, and there was no reason not to make the most of it. I also thought Chirpie was sitting alone in his hotel reading comics, after a lean and sober evening meal. Then he would have a long night's sleep, and get up with his eyes rested and his nerves alert. I planned to have lunch with him and to feed him some light energetic food, like a steak, and some cheese, and maybe even half a glass of wine, although he was unaccustomed to spirits and it might spoil his aim. I would decide that on the spur of the moment. Concerning Chirpie, I may say now I was completely wrong, more wrong than I thought I could be wrong; concerning Nénette and me, I was right: we had a great time.

We began with a Scotch at Le Pont-Royal, a subterranean bar of which I was very fond, and where you can always meet literary celebrities. Well, not meet: catch a glimpse of. But it was not the celebrities we were after: it was the cosy, luxurious atmosphere, the excellent drinks, and the huge-eared barman who was practically a friend.

"Ah! Monsieur Walter! Glad to see you again! Mademoiselle Nénette, do you want your old table? It is free. What shall I serve you? Are you going to have a snack with us or just a drink?"

It was like old times and Nénette and I exchanged a sentimental glance.

We had our drink and we talked about nothings. Nénette never asked me what I was doing, and I was grateful for that. We discussed common friends, and last night's show, and tonight's dinner, and what we would do afterwards.

After a couple of drinks we adjourned to *La Tour d'Argent*. That's the place where, if you order a Coca-Cola, they ask you how to spell it, and then tell you they don't have it. It is a little showy for my taste, but Nénette liked it, and there was nothing to complain about as far as cuisine, service and wines were concerned. For some reason I don't like restaurants full of famous people. Maybe because I'm not famous myself. With bars, it's different. Damn it all, a bar is just for fun, a restaurant is a serious place, and no actors, writers, boxers, princes, astronauts, prophets, skiers, quacks and the like should be allowed to interfere with the mystic and sensual love story that is developing between your taste buds and the contents of your plate and glass. The specialty of *La Tour d'Argent* is duck in its own blood, but we were not so bloodthirsty as that and we had a satisfactory meal all the same: eel pâté for Nénette, pike *quenelles* for me, with a half-bottle of Rhine wine of which I am not a connoisseur at all, but it was good, which the sommelier told us was only to be expected since it was born in '53. After that, having decided we wanted simple things, we had a *carré d'agneau jardiniere* for two, with a Mouton-Rothschild 1961, one of the greatest I ever drank. We finished off with cheese and a half-bottle of a cuvée spéciale of Châteauneuf du Pape '52. After that, coffee, and pear brandy in huge iced glasses.

"Divine," said Nénette.

"What next?" I asked.

It was ten o'clock, time enough to get to one of those delightful cabarets on the left bank, where new singers get launched, old comedians spit their bile at the government (don't forget that the first duty of a government, in France, is to be funny), where you practically have to sit in your neighbor's lap but you don't mind it because your neighbor is another dilettante coming for a good song and a good laugh, where, in short, I had spent many pleasant hours in an earlier life, and where I was happy to set foot again.

The program began at eleven and ended at about two. Nénette

was wisely drinking *citron presse*, but I had gone back to Scotch. When we left the place, Nénette began to cry, because in former days we could have gone on to les Halles, Paris's produce market, such a fun place to explore before dawn, but it had recently been exiled to some crazy place in the suburbs, and no poetry was left. Some of the restaurants, where you could eat the best onion soup in the world, might still be there, but the atmosphere was all lost: you couldn't get abused and pushed around by *les forts* (the heavies) any more. There was nothing to do but to go home.

So we went. When we arrived the telephone was ringing.

And it was not "one of Nénette's" as the vulgar press photographer put it. It was the press photographer himself.

"Hello. May I speak to the American? Quick!"

"Walter de Walter speaking."

"Tell me the truth. Do you have Joyce?"

"Certainly not."

"Well, she must be somewhere."

"Did you look in the shower?"

"This is no joke, Monsieur! Joyce has disappeared."

"Somebody must have listened to your prayers."

"It's no joke, I tell you. Last night she went out for a date and she hasn't come back."

Mistigri's melodramatic warning came to my mind.

"Did you give her my message?"

"I did. She said you were jealous."

"Do you know whom she was supposed to meet?"

"I don't. I thought it might be you."

"It wasn't. Have you tried your friends?"

"They haven't seen her. That's what's so strange, you know! When you get cheated on, it's always by your best friends. But they haven't seen her. They would cheat on me but they wouldn't lie to me, if you see what I mean."

"Try the police."

He sounded shocked. "The police! Really? You think I should?"

"It was just a suggestion. She'll probably turn up in somebody else's shower."

I wasn't very much interested in Joyce's whereabouts. I had more urgent things to think of. So I hung up.

I was precisely in the process of attending to these urgent things, when Nénette gently stopped me and whispered: "Listen."

I listened and couldn't hear anything.

"What is it, Nénette?"

"Somebody is standing by the front door. They are trying the lock."

"Oh! come on, Nénette."

"You know I can hear better than you."

I got up and crept up to the door. We had no lights on and we had been home for some time, so whoever the intruder was, if he didn't know Nénette and me, he could very well think that we were asleep. I stood for some time very close to the door and couldn't hear anything. I was already going to return to more interesting occupations, when I detected a grating sound, like metal on metal, coming from the keyhole. Somebody was obviously trying to unlock the door. It could be some drunk, taking our door for his own. That happens all the time. But why was he so stealthy about it?

I suppose I should have done something intelligent, like calling the police, or arming myself with a saucepan and lying in ambush, but I was in a hurry to get rid of the intruder, and I had had, if you remember, quite a few drinks. So I did something completely idiotic.

I seized the first thing that I found—it happened to be Nénette's umbrella—and at the same time switched the light on and flung the door open. The suddenness of the action shocked the burglar or drunk or whoever he was out of his wits, and my appearance added to his bewilderment. Stark naked as I was, and waving Nénette's umbrella in the air, I chased after the poor man down three flight of stairs, and then returned home, very proud of having routed the enemy. It might not have been the wisest thing to do, but I felt very proud of myself. Nénette was dying with laughter in bed, and I only added to her mirth when I told her that the intruder—I had caught only a glimpse of him—reminded me of a romantic old gentleman whom I had seen roaming the day before in the Cour de Rohan.

In spite of this interlude, I woke up at five, and began thinking. Soon, I thought, the sun would show up, and it was the last time

Serge Saint-Fiacre would see it. There was no pity in me for him. Mistigri's confessions had made it quite clear that Serge Saint-Fiacre was a louse, and in my book lice should be destroyed: the means is of no importance: an insect spray if you can afford it, and your two thumbnails if you can't. Don't taunt me with beautiful arguments like: who is going to decide who is a louse? I've read all about it and I'm not trying to convert you to my faith. If you enjoy lice in your hair, that's all right with me. I just want to get them out of mine.

So Serge Saint-Fiacre was going to die, whatever that means. Rot and stink, I supposed, as far as his body was concerned; as to his soul if he had one, what would become of it was fortunately none of my business. There was another way to look at it. Chirpie was going to kill. Put like that, it didn't mean much. But the fact that Chirpie was going to kill Saint-Fiacre meant something. There was some kind of crazy but satisfactory logic to the fact that the mentally underdeveloped Chirpie would shoot a bullet through the overdeveloped brain of a politician who had begun his career by torturing children. If Chirpie couldn't protect them, he would at least avenge them: there was a kind of savage, romantic beauty in it. Ironically, the myth of Les Enfants de Mai was coming true. . . . I found that rather moving, but you mustn't forget all the drink and the little sleep I had had.

I suppose I was feeling somewhat drowsy so that all these philosophical considerations got blended together into a dream. I remember it vividly. Mistigri (I couldn't see her face, but somehow managed to recognize her interesting features from the rear) was standing naked at the foot of the stake. Her wrists were chained to it. She was supposed to be a very little girl, although she didn't look the part. A brilliant audience was gathered all around. They lounged in armchairs, chatting about the latest Parisian news, sipping champagne. A man began moving toward the victim. He took long, exaggerated steps and swung his arms at the same time. He looked like the Wolf in Little Red Riding Hood. When the people saw him, there was a pleasurable shudder of admiration and expectation. Then silence. He came closer and closer to Mistigri. He had a bundle of rods pickled in vinegar of champagne in his right hand. She cried: "No! Serge! No! Darling, please, no!"

He looked at the audience and grinned as if he had made a point. His pricked ears looked like horns. I noticed he had hairy legs terminating in hooves. He raised his arm and began to work on her. "Daddy! Don't!" she cried the eternal cry. But he lashed her, and lashed her, and trickles of blood ran on her white, defenseless body. The audience expressed appreciation, and the bejeweled Countess, who sat in the first row, yelled: "Give her hell, buddy! Give her sweet hell!" Nobody saw Chirpie enter, but I did. He moved noiselessly, without touching the floor. He had a very stern face and his natural ugliness was somehow ennobled by his expression. He carried a .22 carbine in his hands. He deliberately took his aim. His lips were moving, forming the words: "Thou shalt not miss." I didn't hear the shot, but suddenly the executioner reeled backwards, and I could see, in slow motion, the bullet go through his head. "What a pity I am not Chirpie," I thought, and woke up. That was the limit! That I should be Chirpie? No, thank you. I looked at the alarm clock: it was ten. I should have waked up before seeing that corny dream.

I washed, and shaved, and dressed, and packed. That seemed to be the end of the journey. There really wasn't much more to do besides buying a cello case.

"Where are you going?" asked Nénette trying very hard to look proper in her mini-nuisette.

"America."

"Are you happy?"

"It's a nice country."

"Did you make all the money you wanted?"

"I don't know yet."

"Is it fun, working for the C.I.A.?"

"It isn't that bad."

"Did Fifi work well for you?"

"He's done wonders."

"Well, it's been delightful to have you here, *Darrlene*."

"I've enjoyed it tremendously, Nénette."

"Come back anytime."

"I will."

All right, I won't. I won't! I didn't know I wouldn't, so I said I would. Please, stop pulling my hair. It's not my fault if I was a little dense. After all I had seen you only twice. All right, I take 'only' back. I was just a little slow, that's all.

Sorry for the interruption. There isn't much more to say anyway. I just picked up my bags and walked down the stairs.

She stood on the balcony. She had put something over the nightie. Too bad. She waved. And I waved. I seem to remember I had a lump in my throat, but you mustn't tell anybody. I got into the silver grey Continental and drove off.

If anybody had told me then what lay in wait for me at the *Hôtel des Grands Ducs,* I might have gone in despair to check my mail at rue du Louvre, and then none of the following would have happened. But there was no one to tell me. So I calmly drove on, my elegantly gloved hands lying negligently on the steering wheel, the Ruger dancing its little dance in my trunk, and my thoughts clear and collected in my head. I was master-minding a political murder, wasn't I?

14

No one was waiting for me at the Gare du Nord.

I inspected the *buffet,* the waiting rooms, the rest rooms, went back to the *buffet.* Neither Chirpie nor Fifi were to be seen. The appointment had been for twelve. It was quarter past. I called the Hôtel des Grands-Ducs. A surly waiter answered that so far as he knew Monsieur Watergate had not left his room. Could he be called to the phone? No, that wouldn't be convenient.

Anxiety is not something I encourage in myself, but I must confess that my intestines began playing their Indian cobra tricks again. There was nothing to do but go see for myself. Had Chirpie's watch stopped? Or Fifi's? Or had the police learned about our plans and, in that case, was there a mousetrap waiting for me at l'Hôtel des Grands-Ducs? It would be very foolish to throw myself into it. The Ruger was now in the cello case, and the cello case was in my car, and it is a serious offense in France to have in one's possession a weapon forbidden by law. I had a strong wish to throw that cello case into the Seine. But the merger? I decided to go and have a discreet look at the hotel.

I parked some distance from it and walked the rest of the way. It was the same kind of place as the Cardinal. A little more modern, a little more vulgar still. I walked past it, on the opposite sidewalk, very cautiously, with the most indifferent air I could muster. I didn't see a thing that could help me. Then I walked past it on its own sidewalk and stole a glance into the hall. There were no plainclothes policemen there (you know them in Paris by their mackintoshes and their felt hats); there was just an oldish clerk behind the desk. I went away, but one minute later I was there again. I hesitated and went finally in. The clerk was reading the horse racing page of his newspaper. He didn't look at me. Had I known Chirpie's room number, I might have crept by him without his noticing me. As it was, I had to ask for it.

"Number 13. Fourth floor," he said without looking up.

What did that mean? Was he always so casual? Or were half a dozen police officers hiding in that bloody Number 13. Thirteen, indeed! Why had Fifi allowed Chirpie to take number 13? Didn't he know it was unlucky?

I threw a glance at the door. There was still time to run away. Then I began to ascend the smelly stairs. Everything was very dark above me, and, try as I might, I couldn't see if there was an ambush on the landing or not.

Fourth floor in France means fifth floor in English. I reached it without any trouble except the trouble I was creating for myself by peering into dark halls and darker doorways. Now, was number 13 on my right or on my left? I tried to move stealthily, checking the numbers as I went: 11... 12... 13. There it was. There was noise in the room, voices in argument, moans. I didn't know what to do. There was no reason for a half-dozen policemen to moan or to argue. I was still hesitating when suddenly the door was flung open. I jumped backwards, just as shocked as that old drunk yesterday at Nénette's. It was Fifi.

He also was startled to see me. We recovered simultaneously.

"I was going to the Gare du Nord," he said.

And stood back to let me enter.

"What happened?"

"See for yourself."

I went in. Chirpie was lying in bed, with a rubber bottle on his head. A black-haired woman, wearing only a slip, was sitting on the bed and producing consolatory sounds, something like "There, there, duckie, you'll feel better in a little while." The room was very small; and very little light fell through the curtains covering a window which gave into one of those well-courtyards so numerous in Paris. Besides the bed, the furniture consisted of an armoire with a mirror in the middle of it, of two chairs, a night table and a chest of drawers. On the chest of drawers stood three empty bottles. The gold paper around their necks told me what they had been full of some time ago: *vin mousseux*.

"*Vahn-moo-sur*," moaned Chirpie. "I'll never touch it again, Wally."

"Who is that woman?" I asked.

Chirpie began rolling his head on the pillow. Fifi replied: "Mademoiselle Lili. A *respectful one.*"

That curious phrase is a relatively polite way of referring to a prostitute.

"What happened?"

Mademoiselle Lili, the respectful one, began talking thirteen to the dozen. She had been walking her regular beat yesterday night when she had met this Monsieur. She offered her services. Monsieur asked her where he could find some *vin mousseux.* She had trouble understanding him, but she tried her best, she didn't think all foreigners should be treated like dogs, some of them were rather nice guys, and finally she guessed what he wanted. Well, she took him to a store that was still open, and they bought three bottles. Monsieur kept talking to her in a language which she couldn't understand—she guessed it was English—and she kept talking to him in French, promising him all sorts of goodies, and so they came to the hotel. Although she had put her own room at Monsieur's disposal, he had apparently insisted on taking her here. That was all right with her. The clerk seemed to object; so she told Monsieur—who seemed as innocent as a child—how much to tip him, and Monsieur tipped him, and they came up. He seemed a little surprised that she followed him, but he let her come and invited her to share the first bottle of *vin mousseux.* He explained by gestures that it was the third one he was drinking that day. After that, since she was a conscientious woman, she began doing her job. And just imagine, she had been right in her surmise, Monsieur was indeed as innocent as a child. (Yes, I remembered having guaranteed Chirpie's chastity to an irate Colonel of the American Army.) But she was a clever one, yes she was, and an affectionate one, and a patriotic one! She wanted Monsieur to go back to his country with the best possible impression of French women. So she didn't spare her efforts and Monsieur was really very cute, only so inexperienced, and with the help of the second bottle, she finally carried a total victory, of which she was justly proud, so that the third bottle had been finally consumed among mutual congratulations. Later, Monsieur had been very ill and Mademoiselle Lili had taken care of him, as was only right. She had held his head over the sink and had given him aspirin, and what not. In the morning, she had felt it would be inhuman to leave him in the state he was, although he still had not paid her. So she had gone and brought the ice bottle from her home, and that didn't help much. And then Monsieur's friend had come too, and sworn a lot, and brought Alka-Seltzer and that didn't help either. And that was it.

I looked at Fifi. He shrugged his shoulders. I looked at my watch. Chirpie had about five hours to become a man again.

The first thing was to get rid of that woman.

"Mademoiselle," I said very politely, "I am very grateful for everything you did for my friend. Maybe with the exception of the *vin mousseux,* but, of course, you couldn't have known. He will go back to his country enriched by an unforgettable experience. As far as his health is concerned, I will take over from now on. Please tell me how much I owe you."

She volunteered to stay and take care of Monsieur Watergate; but I objected to that, and asked her again how much she wanted. She was obviously very honest, because she began figuring it out with great precision. She charged so much a night, but she didn't want to charge Monsieur for the time she had been nursing him, that was just a favor she did him because of her good heart. The trouble she took with him previously she wanted to charge extra. Also she .... I finally gave her about two hundred dollars and pushed her out. She thanked me profusely and, on second thought, gave Fifi and me two bits of paper with her address on it: business cards, so to speak. After that, we were rid of her.

I sat on the edge of Chirpie's bed and began talking to him very gently. I knew there was no point in abusing him, although he deserved it. He wept in my arms and begged for forgiveness. It was the *vahn-moo-sur* that had started it, he thought, but he didn't think he was ill because of it. He was ill because of the woman. I tried to persuade him that he was mistaken, but couldn't. Finally, he made a complete confession. It was not pure chance that he had picked up Mademoiselle Lili. The wine had given him courage to do it, but there was a virtuous purpose behind it all. He had heard that love-making a few hours before shooting improved a man's marksmanship, and was so afraid of missing again, that he wanted to have all chances on his side. So, in spite of his fear of meeting Boudin or Snipe, he had decided to walk the streets in search of technical help. That was already his intention when he had had his hair shaved as a disguise.

Fifi and I exchanged glances. It was all very pitiful and ridiculous and unfortunate. We looked at our watches. About four hours to go.

"Get up, Chirpie!" I ordered.

He did get up, but he couldn't stay up. And he felt nauseous again. Some more Alka-Seltzer could help, maybe. Fifi was all for it. We tried. Meanwhile, Chirpie had fallen back into bed. Fifi held his head while I made him drink. Another hour went by. From time to time, Chirpie would say: "I feel fine now." And get up, and take three steps around the room, and then put his hand to his head and whisper: "Not as fine as I thought" and lie down again. At three o'clock he could stand, but his hands shook as leaves in the wind.

"Can't you hold your hands steady, Chirpie?"

"Yes, I can."

He extended them and with all his might tried to hold them steady. They shook all the more from the effort.

"It's no use," said Fifi.

"But I want to bump him off!" rebelled Chirpie. "I want to do it."

"Well, you can't. So you'd better shut up."

Chirpie began crying again. I always had had more patience with him than with anybody else, and Fifi looked on with some surprise as I coaxed him back into bed and held his hand while he fell asleep. Tears rolled down his cheeks, though, and from time to time he would curse Mademoiselle Lili in his sleep, which was really unfair.

"What shall we do?" asked Fifi.

I looked at the dull light that fell through the becurtained window.

"Will you do it?" I asked.

I didn't know if Fifi was a good shot, but who could miss a man's head at twenty-five meters, with a scope?

He stretched his arms and yawned nervously.

"Yes, I'll do it. For twenty-five thousand dollars."

Added to all the expenses I had already incurred it was a pretty steep price.

"Ten," I said.

"I won't bargain, *Mister* Turner. I'm not a professional murderer, you know. It's twenty-five or it's no go. Period."

He stood looking out the window. There was nothing to see there, of course.

I thought about Amarantha's telegram. Good job guaranteed. Merger inevitable.

"All right," I said.

He looked at me and smiled his ironic smile.

"In cash," he added. "Fifteen in advance."

"You're crazy! It's three o'clock, you have to do it at five-thirty. Where can I find all that cash?"

"That's your problem."

If he really meant it, it was a dead end. No pun intended. I had spent most of the cash I had with me. Munchin and Munchin had no account in Paris and anyway would have refused to pay for the murder. Our first idea was that somebody else would pay for it and that we would profit by it, which was somewhat different. I had wealthy friends, yes, from whom I could borrow, or rather from whom I could have borrowed had I not already borrowed all I could in past years. It was hopeless.

"Fifi," I said, "you're being unreasonable. One thousand now, yes. And the rest a year from now."

He burst out laughing, a dry, unnatural laugh.

"Who do you take me for?" he said, mimicking Chirpie. "A moron?"

"Fifi, I don't have the money."

"Well, aren't you supposed to be working for the C.I.A. or something?"

"I'll sign you an I.O.U."

"An I.O.U. for the murder of Serge Saint-Fiacre, signed *Mister* Turner?"

I saw I was making a fool of myself.

"Too bad," I said, suppressing a yawn. "Too bad you won't trust me. You could have been a rich man."

"I was a rich man once," he said meditatively. "I wore short hair and the kind of clothes you wear. Tailored blazers. Custom-made shirts. I'm through with all that."

And then he turned toward me, looked at me sitting on that bed and smiled his slow, languid smile. And kept ironically quiet.

"Well, say it!" I growled impatiently. "Say what you have on your mind."

"Don't you see what I mean? I've already nearly said it. When I had money, I had things done for me. I had my shoes shined for me by little Arab boys in the streets. Now I have no more money; and if I wanted my shoes to be clean, I would shine them myself."

He looked down at his shoes, following my own gaze, and smiled again. They badly needed some shining.

We kept silent for a few seconds. Then he spoke again, very lightly.

"All right, I'll say it. Why don't you do it yourself?"

15

We drove separately, Fifi in the GS, I in the Continental. I parked the Continental near the church of Saint-Julien le Pauvre, about a quarter of a mile from the rue Saint-André-des-Arts. Then we drove to the rue Saint-André-des-Arts together in the GS. Fifi parked it. And we walked over to rue Mazarine. That morning he had parked there a rented van containing the ladder. We carried the ladder into the Cour de Rohan and set it where we wanted it. Nobody stopped us. It was four o'clock.

We left the Cour and took a stroll along the Boulevard Saint-Germain. Everything was pretty quiet. Cars were still passing to and fro. A small crowd had begun gathering. Behind the Faculté de Médecine we saw four black Marias full of grim policemen with helmets, shields and ugly long sticks.

"That's for the counter-counter-manifestation," Fifi said.

I agreed. Some patriotic organizations had announced they would interfere with the plaque business; and if they were asking for a good beating, they would get it.

Uniformed policemen and plainclothes men sauntered along with a casual appearance. Students were selling subversive newspapers: extreme left or extreme right, they were far out both ways. A political quarrel started at the corner of the rue Serpente. Fists flew. Someone was led away with a bloody nose. It was all very ordinary.

"Fifi," I said, "we don't have much time left to talk. Keep the engine running."

"I would have thought of it, *Mister* Turner."

"Did you change the license number of the GS?"

"I did."

"You will return the GS and the van to the renting companies."

"Most certainly."

"Get Chirpie on the first flight to Atlanta, Georgia, via New York. He has nothing to fear. He has done nothing illegal. He will be awfully disappointed at not having bumped off the anti-American bastard, but he won't have lost anything by this trip."

"Except his hair and innocence."

"That's right. Here is his passport. Take it. His return ticket's in it. How much money do you want to tidy everything?"

"One hundred will do."

"Here you are."

We walked back to the GS to which we had transferred the cello case. Then we entered the Cour from the rue Saint-André-des-Arts side, the one by which I would be escaping. As we reached the first gate to our right, we saw a uniformed policeman in the process of closing it.

We exchanged a glance.

"What are you doing, Monsieur l'agent?" I asked.

"Executing orders," he answered politely enough. "If there is any trouble, we don't want those rascals to run away through here."

"Do you mean you are sealing the Cour de Rohan completely?"

"Oh! no, sir. We will leave the Saint-André-des-Arts entrance open. But if they enter through there, they are bagged!"

"An excellent idea," I said.

We left the Cour through another exit, and another policeman locked it as soon as we were out.

"They are doing our work for us," said Fifi.

"Not quite. They have the keys of these locks. You will still have to padlock the gates."

"True."

"Well. . ."

All seemed in order.

"Good-bye," I said. "See you in half an hour."

He smiled his supercilious smile.

"*Macte animo, generose puer*," he murmured. "Which means: break a leg."

I turned my back on him and walked down the Boulevard. The

police were setting roadblocks east and west of the Carrefour. People on foot were allowed to walk by, but cars had to follow a detour.

I entered the target house.

This time something must have been wrong with the TV, because the dishevelled concierge jumped at me out of her *loge* like a jack-in-the-box.

"What do you want? No salesmen allowed."

"My dear Madam, do you really think I look like a salesman?"

She was impressed by my manner but not impressed enough to quell her curiosity.

"Who do you want to see?"

I had noticed some of those names on the visiting cards.

"I'm going to give Madame Thomas her cello lesson. Now will you let me pass, please?"

"Madame Thomas doesn't come home until eight."

"You are misinformed. Madame Thomas is expecting me now."

It's all in the air. I looked so sure of myself that she popped back into her *loge* without bothering me anymore. I took the elevator, this time, although it was difficult to get the case inside.

The elevator stopped at the sixth floor. I got out, and climbed the one remaining flight of stairs. I still had had no time to think about anything. My only worry was of a practical character: had the Alka-Seltzer I had borrowed from Chirpie done me any good or not? Would my hands keep shaking or wouldn't they? As I stated before, I had made quite a night of it, and I was definitely not in the best of shape.

I felt for the key in my pocket and didn't find it. I panicked. Then I remembered I had put it in another pocket, not to mix it up with the other keys. Here it was. And here was Mr. Bobo-Diulasso's door, with a beautifully engraved card on it.

The key fitted the lock. The lock opened noiselessly. I pushed the door and went in.

It was a small room, rather expensively furnished. Period pieces, if you please! The sons of old cannibal kings don't do too badly on French scholarships, I reflected. There was a Louis XV secretary, gilt all around, which must have cost a fortune just to hoist up here. I walked over to the window. Fifi had not lied to me. The statue of Danton was a little to my left, at no more than thirty meters. It would be child's play.

I checked my watch. Five to five.

I had a look around. The walls were decorated with expensive, semi-pornographic posters representing magnificent blondes in varied postures.

I opened the cello case. It contained two things: the Ruger, complete with scope, and the rope. I took the rope and walked out into the hall. I seem to remember that I had a wild hope the door leading to the roof would be locked. It wasn't. Fifi's match was still in operation. I even thought for a second that I could throw the match away and then say I hadn't been able to open the door. Say that to whom? Was I responsible before Fifi? Or was I trying to lie to myself? I opened the little door, ascended the stairs and found myself on the roof. It was windy here. The rumors of the steet came up, but subdued. A cat ran away from me and nearly knocked me down. I walked to the chimney-stack we had selected the day before and tied the rope to it. I'm not very good with knots, I'm not that kind of scout. But this knot was strong, I can tell you that. I kept the end of the rope on the roof, so it wouldn't be noticed by anybody who would happen to look this way. Not that there was much chance of anybody doing so.

I got back into the house and checked the door carefully. It wouldn't lock automatically with that match in there.

On the landing I met a lady: seventyish, old-fashioned dress: it might be the patriotic soul who wanted to kill Saint-Fiacre. Well, I would do that for her. I pressed myself into the wall so as to give her as much room as I could; she thanked me with a courteous little nod. When she had disappeared, I reopened M. Bobo-Diulasso's door and went in. I pondered whether I would lock it from the inside and decided against it. Unlocking it would take a few seconds which might prove vital.

I went to the window and opened it. Then I retreated to find how far back into the room I could get and still see Danton's statue and the ground around it. I determined that, to be able to shoot, I would have to stand very close to the window, but that I could still hide in the shadow on the left side.

I would need something to lean the rifle on. My hands didn't shake; on the contrary, there was a leaden quality to them: they seemed heavy and inert. Nevertheless, I wanted a support for the weapon. I thought that the back of a Louis XV bergère would do nicely. I carried it close to the window.

The people down there seemed at the same time very close and very remote. Close, because I was afraid they might see what I was doing; remote, because I began doubting my ability to put a bullet through one of those small heads. And I had only two shells left. Besides, the Ruger had a bolt action and seconds would be numbered. . . . I took the rifle and propped it on the back of the armchair. It took a great effort of will to do that. I was afraid somebody down there would see what I was doing, although I took great care to remain in the shadow. I put one knee on the seat of the armchair. That felt comfortable. I pressed the butt of the rifle against my shoulder and aimed at Danton's head. Danton wouldn't tattle on me. Somehow I began feeling better. The gun was beautifully shaped, it was pleasant to hold, it was becoming part of me. I put my eye to the scope and saw Danton's ugly head considerably magnified. The crosshairs gave me a feeling of power and precision at the same time: the bullet would go where I wanted it. There was not the least doubt about that. I checked the safety with my thumb and caressed the trigger with my forefinger. I began to feel very good indeed. I chose the silly blond head of a student selling a monarchist paper and aimed the scope at him. It was weird and exhilarating at the same time to feel that that young man's life was in my hands. Then I chose a student who was selling a communist paper: he had dark, unwashed hair, all curly. I killed him. Then I killed a policeman. Then I recognized a reporter whom I had known years ago and who had stolen my girlfriend from me: I killed him. My rifle was inexhaustible, like those you see on TV. I had to lay it down: it would have killed every passer-by on the Boulevard Saint-Germain.

There was nothing more to do but wait.

Variegated images ran through my head while I waited. Bill Bopkins' stupid, overbearing face. Amarantha's sleek, elongated, body. Mistigri's pathetic eyes. Chirpie's figure in bed, with the ice bottle on his forehead. And then a kind of joke: Chirpie had come to France to lose his hair and innocence, as Fifi put it, but I also was going to lose a different kind of virginity. I had never killed a man before.

Suddenly it all appeared completely implausible to me: what? I, a peaceful publisher's scout, an easy-going spendthrift, a rather pleasant good-for-nothing, not a profound character by any means but, all told, a fairly nice chap, I was going to commit murder? In cold blood? And risk being tried for it? And guillotined? Or sentenced to spend the rest of my life in quite undesirable company? How had I got into that situation? I couldn't tell. Of course, it had to do with Chirpie's double failure, it had to do with Amarantha's telegram ("Merger inevitable"), but it also had to do, I didn't know how, with the scene at Le Vésinet. When Saint-Fiacre had offered the cork to all those nice people who had excused themselves, when I had seen him sneer at them, I had partly become an Enfant de Mai myself. And when Mistigri had confided in me, I had gone one step more. Hadn't I come very close to regretting I was not Chirpie? It didn't really make sense, but there it was: I knew I could still refrain from shooting and chuck the whole business, but I also knew I would do no such thing. And as to its being implausible, quite a few prominent men had been shot recently, in South Africa, in the United States, in Rome, and in a few other places. In France, they missed de Gaulle, but they tried. In fact, political assassination was very much the fashion. I didn't have to feel a loner. I was just following the current fad.

A low, rumbling noise began rolling on my left. I stuck my head out and looked up Boulevard Saint-Germain, toward the Boul' Mich' crossing. The noise increased, and it had a particularly dramatic quality, because the police didn't allow any more cars on the Boulevard Saint-Germain: those hundreds of feet hitting the pavement together without observing any rhythm, those whispers, conversations, speeches and cries blended into one indistinct clamor, seemed to fill gradually the eerie silence that had settled over this part of Paris. One felt that a great strength was approaching, senseless and purposeless as all crowds, but still impressive and even a little frightening. For the three or four hundred people who were marching down the Boulevard Saint-Germain, Saint-

Fiacre was a hero, and I certainly wouldn't wish to fall into their hands after I had shot him. The police would be better. That much was clear.

I saw them as they paraded before the School of Medicine. Saint-Fiacre and a fat German gentleman were walking at some distance from the rest of the crowd. Saint-Fiacre held the German flag (not Hitler's one, though) and the German gentleman held the French tricolor. Saint-Fiacre looked better than the German, who seemed to feel ill at ease in the midst of all this flag-waving. Saint-Fiacre, on the contrary, brandished the foreign colors with gusto. A small crowd followed. There were some signbearers: I could read *Parti Européen International* written in gothic red letters on the white calicos.

There were a certain number of pretty women. And then there was the usual intellectual rabble, a little more interesting this time because Italian faces always look nice with a fierce expression, and there were a few fierce Italian delegates scattered around.

I looked at that crowd and felt mainly disgust. The same kind of crowd had sent to the guillotine twenty thousand poor people labeled "aristocrats" because the crowd felt bloodthirsty back in '93; the same kind of crowd had butchered Protestants on the night of Saint Bartholomew, and defenseless prisoners those bloody days in September; the same kind of crowd had acclaimed Robespierre and Napoleon and Pétain and de Gaulle and Lenin and Hitler. Fortunately, I had only a rifle and not a machine gun: I might have been tempted to use it.

Saint-Fiacre took his position at the foot of Danton's statue. He gave the German flag to somebody else to carry and received in exchange a marble plaque which he held very high for everybody to see. Then he clutched it to his breast, and waited for the crowd to make a half-circle around him. Some of his helpers, I saw, linked hands and made the inner half-circle, so he would have some breathing space. Five hundred people pressed against them from all sides. It was not a large crowd as crowds go, but they occupied a good part of the Carrefour de l'Odéon and of the Boulevard.

There was a lot of noise, and he waited for it to subside. Then he raised his arm, and a dead silence fell over the crowd.

"Fellow Europeans!" he began. And I saw him smile as if he had made a point. There was a roar of applause.

The time had come. Saint-Fiacre was standing a little to my left, no more than thirty yards from me. I could see his whole figure, clad in blue overalls, with that marble plaque in its hands, standing in the middle of that empty half-circle. I ran no risk of hitting anyone else: they were keeping away from him, as was only decent: after all, he was the great man, the future President of a Marxist Unified Europe. The time had come.

I took the Ruger in my hands. They didn't tremble. I propped it on the back of the armchair. I got into that comfortable kneeling position. I checked the safety, and began aiming.

It took me some time to get Saint-Fiacre's head in the scope, but once I had him, I held him. The crosshairs centered on his receding forehead. I remembered the rifle had not been sighted in properly, but at such a short distance, it couldn't make much difference.

"Well, Monsieur Serge Saint-Fiacre," I murmured, "your hour has come. You can yack all you like about progress and equality, and underdevelopment, and underprivilege and all kinds of underdogs, it won't help you more than your Napoleon III houses, and your beautiful furniture, and your unequal champagne. You are a subversive bastard and I am going to flatten you into a book with the help of this magic wand." I patted the Ruger.

"Do you remember all those little dancers, *petits rats* they call them, whom you picked up at the Opéra and brought to the Senators and Ministers of the Fourth Republic, for whom you were working with such commendable zeal? Either they were foundlings, or their parents sacrificed them, I don't know; but you sacrificed their poor little innocent bodies and souls to the filthy desires of those disgusting old men. Well, the time of revenge, the time of justice has come. And this is its instrument." I patted the Ruger.

"Come on, you dirty bastard! You can't believe what you're saying! You're preaching for freedom and equality, but what freedom and equality did they have, those poor little mites whom you corrupted and perverted for the sake of a little more money. I'm not a saint either, Monsieur Saint-Fiacre, but I'm going to kill you all the same, and count it as a good deed." I patted the Ruger.

"Oh! now you're preaching against violence! Bravo! How appropriate! Yes, of course, violence is damnable when it is used by the police, or the army, or any part of the Establishment. But when you were playing Father Flogger at the Ballets Bleus, drawing blood from young innocent bodies for the pleasure of slobbering emasculated old vampires that was permissible, I suppose. Oh! I'm going to drive a bullet through this forehead of yours, Saint-Fiacre." I patted the Ruger.

It didn't work. He was still talking to the people, and I was still trying to talk myself into shooting him.

You may have had a comparable experience. She is willing, but you are tired. You don't want to disgrace yourself, but her charms do not impress you enough. So you begin using your imagination, and talking yourself into a more energetic state of mind. It was precisely what I was trying to do.

"You, son-of-a-bitch!" I cried. "There was a girl called Mistigri, and she was standing there and begging you not to do it, but you came at her! You beat her and then you took her! You're going to pay for it!"

My forefinger curled around the trigger, but that was as much as I could do. It was not a physical impossibility: it was much worse, it was a moral impossibility. I hated his guts with all of mine, but I couldn't bring myself to press that little bit of steel. I guess it is a matter of education: I just hadn't been brought up to kill people in cold blood. I despised myself for it, but what could I do?

I made myself think about the merger. It seemed very, very far off. Yes, I loved Amarantha, in principle at least; yes, I didn't want Munchin and Munchin to become a branch of Bopkins and Co.; but there seemed no solid, acceptable, relationship between these two concepts: "Amarantha must not become Billy-boy's mistress"; "my finger must press a little more on that little device."

It was no use. I couldn't do it. Saint-Fiacre could go on blabbering about virtuous peoples and corrupt government, I was neither virtuous nor corrupt enough, I just couldn't do it. That was the long and the short of it. I just didn't have the guts. I was just going to funk out. I cursed myself but that was no help. I knew how I would curse myself a few minutes from now, and that was no help either. I would rather be poor, disgraced and, as far as Amarantha was concerned, a cuckold, than press that trigger. Please understand that I was no more afraid of the police, the guillotine and such like trifles. I had forgotten all about them. I couldn't bring myself to take the life of the little man who was lying his head off down there. I had never been so ashamed of myself, but there was no use going on pretending. I replaced the safety, shoved the furniture back into place, threw a last nostalgic glance at Saint-Fiacre who was still talking and let myself out into the hall. By some strange piece of confusion I left the cello case in the room but I took the Ruger with me. It was sheer absent-mindedness on my part, but that absent-mindedness was to produce strange results.

I carefully locked the room, and I remember that it was a little hard to lock the room while holding the Ruger, but the idea to leave it there didn't come to me. I walked like a somnambulist to the door leading to the roof. Instead of being closed as I had left it, it was open.

That should have drawn my attention, but please remember I was not exactly a professional. Anything but a professional, as a matter-of-fact. And I was thinking about something else. A mixture of things. Amarantha, who would merge with Billy-boy; Mistigri, whom I had failed to avenge; Fifi, to whom I couldn't explain that I had chickened out. . . . I took the match out so the door would close.

I climbed the staircase. I emerged on the roof.

Or, rather, I began emerging. What I saw made me duck immediately, and then re-emerge very slowly, very carefully, just the top of my head and my two eyes protruding above the roof.

About fifteen feet from me, a very feminine figure was lying prone on the roof. Legs apart, tummy pressed against the ground (in this case: the roof), head erect, a rifle pressed against her right shoulder, wearing the little green dress she had had the first time I met her and, of course, her modish octagonal glasses, it was (I have to tell you because you would never guess, and if you guessed you would be wrong anyway), it was Miss Joyce Price.

*

I won't attempt to describe my surprise. What I saw made no sense at all. The hygienic Miss Price—a political murderess? Anyway we seemed to be more or less back at where we started: somebody else would do the killing and I could still publish the book.

No hesitation on the part of Miss Price. Please remember that what I saw of her was just a rear view. The shot rang without my having seen her press the trigger.

Saint-Fiacre's voice which had at that time reached the beginning of his peroration, or so it sounded from the majestic rhythm of his sentences, suddenly stopped. There was a brief and complete silence. Then the crowd exploded into a roar.

Miss Price got up, turned toward me, and then I saw it was not Miss Price at all, but Mistigri. Mistigri with octagonal glasses, dyed hair, and Miss Price's dress. My head swam.

"Now!" said a snappish little voice somewhere behind me.

I looked in that direction. I scarcely could be seen because I was still standing on the stairs: only my eyes were on roof level, but there was nothing to impair my vision of the strange scene which was taking place.

Snipe and Boudin were standing there, between two chimney-stacks. Snipe had just given the order, and Boudin began to advance, a little clumsily. His left leg seemed to hurt him, but obviously Fifi had missed the kneecap: otherwise Boudin would not have been playing acrobatics on that roof. He walked toward Mistigri. She didn't seem surprised to see him, but seemed to wonder at his threatening manner. "Let's run," she said to him. But he was still progressing, slowly and heavily toward her. He was a mountain of a man, and she, as I have said, was a very small girl.

"Don't forget, Boudin. Head first!" cried Snipe.

Then I saw it all. It came to me in a flash, the big things and most of the little details: why Chirpie had travelled under his own name, why I had been invited to Le Vésinet, why Saint-Fiacre had seemed to trip on a banana peel, and all the rest. Or nearly all. Of course, there were still things I couldn't understand, but most of it was crystal clear.

What followed happened in much less time than it will take in the telling.

Boudin rushed at Mistigri like a bull.

But she was a bodyguard by profession. She sidestepped and tripped him neatly just by extending her foot. He fell over it, tried to catch at the smooth roof, couldn't, and rolled into space with an awful cry of terror.

I looked at Snipe. He came running at her. He had been aptly compared to a stick man, he didn't weigh half as much as Boudin, but he was more agile, and his attack came as a surprise. He obviously did not understand what had happened to Boudin: he thought it was an accident. He did not realize that she knew something of martial arts.

He caught her by the arm and tried to shove her off the roof. She fell backwards, drawing him with her, disengaged her arm and rolled over to the side, leaving him to continue on the same trajectory. I saw him dive from the roof, somersault in the air and disappear. Another cry rose from the crowd.

I was a little ashamed of not having done anything to help, but I hadn't had the time, and Mistigri hadn't needed me.

Then a third figure emerged from behind a chimney-stack.

It was the romantic old gentleman of the Cour de Rohan, complete with hat and muffler and neat little moustache. In his right hand he held, of all things, a sling. In his left one, a sizable rock.

Mistigri stared incredulously at him. For some reason she didn't pick up the .22 carbine she had dropped. I assumed they had given her only one shot and she knew it.

She looked around and saw no protection. She could run, but that smooth roof was not very good for running. The old gentleman was standing between her and the stairs. She didn't know about my rope. She was as good as dead.

The old gentleman raised his sling and began pulling at it.

A second shot rang out; the old gentleman let the sling go and fell face forward on the roof. It was the Ruger which I still held. It had fired the shot of its own accord. It must have been as angry as I was.

I rushed onto the roof and ran to the very edge of it.

Down there, it was bedlam. The crowd had had two bodies drop in the middle of it and seemed to be expecting more. The police were trying to control it, but without any success. Some people were running away, others elbowed their way toward the two interesting corpses. Most were looking at the house from whose top they had been dropping.

I was not surprised to see that Saint-Fiacre was still standing at the feet of Danton's statue. Hans Schmidt's plaque was lying at his feet, broken in two.

"You bastard!" I shouted. "You filthy anti-American bastard!"

It is doubtful whether he heard me. But he did see me, and I, through the scope, could read the sheer physical, beastly, disgusting terror on his face.

I saw the skull break and the blood and brains gush out. That's what you get when you use a heavy caliber.

I dropped the Ruger.

"You've killed him," said Mistigri in a strange dispassionate voice.

"Come!" I cried.

"I couldn't have," she added. She was still in a trance.

I grasped her hand. "Come! Quick!"

She smiled. "Where could we go?"

She indicated the stairs. The police were pounding the door from the inside. It was not very strong. It would be broken in a few seconds.

I didn't answer. I dragged her after me. I dropped the end of the rope on the Cour de Rohan side of the building.

"Can you use a rope?" I asked.

She could, much better than I. She wore no gloves but she didn't hesitate to slide down it. From one roof she jumped onto another one and yet another. She had seen the ladder. She was on the ground when I was still on the second roof.

"Hurry up!" she cried. "They're climbing the gates."

I reached the ground at the same time as a policeman who seemed to be more of a sportsman than the rest.

"Stop!" he cried.

In France, the police are not allowed to shoot at people to stop them, and I was confident we could outrun him. I started running in the direction of the rue Saint-André-des-Arts, and Mistigri came after me.

The GS was there, with the engine running and Fifi at the wheel.

He had opened the doors. I jumped in beside him, and Mistigri in the back.

He whistled as he took off.

"So you won a prize too!" he said.

*

The policeman had time to see the GS, not to note the license number.

Fifi drove like a madman. We crossed the Boul'Mich' in the midst of the evening traffic, simply by wedging our way between the cars. To reach the embankment, he used the sidewalk, as the fastest way. He dropped us a few steps from the Continental and continued his erratic way, pursued by a concern of horns. The plan was that he would distract attention from us; then, if he could, he would stop in some quiet side street and change plates. After that, he would be safe.

We jumped into the Continental and drove off at a brisk but reasonable speed.

Mistigri was sitting beside me. She didn't say a word. From time to time she looked absent-mindedly at her hands, burned by the rapid descent. I dared not stop at a drugstore yet and she understood it. Or maybe she was thinking about something completely different, not even feeling the pain.

We had reached the perimeter when she finally said, with a queer little smile:

"So he wanted to kill me!"

I nodded. I knew her relationship to Serge Saint-Fiacre had been a strange one. She had every reason to hate him, yet she had been willing to work for him, and said she could never have killed him. I wondered if she hated me for doing it. But I couldn't ask her that. Instead, I asked:

"You have a passport?"

"Yes," she said in a dull voice.

"Joyce's?"

"Yes."

It would have to do.

We drove on in silence. There was no sign of a pursuit. I finally stopped in front of a drugstore, went in and bought an ointment for her hands. The store next door was a ladies' clothes store. There I bought gloves. We couldn't afford to have her try to leave France under a false passport and with bandaged hands.

I slipped back into the car, took her hands, opened them in my lap and, as it said on the tube, used the ointment *liberally* on them. I thought it was funny that the ointment could also be used *conservatively* and maybe even *radically*. What political animals we have become! I kissed the tips of her fingers and then helped her with the gloves. She looked at me in some surprise.

"You are kind," she said. "I didn't know men could be kind."

I didn't trust my voice enough to reply.

"Especially Americans," she went on. "M. Serge always said they wanted everything for nothing."

"And you believe that M. Serge always said the truth?"

"I suppose not. I'll have to get used to the idea that he was probably lying half the time."

"At least."

"But what he said seemed to make sense, you know. He said the world was split between the haves and the have-nots, and the Americans were the haves, but that it was more generous to stand for the have-nots."

"Yes, the 'Underdog Appeal.' May I ask if S.F. put himself in the category of the have-nots?"

"He put himself in the noble category of the haves who want the have-nots to become haves too."

"I see. And you fell for it?"

"Yes, up to a point." She added with a shy little smile: "Not from the roof though. Thanks to you. . .Walter."

She looked at me and then quickly at her gloved hands, which must be hurting like hell. A tear dropped from her eyes.

I put the clutch in and made the tires hiss on the gravel.

The night was descending on us fast. We were already on the highway. There was really no reason to be afraid of anything. I could not be suspect to anyone. At least not yet. Joyce Price's passport was probably in order, and although the resemblance between the two girls was not striking, the measurements must be about right, and the octagonal glasses would do the trick. At least I hoped so.

"Where is Joyce?" I asked.

Mistigri considered. "He told me she was in the house at Fontainebleau," she said. "The one of the Ballets Roses."

"The one they took Chirpie to the first day, I suppose. It belongs to S.F.?"

"Yes, he inherited it from the Senator, along with the rest. He's never lived there since. He wanted it to be forgotten. But he's used it from time to time for secret meetings, private talks, that kind of thing. And sometimes women. He told me Joyce was there. That she sent me her dress and passport. But now. . . ."

"But now, Mistigri?"

"I'm sorry, Walter. After what he's tried to do to me, I can't be sure."

"Is that what you tried to warn me about?"

"No. I had no idea he would be using her for that. But she looked like a nice enough girl and I thought you . . . cared for her, and I didn't want him to . . . to spoil her for you."

We drove on. She asked no questions. Maybe she wasn't interested in knowing the answers. I was thinking about Amarantha. She still could have the book if she wanted it, but not the author. That much was clear in my mind. It would not be pleasant to tell her how I felt about it, though. And I couldn't help wondering if Munchin and Munchin were the best possible publisher for the book. After all, the murder had been a great success. The news would be around the world very soon. People would want to know, and I could supply them with *firsthand* knowledge. I had gone much further than I thought I would when I had explained to Amarantha how advantageous it would be to work *in vivo* (which means: with one's sleeves rolled up). Most writers describe a murder which has been committed without their knowledge; I had a plan to describe one about which I knew beforehand; I had ended up committing it myself. What an ideal situation! I had felt no emotion while doing the job (except anger), but I could make up all the virtuous emotions which would please the reader and dovetail them to what I actually did. Should I spoil such an extraordinary chance by giving the manuscript to a provincial publishing company? Well, my word was pledged to it. Amarantha had accepted to incur my expenses; she had put her trust in me; I would not betray it. That was that.

As to publicity, I knew I would get now as much as I wanted. As soon as I had crossed the frontier, I would give a ring to the six journalists whom I had already made contact with and who, having already heard about Saint-Fiacre's death, would be sitting very close to their telephones. The next morning I would hold a press conference with a black stocking on my head; I had packed Nénette's in my luggage; everything would go well, I felt sure of it. Les Enfants de Mai would, for a time, be the rage of Europe and the United States. I began adding figures in my head. The book was bound to be a great success in America and Europe. I wondered if I could get the Japanese to translate it: Japan affords an excellent market to those who know how to use it.

Minutes and kilometers sped by. Mistigri was still silent. As a rule, Siamese cats don't talk much, and I was content to have her there, knowing that the time would come when she would explain her part of the story, and I would mine. There was no hurry. We had a lifetime before us. Or, so I felt.

From time to time, my mind would revert to the dangers we were facing. But on the whole they didn't seem too great. Boudin, Snipe, the romantic old gentleman and Saint-Fiacre would not talk. If any other conspirators were involved, they would probably be made to talk but much later. Mistigri's fingerprints were on the carbine, but they don't fingerprint you every time you cross a frontier. I caught myself thinking that anyway Mistigri had not killed anybody and that, consequently, she had nothing to fear, which, at that time, already seemed to me the most important thing in the world. Then I reflected that Boudin's and Snipe's deaths could be interpreted as homicides, although in fact they were nothing but accidents. Surely a good lawyer could make the most of that slippery roof.

For the first time in my life, I think, I stopped at a frontier post without the smallest flutter in my stomach. After all, I wasn't carrying any forbidden liquor, any clandestine cigars. . . .

The officer came up to the window. I rolled it down, extending my own passport, Joyce Price's one, and the car's papers.

"Monsieur de Walter?"

"Yes."

"Would you mind stepping out for a minute?"

"What's wrong?"

"Nothing at all. Just a routine matter."

I stepped out. What could I do? Everything was very dark around us. The Continental's lights and the lighted window of the frontier post were the only bright spots around.

I took three steps toward the window. Suddenly, I felt myself grasped by the elbow on both sides. Tall men wearing felt hats and mackintoshes had appeared from nowhere.

"Gentlemen! What does this mean? I am an American citizen. I demand. . . ."

"Cool it, buddy," said one of the men, in excellent, if colloquial, English.

I looked around. I saw that two other men were extracting Mistigri from the car. Not without trouble. She knew a trick or two, and showed them what she could do. But they were stronger than she, and they knew tricks too.

"You'd better go with them, Mistigri," I cried. "No use hurting the poor fellows for nothing. They are only doing their job."

She submitted immediately, and we were both marched into the darkness by our four guards. The first officer got into the Continental and got it out of the road. He parked it alongside the frontier post, and the last thing I could see were the lights of the big car going out. You would have thought she had closed her eyes.

16

The next few hours count among the darkest in my life. We had been frisked, hoisted into two cars, driven for about an hour at night, in a country I didn't know, brought to a house that didn't look at all like a police station, and separated. After that, I had been thrown into an underground cellar, with no furniture and no light. I had every reason to suppose that Mistigri had been treated the same way, and I sat on the floor, remembering that France has no *habeas corpus* law (*habeas corpus* means: they have a right to torture you only for a set period, generally twenty-four hours). Next time I plan an assassination, I thought, I would choose a civilized country.

After some time spent in gloomy regrets rather than remorse, I noted one curious little thing: I was giving much more anxiety to Mistigri's plight than mine. It was the first time in my life, I believe, that another person's interests concerned me more than mine. Well, that didn't tell me anything about the state of my feelings which I didn't already know or suspect, but it did tell me something about my inner nature, something that came as rather a pleasant surprise. And so, from time to time, I found myself thinking of a middle-aged couple who, on retiring from prison some thirty years hence, would lead a simple and sentimental life in some cosy nook for the few years that would remain of their earthly existence. I must confess, conceited as it sounds, that the idea that Mistigri might not love me as I thought I loved her never crossed my mind. My conversion to virtue, as you see, did not go as far as humility.

The rest of the time, I devoted to preparing the story I would tell whoever would question me. I decided not to deny anything, but, at the same time, to try and take all the guilt on myself. There was no need for Chirpie, Fifi, Nénette and Amarantha to be involved. Or so I fondly imagined. I found a certain noble and melancholic pleasure in thinking that I would be protecting someone although I was in such a dire situation.

I had no way to measure the passing of time, but I guess about four hours must have elapsed while I was sitting in that dark dungeon. Finally, I heard steps, the door opened, a dazzling light blinded me completely, and two men took me to what they called the Interrogation Room. I didn't like that name at all, but I tried to cut a decent figure nevertheless. If they wanted to see me cringe, it would at least take them a few more hours or a physical effort or two.

The Interrogation Room held no frightening devices of any kind. Maybe they were next door. There were no windows; there was just one door, one table behind which two men were sitting on two chairs, and one stool for me. I sat on it without being asked. If they started beating me, I might reconsider and become polite, but before that I had to check out one chance that still lurked in my mind: perhaps we had not been arrested for Saint-Fiacre's murder but for some other frivolous reason.

"What are you keeping me under arrest for?" I asked querulously.

The two men looked at me. The one on the left was fiftyish, with silvery hair, a clean-cut face and watchful eyes. He wore a grey suit that had been cut by quite a decent tailor. He held a silver pencil in his hands and tapped gently with it on the table. His partner was younger, bigger, redder, with a meaty face, and shiny maroon eyes. He wore a brown suit, more expensive than what policemen generally can afford. He was in charge of the tape recorder.

"You are mistaken," answered the older one in a very gentle voice. "You are not under arrest."

"What do you call it then? You grab me, you shut me up in a dark cellar, you take my possessions from me, you. . . ."

"Precisely. If you were under arrest, you would have been treated quite differently: advised of your rights, measured, photographed. No, sir: you are not under arrest."

"What am I doing here then? And who are you by the way?"

"Please," he said still more gently and with a deprecating gesture of his quite handome hand. "Let's not play tin soldiers'
games. We are in a position to question you, and you are in a
position in which it would be wise to answer our questions. Isn't
that enough? I thought you were a man of the world, Mr. de
Walter. Oh! yes, I know your name. We've been through your
passports. Both of them."

All right. So they were some kind of "parallel police," not
bound by usual restrictions. These gents don't generally arrest you
because you've been speeding on the highway. Saint-Fiacre it was.
I decided to make a clean breast of it, with the above-mentioned
restrictions.

"What do you want to know?"

"I knew you would be reasonable and we could settle all this in
the most pleasant way for everybody concerned."

For some reason, the way he pronounced the word *pleasant* sent
my stomach somewhere it had no business staying. With an effort
of will I put it back into place. The polite policeman went on:

"Now your friend is much less reasonably inclined. We have
been dealing with her at some length, and she has insisted on
telling us some very silly lies. We hope you won't try anything of
the kind. This could make it very *unpleasant* for everybody concerned."

"You haven't touched her?" I cried as savagely as if I had been
Sir Galahad reincarnated.

The man smiled. "You have been reading too many spy stories,
Monsieur. Most government officials still prefer *not* to be driven
into resorting to cruder methods."

"What has she been lying to you about?"

Strangely enough he seemed to fall into that trap.

"Well, for instance, she told us that she had killed M. Saint-
Fiacre. But that was impossible, you see, because we do have a
photograph showing a man shooting at M. Saint-Fiacre with a
high caliber rifle, and we also know M. Saint-Fiacre died from a
high caliber bullet. Now your friend definitely does not look like a
man."

She definitely doesn't.

"The man was I," I said.

He nodded. "Yes. We thought as much. Miss SNP must have been protecting you."

The idea that Mistigri had lied for me brought my blood to my head. But how had he called her?

"Miss SNP. *Sans Nom Patronymique*." (Without family name.) She told us that was her official surname, as is usual for found children. Isn't that true either?"

"I suppose it is."

"You don't know?"

"I've always called her Mistigri."

"I see."

"What else did she lie about?"

"Well, for instance, she told us that she thought you were working for the C.I.A. or for some other American intelligence unit. Is that true?"

He watched me warily.

For a second the idea of bluffing my way out came to me, but I decided to abide by the plan I had prepared earlier.

"No," I said. "She may believe it, but it isn't true. I'm a publisher's scout, and I happen to be a fairly good shot. Those are my two connections with Saint-Fiacre's death."

"Good, good. I thought you would prove quite reasonable. Now would you mind telling us your own story in your own words?"

The difficult moment had come. I had to serve them a credible cocktail of truth, untruth and surmise. I was supposed to be rather good at cocktails. We would see in a minute.

"All right. I work for a publishing company called Munchin and Munchin, in Atlanta, Georgia. As I was looking for manuscripts for that company, I began thinking that I would make more money if I wrote one best seller than if I found one. At about the same period, I was contacted by two private detectives called Snipe and Boudin, who, having heard that I was a marksman of sorts, offered me the job of killing Saint-Fiacre. They didn't tell me for whom they were working, and I didn't care. I thought I would fulfil the contract, then disappear and write a book about it. Of course Munchin and Munchin knew nothing about my plan."

"Of course."

"I came over under my own name and followed, up to a point, Snipe and Boudin's instructions. I sighted in the Ruger that I had bought at a property near the forest of Fontainebleau. I checked in at the Hôtel Cardinal, and, at a time when Saint-Fiacre was coming back home for lunch, I shot at him. To my surprise, I missed."

"Under what name did you check in into the Hôtel?"

"Oh. . . . I don't remember."

"Go on."

"It was some time before I understood that I had been intended to miss all along. Snipe and Boudin, who were in charge of the rifle, changed the position of the scope on purpose. The whole plan was the product of Saint-Fiacre's own imagination. As you know, he was of strongly anti-American inclinations, and he thought it would prove him right if the Americans tried to assassinate him. Incidentally, arranging an attempt at one's own assassination is nothing new in France. François Mitterand, the President of the Republic is thought to have done so himself a few years ago. So Saint-Fiacre recruited two Americans—the name of one of the two seems to indicate that he was of French origin and could have connections in France—and made them find him an American marksman with an American rifle, who would shoot at him, and then be caught by the French police. You can imagine the international scandal that would create, and how interesting it would make Saint-Fiacre, his party and his newspaper. You will note that the assassination attempt was to coincide with the Convention and the launching of *Le Haut-Parleur*. So when I shot at him, Saint-Fiacre heard the shot because he was expecting it. Instinctively, he fell to the ground so as to protect himself, although he knew that I would miss. But is is not very easy to stand cooly when you are being shot at. I happen to know."

"After that?"

"After that, there was a double mess. I ran away because I didn't want to be rescued by Snipe and Boudin; I wanted to be free and write my book. You see, I thought I had killed him. On the other hand, Saint-Fiacre was disappointed: an attempt at assassination without a corpse and without an assassin wouldn't look serious. He decided he would have to try again. And I also, when I learned he was alive, decided I would try again."

"Where were you staying?"

"Oh. . . . With a friend of mine."

"Name of. . . ?"

"Nénette Cordier. Of course, she knew nothing about my plans."

"Of course."

"Now I have to explain two incidents. I had been to Saint-Fiacre's house with an American friend of mine, who was fascinated by him. He and I had an altercation. I think he was looking for one with an American, so that people would quote what he had said that night, when the Americans would try to assassinate him. Then, after the first attempt missed, he changed his mind. He thought it would make the Americans look much worse if he expressed a friendly attitude toward them, and they bumped him off. So he invited me to his house and apologized to me. Photographs were taken. At the same time he asked Mistigri to make a demonstration of her shooting talents in front of the same audience so that later no one would doubt she really could have murdered him. You see, he had chosen Mistigri to replace me as the American killer."

"Why?"

"Well, he couldn't find a real American in a few hours. So he decided he would fake one. Mistigri had just come back to him after a few years in a convent; she was not widely known; he intended to use her as a cute bodyguard, but now he found he had a better use for her."

"She told us that he had wanted her to . . . become his mistress and that she had refused."

"All right, that's one more reason. He didn't want her around any more, and he thought she could be useful to him by dying. So I assume he asked her to do him a favor. She would pretend she was Joyce Price, whom nobody knew. She was the same height, the same passport description. She would demonstrate her shooting talents and then she would shoot at him during the plaque ceremony. In fact, she would shoot at the plaque, which would be sure to protect him against such a small caliber as a .22. The attempt at assassination would be very spectacular. Of course, if Mistigri were arrested, the police would find out very soon who she was.

So two plans, I suppose, were invented. The first one Mistigri must have known: she would escape to another country with the help of Snipe and Boudin and there resume her real name; Saint-Fiacre would make it look as if he had been shot at by Americans, and she, having been raised with rather anti-American feelings herself, didn't mind helping him with his politics. I don't know what she had been told about the real Joyce Price. Maybe that she was an American leftist ready to help. . . ."

"No. That she had become Saint-Fiacre's mistress and was ready to help for that reason."

"Good. That fits. The second plan was different. As soon as she would have fired her shot, Boudin and Snipe, instead of helping her to escape, would throw her, head first, on the pavement. She would be found dead, practically unrecognizable, with an American dress, American underclothes, American glasses on, and an American passport in the name of Price. The scandal would be lovely. The only person who knew both Joyce and Mistigri and could have some doubts was I, so I had to be taken care of. Once S.F. had my brakes sabotaged. When that didn't help, he sent a professional murderer to Nénette's flat. Fortunately, I was rather drunk that night and managed to frighten him out of his wits. You must have found him very dead. He was a romantic looking old gentleman."

For some reason the two men exchanged an amused glance.

I went on. "I don't know what was the plan concerning Boudin and Snipe. I rather think that the nice old gentleman would have disposed of them after they had disposed of Mistrigri. That would have given the public three American corpses instead of one."

"Are we to assume, Monsieur, that you prepared the second attempt without any help?"

"Oh! yes. I couldn't confide in anybody, of course."

"Of course."

The silver-headed gentleman had a way of saying *of course* which got on my nerves, but there was nothing I could do about it except smile pleasantly. I tried.

There was long silence. The meaty-faced fellow who slumped in his chair scratched his head. The silver-headed teased his ear with the end of his silver pencil. Finally he said:

"What was the book going to be about, Monsieur?"

There was no reason to lie about that.

"About Les Enfants de Mai," I replied readily.

They exchanged a glance of astonishment. They reflected a second and then both looked very pleased. The reddish one grinned. The silver one smiled thinly.

"Well, that's good," said the reddish one in a thick, American drawl. "That sure is good."

"An excellent initiative," commented the other one, keeping to French. "Am I to understand that the organization Les Enfants de Mai does not exist at all?"

"It doesn't."

"You invented it?"

"I did."

"You sent the letters?"

"I wrote them and sent them."

"The two other murders. . . ?"

"Are entirely unconnected."

Another exchange of congratulatory glances.

"Excellent," said the Frenchman. "What were you going to do about publicity?"

I explained about the six journalists and Pavillon Saint-Hu;

"Of course," I added, "Gerhard Crommlinckx didn't know what I would be using his hunting lodge for."

"Of course," assented the Frenchman gravely.

"Who were you going to use as kids?" asked the American.

"That was rather ridiculous: I had no one. I was going to put on a black stocking on my head. Now I had Mistigri with me I thought she might be willing to help."

"You don't look like a teenager, Monsieur, and Mademoiselle certainly doesn't look like one either."

"She sure don't," assented the American.

"I know. This was the weak point."

Glances exchanged.

"Yours could maybe help them out," suggested the American. "And maybe mine too, if they don't have to speak up."

"That sounds like a good idea," said the Frenchman.

"Of course, it could create some problems later on. If they are asked to talk big and revolt for fun, they might consider doing it for real? What do you think?"

The Frenchman shook his head. "I don't think it would create any problems that a good thrashing or two couldn't solve," he said very gently.

"Well, I'm game if you are."

"Certainly. Monsieur, I thought you would be interested in seeing this, so I brought you a copy. It is a rarity, of course. Five hundred thousand of them have been confiscated."

It was a newspaper. Its title, printed in enormous capitals: *LE HAUT-PARLEUR*. And under it: *Numéro 1*.

I didn't read it through. I read only one boxed item on the first page. Here it is. Above it was a photograph of yours truly shaking Saint-Fiacre's hand.

"LAST MINUTE. This sheet was going to press when the most abominable piece of news reached us here at the office. In spite of the Leader's renewed expression of friendship toward the American people as represented by one of that perfidious country's citizens (see photo above), the American Establishment, following its worst traditions, has made up its mind to resort once again to violence and to get rid by means of assassination of the one man who, in Europe, has dared defy it. After shooting the Leader during the touching plaque ceremony at the Carrefour de l'Odéon, an American agent, Joyce Price, a pretty female who had managed to become S.F.'s bodyguard, toppled from the roof on which she was lying in ambush. We have no further details besides the most important one: the Leader is alive. His life was saved by the symbolic plaque which he was carrying in his hands. History needs Serge Saint-Fiacre. He is not going to be disposed of so easily. He will yet lead us to a Unified Europe of peoples not of governments. Long live Saint-Fiacre!"

I raised my eyes to the Frenchman's. He was smiling gently.

"A little hasty of them, wasn't it?" he remarked. "Oh! I have something else for you. I apologize for having had to raid your general delivery mail at the rue du Louvre. There was this."

It was a cable.

I opened it.

It read: *"Merger consummated. Adieu. Amarantha."*

I smiled. The Frenchman was looking at me with some concern.
"It didn't read like good news," he observed.

I sighed. As a matter of fact it was rather good news. I hate jilting women. Or, rather, I hate telling them I've jilted them.

"Oh! it's nothing," I said. "It means I will have to look for another publisher. That's all."

He didn't press me, although my reply couldn't have been really very satisfactory. So I decided it was my turn to ask him a question or two.

"How did you know it was me?" I asked.

The American with the meaty face chuckled.

"Oh! we do know a few things," said the Frenchman modestly. "We know, for instance, that you couldn't have done all that single-handed. Someone had to be driving that GS, don't you think so? And it does sound a little curious that Saint-Fiacre should have invited you to his house and made a scene of it, when he *knew* that you *knew* that you were to murder him. But those are minor points. As to your identity, and a few other details, like the make of your car, we really had no trouble learning them. You see, a certain press photographer called the police to complain about his girlfriend's disappearance. He didn't seem heart-broken, but he said he felt it was his duty to call them." (I noticed he didn't say *us*). "He gave us your name and told us you were living at Mlle. Cordier's. So we went to see Mlle. Cordier and asked her a few questions."

"You don't mean she answered them?"

I had every confidence in Nénette.

"Oh! yes, very readily. She was most cooperative. As soon as my friend here told her he was working for the C.I.A., she said 'Oh you must be a pal of Walter's; he works for the C.I.A. too' and told us everything she knew."

"What a dirty trick!" I cried. There was Sir Galahad riding again!

"I don't think so," replied the Frenchman very gently. "You see, it happens to be true."

I gazed at Meaty-Face who suddenly looked very serious.

"And I," went on Silver Head, "work for the French D.G.S.E. Sometimes we work hand in hand, the Americans and we. Like, for instance, on the case of the Soviet agent Saint-Fiacre, who had been giving us trouble for some time."

"Saint-Fiacre was an agent!?"

"Yes. What is known as an *influence agent*. He was not gathering intelligence. He was working on public opinion."

"You know the kind," interposed the C.I.A. man. "We have plenty of them back home."

"Europe is a very difficult country to unify, but it will be done eventually. And there is nothing the Communists fear more. So the International European Party was created to disrupt the schemes of the men who are really working for a unified Europe at the only level at which it can be done: government level."

I was quick to take advantage of what they were telling me.

"So in fact you're rather glad I did what I did?"

"Yes, we are very glad," said the French officer gravely. "Whatever you may think about the matter, assassination is not something democratic governments go in for very often. And we could prove very little. Fortunately, all that has been changed by you. The romantic old gentleman whom you killed had some correspondence on him which identified him very clearly as the Soviet agent in residence. He was Saint-Fiacre's case officer, you understand. It was he who wanted the Americans to make an attempt to assassinate Saint-Fiacre, to make him a more credible character. It was he who told him to apologize to you; and Saint-Fiacre had to comply, but he must have hated it. He really didn't like Americans at all. My guess is that it was also the romantic old gentleman who killed Joyce."

"Killed Joyce?" I exclaimed.

The American said: "She was found two hours ago in Saint-Fiacre's Fontainebleau estate. Strangled."

What do you say when you learn a nice, silly little girl, has paid a very high price for a little foolishness? I said:

"I'm glad I killed the bastards."

"Amen," said the Frenchman.

17

All the rest was really very easy. Mistigri and I were asked to proceed straight to Pavillon Saint-Hu. The next morning several young teenagers were delivered there: they were the French commandant's and the American captain's children. I briefed them for a few hours and succeeded to make rather convincing rebels of them. You have read all about it, I guess, in my best selling book *The Children of May*. They had great fun wearing stockings on their heads and declaiming against adult chauvinists.

The journalists came. There were seven people instead of six. The seventh one was a scout from a great European publishing house. He wanted to know if a book couldn't be written about Les Enfants de Mai. We discussed business with him, I posing as their business representative. The contract was signed a few days later. The French D.G.S.E. provided all the legal help that was needed.

The night of the press conference, when everybody left, I kissed Mistigri and she kissed me too, but when I tried to press the advantage, she shook her head.

"I'm not a prude," she said, "but, darling, you must remember how I began life. In the Ballets Roses. And after that I spent a few years in a convent. It wasn't very funny there, but they taught me to treat serious things seriously."

"How very un-French!" I exclaimed.

"Am I not going to become half-American then?" she asked a trifle sadly.

"Of course, I'll marry you, if that's what you mean. But I thought you hated Americans!"

"That's what I thought too!" she said, and kissed me very chastely indeed.

The French were helpful with all the red tape. We flew to Spain and were married there, because we wanted a change, and the weather was beautiful, and the authorities wanted us out of the way, and I thought it would be romantic to have our honeymoon there. Mistigri wanted a religious marriage and she got it. She wore a very pretty dress. Not white but pink, as they sometimes make wedding dresses there, which is, if you ask me, a very sensible way of doing things.

The dress had about forty buttons.

"That's on purpose: to tease you," she explained.

The book was published and sold beautifully. You've probably read it. It was translated into twenty-one languages. Even the Russians bought it to show their own children how badly Westerners treat theirs, and what's more, they paid me royalties!

We went to the U.S. and lived there for some time, and Mistigri loved every minute of it. I reimbursed Amarantha for all the expenses she had incurred. Of course, she was disappointed not to have published *The Children of May,* but I hear she is making a fortune publishing cartoons.

Chirpie has gone back to security patrols; I have invested his ten thousand for him; he tells me he has a satisfactory girlfriend— nothing to compare, though, with the one from Paris.

Then, one day, Meaty-Face came to see me and said:

"You better get to some quiet country. We'll take care of the passports and so on. And you'll write another book and tell the story the way it really happened. You can change some of the names if you want to. But you have to prove The Children of May never existed."

"Why?"

"Well, the 'Underdog Appeal,' as you called it, is too powerful a thing to play with for long. We have reliable information according to which organizations patterned after your Children of May are sprouting in France, Germany, England, and the U.S. That might become dangerous. So . . . you'd better tell it how it was."

So I did.

FINIS CORONAT OPUS

which means
(approximately)

THE MEANS JUSTIFIES THE END